She Made Herself a Monster

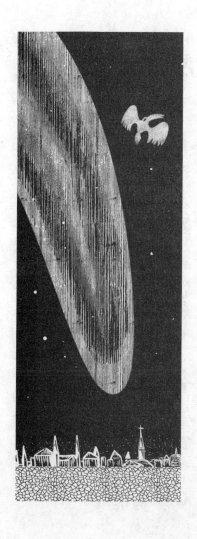

She Made
Herself
a Monster

a novel

ANNA
KOVATCHEVA

MARINER BOOKS
New York   Boston

HarperCollins books may be purchased for educational, business, or sales promotional use. For information, please email the Special Markets Department at SPsales@harpercollins.com.

The Mariner flag design is a registered trademark of HarperCollins Publishers LLC.

hc.com

FIRST EDITION

Interior design and art by Jackie Alvarado
Endpaper art by Jackie Alvarado

Library of Congress Cataloging-in-Publication Data has been applied for.

ISBN 978-0-06-343637-4

Printed in the United States of America

25 26 27 28 29 LBC 5 4 3 2 1

For the survivors and the slayers,
and for my grandfather—my first and biggest fan

She Made Herself a Monster

prologue

THERE IS A brick, and there is a mouth. In a dim root cellar smelling of dirt and brined cabbage, people cluster anxiously close. The whole village has come to watch a gruesome transformation. On the worktable, under a low ceiling, the body waits. They crane their necks to see it.

"Listen," Yana says, and the villagers swallow sour breath. The earth here is warm with a cloying, unwashed sweetness.

"Be soft," she says. "He could wake at any moment."

Not a week ago, this body was a man. He was the stable master. His crown had grayed and his face was well lined when he died, but his arms were strong like ropes, thick and bristled with wiry hairs. He tamed some hundred horses in his life. Now his fingers are blue and swollen, his nails pressed into the putty of his skin like yellow shells. When Yana pulls his dry lips apart, his teeth grind together as though his body knows what is coming. A human mouth is much smaller than a brick. Most open only four fingers wide.

Yana reaches for a knife in her belt. She circles the table so all of them can see it: a short, intimate blade, no longer than her finger. When she cuts into the man's smile, his flesh is stiff, resistant, like cured pork. Carefully, she splits him from gill to gill. Near the pickle barrels, somebody coughs like they're trying not to be sick.

Yana's mother trained her years ago to look at a body and see an object. Usually, she manages. With her fingers on his chin, Yana tests the dead man's jaw. His head lolls against the wooden table, but his teeth stay clenched. From her bag, she lifts a blacksmith's hammer and a long iron spike, the sort used for fixing rails to the earth. A murmur from the crowd—she raises a hand for quiet.

It's easy here. Along the pockmarked road into the village, she passed a dozen pyres still glowing with half-burnt animal bones, the sheep and pigs shriveled by some cloven-foot plague. The village smokehouses stand empty while winter creeps closer every morning. Without a spark of hope, none of them will survive the snow.

Yana levers the spike between the man's lips. With one hard smack of her mallet, his jaw breaks. Muscles pop, the crunch of bone chews the air. At the front of the crowd, jaundiced by gas lamps, the mayor and his wife clutch each other's sleeves. He drags a handkerchief over his upper lip and balding skull, and his gaze darts around the room, unwilling to linger on the table.

"I'll take it now," Yana says softly to the stable boy. He looks younger than her, light-haired and round-eyed. She thinks he must be stronger than he seems, if he can manage the horses alone, but fear shrinks him. He offers her the brick with two quivering hands. The weight of it could snap his white wrists.

Steady, whispers her mother's ghost. Yana receives the brick with one open palm, and she does not tremble.

The man's broken jaw yawns wide when she tilts his head back, his chin falling to his chest. She balances the brick delicately against the crooked fence of his teeth and takes her hammer by its worn oak handle.

While her mother was alive, Yana watched her perform this ritual from where the villagers now stand. The vampire hunter raises the hammer high overhead and lets it dangle. In that moment of waiting, the watchers become like the body: utterly breathless, utterly still. Yana's mother looked like any woman, and they loved her for it. She could have been their own mother, their sister, their wife—and yet, what a thing she could do. She was so ordinary that she captivated them. For Yana, it's different.

"People will think things about you," her mother told her when she was a child, long before they lived by uprooting nightmares. Kneeling over their wooden washtub, she brushed the thick hair back from Yana's face, dragged a wet cloth over her arms and legs, lingering where brown skin gave way to pallor, where she looked as though she'd been splattered by a broken jug of milk. She traced the crooked line down Yana's face with a tender finger. "When they do, they give you power. You can use their thoughts against them."

When Yana enters a new village, she makes sure the people see her. She takes off her hat and holds her chin high. "I have walked in both worlds," she says, voice a low rumble. "I see creatures you cannot—those shades that make the winds cry, those monsters that chase the running rivers." And with a glance at her uneven face, with the stories they know of demons and their slayers, they believe her. The simple fact is: they want to believe her.

When she is traveling, in between places, Yana sees the world stretch out ahead of her like a gray, fallow field dotted with hopeful pinpricks of light. Tall stalks of chimney smoke draw her eye across the horizon to places, to people, who need her. Every village is haunted in its own way. All of them want her to banish something without form.

In the root cellar, Yana lifts the hammer to her brow. The line down her nose disappears, and the villagers see two halves of a girl: one pale, one dark. Sweat slithers down her sides. The room holds its breath.

The muscles in her arms strain as the moment pulls taut. The handle threatens to slip through her palms. *Don't miss*, she thinks, and brings it down.

Iron slams hard against clay, and clay rasps chalky over breaking teeth. The stable boy heaves his breakfast onto the dirt floor. Yana lifts the hammer again, clipping the low ceiling and raining grit onto the table. With the second blow, she drives the brick firmly into the dead man's throat.

People are praying. The cellar fills with sour bile, the sting of urine, coppery fear. Yana lowers the mallet to the ground and holds the railroad spike out to the mayor. Its sharp end is gummy with flesh gouged from the root of the dead man's mouth.

"The beast tethered to this man has done you all great harm," Yana says quietly. "Your harvest has suffered. He has sucked the life from your livestock. You must bury him outside the village. Pin him down with this." She taps her breastbone to show where to drive the spike. "Plant thorned bushes around the grave, and once the earth settles, he will not trouble you again."

Behind the mayor, the stable boy staggers sideways with an outstretched hand, as if to brace himself against the wall. He slumps to the floor with shuttered eyes and open mouth, having fainted.

one

ON HIS WEEKLONG journey home, Kiril rides through the nights. He can't sleep. In the city, there was always noise: drunkards singing in the alleys, wheels on the cobblestones, the unconscious shifting of the other boarding-house boys with their grunts and snores. Outside the ramparts, there is only the dying chirp of autumn insects, the light rustle of falling leaves. Night after night, Kiril is alone on the overgrown road, passing no other travelers.

When he lets his horse stop to rest, the silence leaves too much space for the ringing in his ears. At thirteen, foolishly brave, he dove into a frozen lake. After, when he complained of phantom chimes, his neighbors feared a haunting, or that Anka was somehow to blame. It wasn't until he went to the city, almost a decade later, that he came to understand the workings of the ear and the damage he'd done to the delicate, cochleate pathways in his head. In this way, he is never alone: a tolling bell follows wherever he goes.

Vicious winds rip through withering fields of sunflowers, and he takes shelter in an abandoned barn. Someone has tried to burn it down and failed. Cinders paint the floor, and the punctured roof sags. Lying on his back, he can see the sky through the splintered ceiling. Still awake after the hazy moon has arced by and begun to set, he gets up and keeps riding, the wind freezing his hands to the reins, the horse kicking as he forces her on. Already, the past year away from home feels impossibly far, a dream unspooling in coils of smoke.

On his last night in the city, he sat with Hasan on the high stone wall of the hospital with a brass spyglass and the last bag of late-summer cherries between them. The street was dark beneath their dangling feet, the sky muddled overhead. Somewhere, music spilled from an open window. Hasan held a pad of papers in his lap, searching the breaks in the clouds.

"I do think I've changed," Kiril said. His teeth scraped the pit of a cherry and he twirled the stem. On the street below, a prostitute slouched in a doorway, calling to the men who passed by. Her words didn't carry, but Kiril could guess what she was saying. He leaned back and shot the stone through his teeth. Maybe one day it would sprout a new tree where it landed. They could have planted hundreds in the last month alone. "I'm different from that boy who left home." It was true; something had shifted. That afternoon, as he packed his bag with gifts for his family, he had trouble recalling even the most important faces, though he closed his eyes and strained to picture each of them in turn: his uncle the Captain, his orphaned cousin Anka, his beloved Margarita. He exhaled into the dark. "I'm a different person here."

Hasan hummed, his pencil hovering over the paper, his meticulous diagrams of orbits and angles. His heel tapped the wall, keeping tempo with the urgent violin below. "Is it a good change?" he asked.

Kiril rolled a cherry over his tongue, thinking. Overhead,

the clouds opened, and Hasan gave a sudden, triumphant yell. He waved his drawing pad in greeting. A page slipped free and fluttered down to the alley, but he ignored it.

Among the stars, something was new. There was a rip in the sky, bleeding light. Hasan pulled open the spyglass and pressed it to his eye, his spectacles digging into the bridge of his nose, then passed it to Kiril and began scribbling on his paper. Through the glass, the star looked like a mistake in one of Hasan's night paintings, a smudge with a long white tail.

"What did you call this?" Kiril asked. "A comet?"

"I don't call it that," Hasan said. "That is what it's called." With an outstretched finger, he sketched an invisible path over their heads. "It's magnificent, isn't it? The orbit of this particular comet takes some three hundred years to complete."

"You could be more specific," Kiril suggested.

"Two hundred ninety-six," Hasan conceded, adding something to his notes. "And twelve weeks. The object we're looking at right now—it could be older than anything on this earth."

The evening wore on. As the music died away, Kiril felt in the bag and dug out the last cherry. "You've hardly had any of these," he said. He held it out, but Hasan just hummed, chewing his pencil. The longer they looked at the comet, the brighter it seemed to glow. The other planets and stars faded away one by one.

From the street, there came the sound of a door opening and closing. The prostitute had gone inside. The city was asleep. Somewhere, a gentle ringing. Hasan shut his pad and adjusted his glasses. "You don't need to go back there," he said, like he'd been mulling over the thought for some time, like it was one of his equations. "You said yourself you have more to learn here."

Around them, the night had grown cold. Kiril fastened another button on his coat and dropped the cherry into his pocket. He crumpled the empty bag in his fist.

"I came to study medicine because they need someone," he said. "There's no physician there at all, just an old apothecary who still believes in balancing humors." Was that true? He felt shame as soon as he said it. Margarita's father wasn't to blame for the villagers' superstitions, for the many stillborn children and those who couldn't survive their first nights. How to explain that he had to return to help them, and to save Anka from their bile? It felt too grandiose. He twisted the cherry stem around his finger. "It's not just the village," he said at last. "I have to go back for my family, too."

Hasan smiled. "How noble," he said. He nodded to the sky. "Write and tell me how well you can see it from home. How long it stays visible—it'll be around forty days, I think, before the sun is too bright for it. Write me—I'd like more data."

"I'll make careful observations," Kiril said, though he knew he would never send a letter.

Hasan put a hand on his shoulder and gave it a warm squeeze. "We'll meet again," he promised. "Travel safely, my friend."

His feet were quick along the spine of the wall as he went. His shadow stretched long and thin until it became just another piece of the city, another spire or minaret cast along the ground. Kiril listened to his steps growing distant. Then he took the last cherry out of his pocket and swallowed it without chewing, pit and all. It hurt, burrowing through his chest.

He's trying to sleep beneath the wind-bent crown of a dead willow when he finally marks the comet again. This time, he's close to home. It is the final night of his journey: he recognizes the rocky ridge ahead. He'd begun to wonder if he could even discern it again with naked eye, without Hasan's guiding hand. Maybe he'd traveled too far; maybe he'd dreamed it. But all at once, there it is: a small blur in the sky, bigger than it looked in the city.

The peak of the Witch's Hump is in sight. He wonders if Anka sleeps any better than she used to, or if his cousin is awake and watching the stars, just like him. He could explain it to her—*a comet, circling every two hundred and ninety-six years.* He imagines the two of them cloaked in blankets and leaning halfway out her bedroom window, close to falling. He'd hold her tight. The night before he left for the city, Anka had been furious with him. She begged him to take her along, and when he insisted he couldn't, she stood in the open second-floor window, her face twisted red, and sobbed, *Just push me out, then, if you want to leave me to the wolves.* Eventually, she came down.

In the morning, as the sun crests the steep, blank face of the cliff, Kiril's horse gives a whinny of exhaustion, and the earth levels beneath her hooves. The wind exhales. Nailed to a tree beneath a swatch of red paint, an old wooden sign names the village. Just like that, he's come home.

ANKA'S BLACKBERRY BASKET is light as her path through the brambles winds nearer the stranger's campsite. Her belly is full, and her hands are bloody with juice, though she's meant to save the fruit for supper. Yulia will scold her for the mess—she's left stains all down her front and on Kiril's letter in her apron pocket.

She took the letter when she left the Captain's house this morning. Kiril wrote only once all year, to announce his return. He addressed himself to their uncle, who chuckled as he read and then passed the paper across the table. The note was short, the page bumpy where Kiril had dug in hard with his pen, and it made no mention of Anka at all. Still, she keeps running her purple fingers along its tortured back as she picks her way through the woods. She has no idea she's being watched as she rustles towards the hidden camp.

Who will Kiril be when she sees him again? The letter gave nothing away. She shouldn't hope that he suffered in the city, but she imagines him heavy and humbled with regret. She discards a knuckle-sized pine cone that's snuck into her basket and puts another berry in her mouth. Seeds crunch and fill her back teeth; she likes the challenge of picking them loose with her tongue. Maybe she should have fled again this summer, when she had the chance. If life was like this, just a cool breeze through sweet trees, tart juice on her tongue, then she might want it.

She could leave, she thinks, watching a fat caterpillar inch over a branch. It creeps onto her hand, over her raw nail beds, and tickles her skin with green fuzz. Soon, Margarita won't need her anymore. She could run now, and it would be nightfall before she's missed. Even the Captain no longer worries about letting her wander alone. For a month, illness drained him so weak he couldn't lift his head, and still, she stayed. Like a horse that no longer needs a fence, she's been domesticated. With Kiril's return, her invisible tether grows tighter.

Anka stops short by a cluster of glossy, black berries with flat, green leaves. She was very young when Yulia first taught her to avoid belladonna, and she has always wondered about the taste. She's heard the fruits are sweet, dangerous especially to children. It would be easy to secret some away in her pocket. She kneels, about to touch one bell-shaped flower, when a loud, animal huff startles her from beyond the trees.

In a clearing guarded by nightshade, she finds a donkey hitched to a cedar. He chews fallen needles outside a makeshift tent: over a soft bed of pine, someone has laid a woven mat and strung waxed cotton on a cord for shelter. Anka creeps in close to the remains of a fire, hemmed by stones and recently snuffed—the coals are still warm under a handful of dirt.

She peeks over her shoulder, then into the tent. Stored inside, she finds four leather saddle bags. The first contains a change of clothing: a folded shirt and pants, a woolen blanket. The second, some food and supplies for cooking. The third—a whetstone, oil, and a lumpy leather bundle. It clinks as Anka unrolls it over the ground and reveals a dozen sharp blades. One corner of the leather case is stained dark.

Gooseflesh rising on her arms, Anka tugs a dagger free of its rawhide loop. Its handle is hammered brass, and the point of the blade is dull, the tip broken somewhere long ago. The edges are still sharp, well cared-for and gleaming. Who wields this knife? She grips the handle and imagines how much larger its owner's hands might be. A trapper, who uses these blades to slash and dress their prey? A woods witch, flaying the tender flesh of her victims, catching her knives in hard bone? What stained the case that color? Not blackberry juice.

Across the clearing, the donkey brays. Anka goes still, her fingers tightening around the dagger's hilt. Nobody ever comes to Koprivci. She could stay and wait, hide among the leaves and see who this stranger is—but then what would she do, cornered until they left again? What would they do if they found her?

At her back, a branch snaps. A hooded crow caws, and the tree shakes loose a flock into the gusting wind. *Get out, get out*—the birds vanish with the beating of wings. Anka hooks the basket on her arm and flees. She loses her harvest as she runs, berries rolling on the ground.

She doesn't stop until she's passed the tree line—her pulse runs quick until she's in sight of the Captain's house. When she reaches for the door, at last she remembers the stranger's broken dagger. She still has it clutched tight in her hand.

THE SQUARE IS crowded. Kiril thinks he may have lost track of the days, that his neighbors are gathering for Sunday service, but nobody is going inside. A half-moon of people butts against the wide, flat steps of the church, pulled towards a lodestar he can't see. Their feet stir yellow dust into a low fog. He catches fluttering glimpses of their expressions, disgusted and afraid.

His horse parks herself in front of the first trough. She gives an irritable swat with her tail when he tries to urge her on, so he dismounts and hitches her in place. His spine clicks as he wrings out his traveler's hunch. Nobody looks interested in his arrival.

"Step back," someone is saying. "Really, there's no need to panic." Kiril recognizes the priest's nervous voice. Ivo is a tall, reedy man whose anxious habit of pulling at his beard has left him with a patchy brush of whiskers that trembles from the tip of his chin during sermons. Around him, the crowd is a frantic hive.

Kiril pushes to the front, ignoring the looks that land sourly on him, then turn confused as they try to place him. As rare as strangers are in Koprivci, rarer still are men who return once they've left. He steps around two women praying side by side, their faces tear-streaked and their hands clasped so hard that their chapped knuckles are turning white. A breeze curls something like dandelion fluff around them. The priest raises his voice; his wide black sleeves drape him like a bat when he lifts his hands. "Please," he cries, "we will resolve this calmly." But his long face is scrunched, and the large brown mole on his cheek quivers like an agitated housefly. A toothless old man turns from the scene in disgust, and through the gap he makes, Kiril sees that the stone steps are strewn with white and brown feathers. Unnaturally flattened onto its back, in a circle of down, lies a dead chicken.

The chicken's wings have been broken to stretch wide, as if it could soar. Someone has taken a blade to its breast. Its chest cracks open, ribs reaching for the sky like a parishioner's hands, splintered fingers of wet meat and bone. On the next step up, the bird's severed head has rolled onto its side, beak knocking against the stone. He can smell its uncooked flesh when he kneels to examine the carcass.

"She took its heart," a man says gruffly to the stern woman beside him. The woman squints. She covers her nose and mouth with her hand.

Kiril recognizes the man—a farmer often brought before the Captain for failing to repay personal debts. He gestures to the bird. "Was this one of yours?" he asks.

The farmer gives Kiril a sharp, searching look. He crosses his arms over his round chest. "Taken from my coop in the night," he says loudly.

How big could a chicken's heart be? Behind its opened ribs, the bird's insides have been slashed, and Kiril can make out a dark, empty space where he supposes it must belong.

"This seems like a poorly considered joke," he says, getting to his feet and brushing dust and white fluff from his knees. It's a futile gesture; he's covered head to toe with road dirt. He studies the farmer's petulant face. "What do you mean, *she* took its heart?"

"A baseless accusation," the priest interrupts. His black robe ripples down the steps and curtains the bird from view. "The Captain has already found the young widow innocent of any unnatural wrongdoing, and she has been under lock and key pending her release today. To assume that she had any-thing to do with this—"

"Kiril?" A hand touches his arm, and when he turns his head, the farmer takes the opening and elbows him aside. Margarita beams as she tugs Kiril away from the crush. "I thought that was you."

He is suddenly parched from the road, tastes the cracks in his lips. He tries to smile. "Hello, Margarita."

"Come on," she says.

He follows her through the forest of craning necks and into the sun-washed square. The shade of the church falls sharp and blue across the pavement. She pulls him along by one wrist.

"I wasn't sure it was you at first—you look different."

"I'm a bit taller," Kiril admits. He's grown broader as well, body changed bit by bit with every heavy load carried, every shovel of earth overturned. "You—" He hesitates, shielding his eyes from the glare. "You look as well as ever."

Memory is weak, a liar. Seeing her again catches him off guard: her soft-gloss hair, her cream-white neck. They were the last of the village children to grow up with friends their own age, before the bad streak of stillbirths and fevers: she and Anka, he and Simeon. They were always together, a quartet of sharp-elbowed brats with dirt-skinned knees. Then one day he happened by Margarita kneeling alone among the sweetgrass at the riverbed, watching the fish with a pile of freshwater roots in her apron. The sun was burning her neck. When she heard him coming, and turned, and smiled—he realized they were grown, and he'd been in love with her for a long time. He gave her his hat. By then, he was already too late.

To keep from staring, he looks instead around the bone-bleached square. The red flowers Simeon's mother keeps in the bakery's window box have shriveled. "When was the last time it rained?" he asks.

Margarita's nose wrinkles. "It's been a poor season. They're afraid. But the old woman up the hill thinks it will rain soon. Today, even."

They both look up, to where the sky is thin and empty.

"It doesn't look like rain."

"I don't want to talk about the weather," Margarita says, and embraces him. She's tucked a sprig of lavender behind her ear. Kiril makes himself let her go quickly, but she holds on to his arms and smiles at him with crushing goodness. "Did you just arrive?"

"You're the first person I've seen." Kiril casts back at the crowd and lowers his voice. "Margarita, what's happening here? I understand they're nervous about the harvest, but . . . they don't really mean witchcraft?"

Across the square, the squat, barred door of the jail swings open. The jailer holds it wide for a woman with dark hair. She walks into the sun like she's forgotten how, and Kiril recognizes her: the blacksmith's wife—now a widow, the priest said. The men in town had always watched her. She was an outsider, attractive, and they liked to follow the movement of her hips, liked trying to earn her laughter. Kiril never knew her well, but he can see that confinement has worn hard on her. She has no shoes, and a large, pregnant belly drags on her like an anchor.

"How long has she been in there?" he mutters.

"Almost four months. They said she corrupted men for the devil—married men." Margarita is watching the jailer with distaste. He bolts the door and walks away swinging his keys. "Your uncle was furious when he heard. He was ill, you see, for a long time. Anka thought of writing to you, in case he didn't recover, but she decided that you . . ."

"That a letter wouldn't find me in time," Kiril offers. An uncomfortable blush pinks Margarita's cheeks, and she nods. "How—how is Anka? If they're afraid of witchcraft—nobody's tried to hurt her, have they?"

"No. She kept to the house, mostly. She'll be so glad you're home, Kiril."

The pregnant woman squares her shoulders for a battle-field march. The crowd watches. The tavern keeper shoves her way to the front, and the witch's posture relaxes. Often, these two would stand gossiping and giggling behind the bar, forgetting to turn the spit until the meat charred. They were maids at each other's weddings, inseparable halves.

"And the Captain's recovered now?" He can't imagine his uncle bedridden, infirm.

Margarita doesn't answer. The widow opens her mouth to speak, and the tavern keeper slaps her hard across the face. The witch withers like a lightning-struck tree.

"Kiril," Margarita warns. She knows what he'll do before his feet start moving. But he can see how this first blow shakes the crowd loose: the farmer leans forward like a bull. His neighbors leer. Kiril breaks into a run.

Shame-drenched, the pregnant widow tries to step back, but bodies surround her. The earth rumbles. A thick hand yanks at her dress, ripping her sleeve at the socket. She looks up just in time to see the farmer charging to knock her off her feet.

Kiril is too late to break her fall. He catches the man's arm instead. The farmer wheels around, and Kiril slams a fist into his nose. A crunch, a yell—the man tries to punch back but swings wide and loses his balance. He hits the ground hard, sending up dust.

In the hush that follows, Kiril extends his hand to the pregnant woman. He can hear the wet whistling of the farmer's breath. There's blood on his knuckles, and the widow hesitates before she accepts. He hauls her to her feet as gently as he can.

"You're all going to leave her alone," he declares. He does his best imitation of his uncle's threatening boom.

"Is she your whore, too?" spits the farmer from the ground. He's swiping painfully at his bleeding nose. Already, it's blackening under the blood. "You're fucking the devil's bitch?"

"You're a fool," Kiril says.

The farmer curses him. "She starved my pigs! When we didn't burn her, she slaughtered my bird! And that little boy—"

"She hasn't done anything to your stock. You're a miserable farmer, and that's the end of it."

A few people snicker. The tension cracks, a hairline fissure through the ice.

"He misses that sow is all," another man shouts. "Best he could get, now that his wife's done with him."

Kiril regards the farmer's face. "That looks like a nasty break," he says, tapping his own nose. "I'll be opening a medical salon in the square soon. Come have it reset, if you like. I'll offer you a good price."

He holds out his arm to the witch. Grudgingly, the villagers make a path. Back at Margarita's side, one eye over his shoulder, Kiril lets the pregnant woman's elbow drop. Leaning in, he says, "I can walk you home, if you like."

"No. Thank you." She straightens her crooked dress. Up close, he sees the cloth is filthy, threadbare. Her hair is matted with dirt. She makes an awkward curtsy, then hurries off towards the smithy, disappearing between the apothecary and the butcher. Behind them, the priest appeals to better angels and tries to disperse the crowd.

"I'm not sure that was wise," Margarita says, but he can tell she's pleased.

"They can't do anything to me. They know who my uncle is."

Margarita lifts her eyebrows. "They could refuse to visit your salon. Or they might decide you're a witch, too—who knows what you've been off studying."

"Your father can't heal them all on his own. They'll come to me when they realize that."

"I suppose so." She rakes her hair behind her ear, and the lavender tumbles to her feet. "Listen, I was on my way to the bakery. Will you come? I know Simeon would love to see you."

Kiril almost winces when his name crosses her lips. It's like the farmer's punch has finally landed.

"Not today," he says. "I rode through the night. I need to sleep."

"Of course. Tomorrow, then?"

"Tomorrow."

The crowd thins, people breaking away in clusters of twos and threes, their heads knocked together. A tall, broad man plants himself at the top of the stairs: the Captain, powerful and steady beside the priest's quaking figure. Kiril is too far to make out his expression, but he raises a hand in greeting and thinks he sees his uncle nod in his direction.

The Captain guides the priest into the church by the shoulder, leaning in close. On the steps, the priest's wife wraps the dead chicken's remains in a rag and starts scrubbing feathers and flesh from the stone.

THE CAPTAIN'S HOUSE is empty when Kiril arrives. Inside, it smells like trapped sunlight, and the floors creak in the same places he remembers. A young shade of himself chases Anka down the halls, up the stairs. As children, they shrieked with laughter, crashing through doors. Later, it was fury, each of them after the other's blood.

At Anka's bedroom, he pauses. The door is open, and he looks for a while at the bed they shared as children, until the Captain decided they were too old and had a new frame built. When Kiril first started sleeping alone, just down the hall, he feared his new room's size, the way it swelled and filled with night. Now he has to bend his head to enter. The walls look tilted the wrong way.

He sets down his traveling bag and strips off his dusty clothes. At the sight of a real bed, the sleepless hours collapse into him. He finds a clean nightshirt under the pillow, where Yulia must have left it months ago. He falls asleep on top of the covers as soon as he pulls it over his head.

He wakes to the sound of rain on the windows. It's dark, and a ghost is standing at his bedroom door.

"Yulia told me to let you sleep," Anka says. She hovers just outside. She's wearing a pale gray dress, and her eyes are black in the blue evening. Her face has lost its roundness while he's been gone.

"It's rude to sneak up on people," Kiril says. He yawns into his palm and finds creases from the linens pressed into his cheek.

She takes a step over the threshold. "It's time to eat. I came to wake you for supper."

Kiril pushes himself up to sit, then to stand. The floorboards are cold. A basin and washcloths have appeared on the bedside table while he slept. Anka watches him like she's trying to spot the secret to a street magician's trick.

"I didn't know if you'd come back," she says.

"Didn't I promise I would?"

When he hugged her goodbye a year ago, she stood with her arms limp and refused to look him in the eye. There was still paint from the windowsill stuck under her nails. *Just push me out, then.* This time, when he offers his embrace, she rushes to him. She winds his shirt around her fingers and holds on. Her head tucks under his chin.

After a while, she says, "You smell terrible. And you snored all day."

He laughs into her hair. "I had a long ride."

"I left you some water. Yulia had me bring it earlier. It'll be cold by now."

"It'll do."

Anka waits in the hall while he washes and changes his clothes. The water is soft with rose oil. It's strange, after so much time spent fighting with two dozen other boys for the first turn at the washtub, before the water turned vile and brown. He smells so delicate when he's done.

Kiril unearths two parcels from his bag and follows Anka downstairs. In the dining room, Yulia has already laid out their plates, and the Captain is lighting the candles for dinner. It's his favorite ritual. He crouches by the burning grate and lifts a flame from the logs with a spill, then carries it behind a cupped palm to the table. Anka stops in the doorway to watch.

Margarita's mention of illness hasn't prepared Kiril. He couldn't tell from a distance, but by the light of the fire, shadows dig hard into his uncle's face. His deep-set eyes have hollowed, and his hawkish nose has grown more prominent as his cheeks and beard have thinned. His once-taut clothes slouch from his frame.

Even so, he cuts an imposing figure. The long spill is a needle in his hand. Bent over the candlesticks, he handles it like a delicate, precious thing. The Captain watches the flame with pleasure, and the fire, in return, lights him like a lover's presence. It flares to the wick and flashes warm in his eyes. Kiril has never seen him look at anything as tenderly as burning candles, except perhaps Anka.

Like the rest of the house, the dining room is unchanged. One long table runs the length of the room, a full eight chairs around it, though it's hardly ever more than the three of them eating here, sometimes four if the priest has business to discuss. The fireplace dominates one wall, and above it hangs an oval-framed portrait of a woman with Anka's brown hair, large eyes, and lightly upturned nose.

"Hello, Mama," Anka mumbles as she passes the picture on her way to her seat at the table. "Hello, Uncle."

He smiles. "Good evening, little bird." He blows out the glowing tip of the spill and plants it in its tall vase on the mantel. Then he pulls Anka's chair out for her. Once she's seated, he offers his hand to Kiril. "Welcome home," he says.

There's a thick strip of scar tissue across the Captain's palm, an injury from his youth; Kiril can feel it when they shake. His uncle's grip is solid, and its assurance relaxes him. "Well met. I'm glad to see you up and about, Uncle—I heard you've been ill."

"It nearly killed me," the Captain says grimly, taking his seat and gesturing for Kiril to do the same. "Perhaps Yulia wishes it had. There would be a lot less work for her to do without me here causing trouble, wouldn't there?"

"Not at all, Captain," says the housekeeper. She sets a jug of wine and a large loaf of bread on the table, then disappears back to the kitchen. She's served the Captain's house for almost fifteen years, raised Kiril and Anka from children, and yet Kiril often feels he knows nothing about her. She is a curiously invisible woman: so thin she could disappear into a harsh ray of sunlight, her hair almost white though her pale face is unlined, a smoothness to it like the perfect drops that harden at the base of used candles.

Outside, the rain has turned to a steady downpour. Kiril watches his uncle's large hands tear the bread to pieces, setting one on Anka's plate and one on his own. The Captain has firm fingers with square nails, sharp corners that would catch in Kiril's shirt collars when he was younger.

"I brought you something," Kiril says, and holds out a package to each of them. "Just small things—from the city."

The Captain's mouth smiles. "I didn't expect much left over from the money I gave you." He brushes flour from his hands and takes the gift.

Kiril straightens his shoulders and begins to pour the wine. "I found a position with a surgeon soon after I arrived. He paid me well—and truthfully, I learned more from him than from the university. Go on, open them."

Anka pulls loose the string and unwinds the newspaper. A silver hair comb tumbles onto the table. Engraved roses spill over its crown. Bursting up through the field of flowers, a bird takes flight. Its tail feathers melt into the comb's sharp teeth. She picks it up and stares at it in her hand.

"It reminded me of the story," Kiril prompts. "The girl who forgets to bring gifts to the witch. I know it's your favorite. I'm sorry I missed your birthday."

The Captain peers over the wine jug. "A little bird for our little bird."

Anka turns the comb over between her fingers. "Thank you," she says finally. She straightens her shoulders against the rigid back of her chair. "It's beautiful. It will be perfect to wear at Margarita's wedding."

Kiril has just picked up his wineglass, and he sets it back down again. "Her wedding?" he says. "Is she . . . to Simeon?"

"They agreed upon it just this week," Anka says. "You know her father wanted her to marry into another village, but he never could find a suitor. After all this time, he relented— just a few days before you came home."

The Captain takes the comb from Anka and examines it. "Finely wrought," he notes. "You'll need to be careful with this, Anka. It's quite sharp. Here." He tilts her chin towards him and fixes the comb in her hair.

"It looks lovely," Kiril says, feeling hollow.

"Everything looks lovely on a lovely girl," says the Captain.

Kiril nudges the second parcel. "Uncle, open your gift."

The Captain tears off the smudged newsprint. "What is this?" he asks. It resembles a squat bottle, but its shell is metal instead of glass.

"A new invention, quite remarkable—here." Kiril reaches over and flicks a metal lever on the bottle's side. There's a click. With a hiss, a flame blossoms from its throat. "A fire lighter—you don't need a grate already burning to use it. It's built around a flintlock, like a rifle."

The Captain tests the lever himself. Twice, the flame blooms and then dies at once when he releases the button. "Almost too simple," he says, with a small laugh.

Kiril clears his throat. "I thought you would find it amusing."

Anka's smile is limp with pity. The Captain sets the lighter aside. "It wasn't too costly an amusement, I hope."

"No, no." Kiril gathers the loose newspaper from the table and crumples it. He tosses the ball into the grate.

Yulia comes in with a large clay tureen of stewed meat and lentils balanced between her arms. "Your favorite mutton," she says. "To welcome you home."

"I went looking for berries today, for the sauce," Anka says. "But it was too late in the season."

Kiril catches Yulia's hand and kisses her cool knuckles. She gives his fingers a maternal squeeze, then ladles food onto their plates. She retreats to her post by the dining room door.

For a while, they eat without speaking, the only sounds the crackle of the fire and their spoons against the plates. That must have been why Margarita wanted him to go with her to the bakery, Kiril thinks—so she and Simeon could tell him about their engagement together.

"It was quite a scene in the square this morning," he says.

The Captain drains his wine and refills it from the jug. "The villagers are very angry to see the widow released. She was arrested while I was ill. Ivo thought it best, for her own protection. He tells me somebody tried to burn down her husband's shop. Lucky they failed, or the whole town could have gone up."

"Does the priest know who did it?"

"One of her accusers, he thinks; there were three of them. But he has no proof."

Kiril soaks a piece of bread in juice from the mutton. "That farmer, the angry one. He accused her?"

"He was the third of them." The Captain points at Kiril with a forkful of meat. "What you did was rash."

"He presented a danger to those around him."

His uncle's lip twitches. "That may be," he says, "but you must realize that the people here will look on you differently now. You're a stranger to them."

"I've hardly been gone a year."

"You left—that's what matters."

I think I'm different now—wasn't that what he'd said? Different from the boy who arrived in the city, different from the boy he was at home. Just a week ago, he'd been proud of it.

Cheeks warm, Kiril says, "Who do you think killed that chicken?"

The Captain grimaces. "Maybe somebody trying to hurt the widow on the day of her release. Maybe even the farmer himself. Do I believe it was witchcraft? No. But it's not hard to see how a simple mind could look at such a woman, such a deed, and a strange apparition in the sky—and then decide they must be linked somehow."

"You saw it here as well, then?" Kiril says eagerly. "I watched it from the road. I have a friend in the city who studies these things. He explores all manner of astronomical phenomena—a serious man of science, not at all like our old women divining fortunes by the shapes of clouds."

Anka pushes her plate away. She's barely eaten anything.

"Did he have a name for this apparition?" asks the Captain.

"A comet." Kiril sketches an ellipse with his spoon: "Different from a star—it circles the sun at tremendous distance, over hundreds of years. I admit I haven't retained much of what he said, but he showed me his writings. He was calculating its path."

"Maybe you'd remember better if you could read them," Anka suggests.

The rain rolls against the windows. She tears off a piece of bread and squishes its soft insides between her fingers, watching him closely. She's still angry, then. Or angry now that he's come back changed, better for having been gone.

The Captain snorts into his wine. "Our little bird has been sharpening her beak."

"Indeed," Kiril says. His collar is hot. "She seems to have grown quite a bit since I left." He glances at the portrait above the mantel. The painting is far too small for the wall that it occupies, but Kiril can't remember ever seeing anything else in this place of honor in his uncle's house. She is the Captain's vision for what Anka will one day become: a replacement for the woman he couldn't have while she was alive.

Lightly, Kiril says, "She looks more like her mother than ever."

Anka drops her bread. A cruel, familiar feeling runs through him. It's calming, like a cool cloth on a fresh burn. He takes a drink of wine. "I mean to say," he tells the Captain, not looking in Anka's direction, "that if she still has not achieved menarche at sixteen, perhaps she should undergo another examination."

The Captain tips his head, tracing the rim of his cup with his thumb. "Anka would tell me at once if she were ready for us to marry. We all have our obligations."

"Yes, Uncle," Anka says. She bows her head. The silver comb glitters in the candlelight.

"We don't have a midwife anymore," the Captain ponders. "She passed last winter. What did your physician's training teach you in this matter?"

"I learned about birthing," Kiril says, "but little about this. Some men who stayed at the university longer could choose to specialize in this area, but few of them did."

Yulia refills the Captain's wine. "There is the old woman on the hill," she says. "She was midwife to her people, once. I believe she has even tended to our women from time to time. I could take Anka to see her tomorrow."

Anka bites her thumbnail, watching Kiril between the burning candles. They've practiced this dance before: twist your ankle, keep going, wrench your partner's wrist. Perhaps nothing has changed after all. He drinks.

"Fine," the Captain says. "Very well. Yulia, you will take her in the morning. See what the old woman can divine about our girl."

He tips his cup to Anka, finishes the wine in two swallows, and rises from his chair. He gives her neck a pinch by way of bidding her good night, then leaves the dining room without saying anything more.

Anka goes out soon after, her shoulders rigid and her eyes on the ground. She disappears into the hall and slams the door.

"She's angry with me," Kiril observes to Yulia, who is collecting the plates.

Yulia takes her time before responding. Conversations with her often stretch long with silence. People who meet her sometimes think she's simple, but Kiril knows it isn't true. Words take longer to reach her, but she's as sharp as any woman once they do. "I believe she's been lonely with you gone," she says.

I was lonely, too, Kiril thinks bitterly, but it feels wrong to say. Was he lonely? He thinks of Hasan, suggesting that he stay. He imagines his friend alone on the wall with his spyglass and his notes. He feels sure he knows exactly where Hasan is at this moment, and at the same time, it's impossible that such a person exists at all.

Yulia balances their plates on her arm, and Kiril holds the door to the kitchen open for her. She wishes him good night. He lets the door close, then crosses the dining room to the west stairs.

In the unlit hallway, he doesn't see her coming. When the door shuts behind him, Anka lunges forward and smacks him hard across the face.

His cheek buzzes with the imprint of her palm. A thread stretches between them, the humming strand of a spider's web. Bells ring in his ears. Anka raises her arm to strike him again, but now his eyes have adjusted, and he sees. He catches her blow before it lands.

"Let go," she hisses, but he holds her fast. "Do you have any idea what you've done?"

"*You* did it," Kiril growls. He hears their uncle in his voice, more real than his weak imitation this morning. It makes him feel stronger.

Anka's left arm is still free. She swings, and her fingernails dig into the skin of his neck. Kiril curses and grabs at her. He holds her by both wrists. For the harvest, the villagers gather and watch farmers string up pigs like this, for bleeding.

"Did you plan it?" he demands. "Did you decide, the two of you, before I got back—you'd reject my gifts, tell jokes about—" He can't even say it, shame hot in his throat. "Did you sit here, the two of you, and gossip about how the idiot boy went off to study, how you'd teach him not to be so proud when he came home?"

"I never talk to him if I can help it," Anka snaps. "I never want anything to do with him." She tries to free herself, but he holds tight.

"He *loves* you." It hurts to say it. His own voice sounds pathetic, starved. "Don't you understand that? He even respects you. I've never—"

Anka wrenches her head to the side and bites his hand. The pain startles him—it's enough for her to pull away. She runs for the stairs. Kiril throws himself after her, grabbing for her skirts, and she trips. She breaks her fall against the second step. He pins her down, wrestling her around so they're face-to-face. Her head knocks loudly against the lip of the stair and she yelps. For a moment, they both listen, but no footsteps come. Yulia must be back in the kitchen by now, and their uncle is off in his rooms, in the other wing of the house.

Anka is breathing hard. She doesn't look afraid.

"If I scream," she whispers, "he'll come running. He'll kill you."

Kiril's anger makes him shaky. He hears the echo of his uncle's laughter, and his hold on himself grows brittle, self-control slipping from the tips of his fingers.

Anka sucks in her cheeks and spits in his face. The moment shatters. Kiril smacks her across the jaw and grabs her by the neck. The skin of her throat is damp with sweat. Small cartilage pearls grind together under his hands.

He can hear the rain thrashing against the windows and walls, but inside his head, the ringing stops. The silence lifts a weight from his chest. Kiril's shoulders burn and his knees dig painfully into the stairs. Anka's eyes fall shut.

His arms tremble. His nose is close to hers, the bite on his hand throbbing. He hisses: "The old woman can march you naked through the streets, for all I care. You deserve what you get." His fingers spasm tighter. Then he lets go.

Anka's body bows, gasping for air. Kiril falls back onto his heels, hands at his sides. His fingers tingle like he's just come in from the cold.

Anka scrambles backwards up the stairs. In the dark, he can't make sense of her expression. Her slipper falls from her foot as she stumbles away, and she leaves it behind. He doesn't try to chase her. He runs his shaking hands through his hair and rubs his face, the still-warm place where she struck him, spittle on his cheek. Overhead, he hears a door slam shut, and the click of the tightening lock.

two

W HAT ANKA FEARS is blood. Not all blood—she would have liked to see the chicken in the village square that morning, but Yulia forbade her to go looking, chiding: *Whatever it is, you don't get involved*. The villagers are already suspicious of her. But it's not them that Anka worries about most times, even when they glare as she passes. Blood, her own: not from a poorly placed needle or a cut from a kitchen knife; not the blood of an accident, quick with excitement. What scares her is the wound in her that never heals, that opens with cruel regularity, staining her bedsheets and clothes. The month grows old, and some invisible hand forces its way into her body to squeeze her insides in an angry fist, twist her guts through its fingers, leave her sore and bleeding between the legs. At dinner, under the Captain's watchful eye, Anka bites the inside of her cheek to hide the pain.

When it first began, Yulia helped her chart the days on a scrap of muslin disguised as a sampler, dotted with small flowers. They found the rhythm unflinching. Some women never have such certainty, Yulia told her. Margarita sometimes goes entire seasons without a single red spot. Yulia herself hasn't bled in years, though she hardly looks that old. But Anka's body is a perfect, diligent clock.

Even knowing this, she is cautious. For days before and days after, she wears a leather belt under her clothes, a sling for a woolen pad that soaks up the spill. The straps rub her hips raw. In her nightmares, the pad flips like an upturned boat, the pins that hold it prick her thighs, and the day's blood smears her skirt, seeps into the cloth of her dress, paints her skin and hair. If the Captain catches even a glimpse of it, he'll know. She can't imagine his anger at being so deceived. Whenever she sits with him for dinner, Anka's body tells her anxious lies: she feels a red wetness sliding down her legs, pooling in the seat of her chair. She'll be soaked when she stands. When Kiril knocks her down in the hallway, she's sure that he'll smell it. Any moment, he'll rip up her dress, and he'll call for the Captain.

Once, when she was young, Anka fell into the frozen lake at winter. They were sliding gleefully over the ice when a thin patch cracked beneath her feet with a sound like ripping cloth, and she dropped into the cold below. The water crushed the air from her lungs. The world sealed itself against her: above her was hard ice, above her was black water. She was lost inches from home, thrashing against a locked door.

Was that how the demons felt? Clawing at the walls of the world, desperate to cross? The movement between was jarring, the passage painful and cold, something they couldn't possibly survive. Even when her hands dug into the grit of the far shore and she coughed up her burning lungs, some piece of her was left behind.

It was Kiril who pulled her out. He broke through the ice with a rock and dove in to save her while Margarita was still looking for a strong branch. He dragged her onto the frosty lip of the lake and wrapped her in his coat, held her while she cried and shook and Simeon ran for help. Her gulping breaths rose in desperate white mist around them, and she was safe. He saved her. He loved her. The memory returns to her at the strangest times.

Anka is floating underwater, in a dark world split from her own by thinnest ice. It sounds like hard rain against glass. Her lungs are empty. Kiril leans over her, and he looks like the Captain.

"You deserve whatever you get," he spits, and his voice reaches her from far away.

When she surfaces, her head is still swimming, and her hem is below her knees. Her vision clears, and she realizes it had begun to go black. The stolen dagger is heavy in her pocket, but she never reached for it. She pulls herself up by the railing, and Kiril watches her stagger to her feet, watches her trip up the stairs. One shoe slips off her foot, but she doesn't stop to pick it up.

At the top of the stairs, her bedroom door crashes open. She fumbles the key in the lock until it clicks. Giddiness bubbles in her chest.

"Anka."

Kiril sounds wounded. She pictures him leaning his forehead against the door, holding his wet, battle-torn insides with both hands.

"Anka, open the door."

There's a slapping noise: not his knuckles knocking, but the flat leather sole of her abandoned slipper. The pause is full of splinters: her ice-burnt lungs reinflating, the softening of her spiked pulse. Anka presses her fingers to his handprint through the door and closes her eyes. He really has come home. The strings to pull, the tender spots where she can dig—those are still the same.

He knocks again, less certain. Anka stays quiet with the crumpled in-and-out of her breath. She wants to laugh and cry all at once. Instead, she touches her hand to her throat and squeezes, just enough for it to shine. Somewhere in her, a hidden lock clicks.

In the hall, Kiril drops her shoe to the floor with a soft thump. His footsteps drag away.

Anka leans her back against the door. Yulia has lit a fire in the grate. The sparks crackle in her skin; she floats. She feels the pressure of the marks on her neck, the ridges of the stairs that ladder up her spine, and a crab-apple bruise ripening on her thigh where she fell on the dagger's hilt. She wrapped the blade before putting it in her pocket, but the pommel dug in when Kiril pushed her down.

Carefully, she unlaces her dress and unpins the heavy wool rag between her legs. She hides it in a chamber pot pushed beneath the far corner of her bed, and finds a new pad folded into the sheets by her pillow. She stows the dagger in her wardrobe, behind her summer dresses.

Yulia has laid a coal pan in the bed for the brisk night. Under the covers, the darkness is orange and warm. Anka squeezes her eyes shut and sucks a bruised finger into her mouth. In the curves of her nails, she can taste the blood where she clawed at Kiril's neck. She breathes deep, until the air under the blankets runs out, and she has to unwrap herself to the chill of the room.

They'll reconcile tomorrow. They always do. Maybe she'll be in the kitchen, helping Yulia with dinner, and he'll come and ask for a cup of water and she'll pour it for him, and when the cup passes from hand to hand, that will be enough. Or he'll find her in the parlor while she's bent over her needlework, and he'll kneel by her feet and bow his head into her lap and ask for forgiveness in the loudest whisper he can muster, and she'll touch his crown with her hand to say, *Of course*, and for a while after, he'll stay like that, like he's praying into the folds of her skirt.

It won't take long. Kiril is quick to anger, but desperate for love. She has always understood him, how he works. She still does.

When she falls asleep, her fingertips still wet between her lips, it's with one bright thought in her: when she's ready, if there's no escape, she can make him drown her for good.

THE OLD WOMAN who Yulia knows lives up the hill and by the stream, a walk that takes most of an hour. Yulia wakes Anka early, rapping impatiently on the locked door. When Anka goes out, a thick shawl hiding the ring of bruises around her neck, she finds her abandoned slipper on the ground where Kiril dropped it. His own door is open, room empty, the twisted bedsheets the only sign that he ever came home at all.

The shawl quickly becomes too heavy as they climb the hill, even as their breath clouds the morning. Sweat gathers at her collar and under her bodice.

"You needn't worry," Yulia says. "You're angry with your

cousin, I understand—but Minka won't hurt you, and she won't expose you. Our coming here is just for show."

"The last one didn't hurt me, either," Anka says, remembering the late midwife's clawed fingers pinching at the flesh of her belly and thighs, prodding her breasts, examining where her body grew hair, all while the Captain's shadow pressed against the flimsy curtain the old woman had drawn across the room. She tugs her shawl tighter. "I mean, not really."

Yulia doesn't answer, but Yulia often doesn't answer. She shifts the basket she's carrying from one arm to the other, and pats a loose lock of pale hair behind her ear. The narrow footpath through the grass meets a beaten road, seldom traveled and overgrown. A cluster of houses slump tiredly against one another. Out front, green moss paints the sides of a broken horse cart. The serrated leaves of nettles twist through the spokes of its wheels.

Anka has never been this far up the hill, but she knows that the people who once lived here have all been dead a long time, since before she was born. The villagers sometimes talk about the ghosts. As children, they would play a game to see who would dare go farthest up the slope, but they never made it too close before a snap of wind or a wolf's howl sent them scrambling back.

"Not all of them died," Yulia says, when she asks. "Most left. Some to the war, some to escape it. They were nomads to begin with."

"Then why is the old woman still here?"

Yulia lifts her skirt to step over the shell of a thick tree lying across the path, blackened with age. "That's her business. You can ask her yourself, if you like. Here, boy!"

A dog dozing on the slanted porch of an empty house lifts his head and regards them suspiciously. "Suit yourself, then," Yulia says, but after a moment, he stretches his bones and trots after them towards the stream.

The old woman's house is better kept than its neighbors. Nothing tilts or sags. It stands so close to the water that it was built on stilts, which after the long, dry summer are exposed and feathered with flakes of white mushrooms, like a chicken's legs. The ground has greedily drunk last night's storm, leaving just a few puddles behind. The dog overtakes them, splashing through a wagon rut, and darts up the steps to the front door, letting out a bark of greeting.

Despite Yulia's promises, Anka's heart seizes as the door opens. But the woman on the other side isn't what she expected. There's nothing of the dead midwife's animus in her. She's very old, and shorter than Anka by a full head. Her face is brown and wrinkled like a walnut, and her gray hair falls long to her waist.

And she isn't alone in the little hut. Before the midwife can greet them, Margarita steps through the door, blushing. She tucks a bundle of leaves into her basket. "I'll leave you to your next guests, then," she says. The old woman squeezes her smooth hand between two rough palms. "I'm sorry to have called on you so early."

"You're always welcome here," the old woman says. She shows Yulia and Anka a smile punctured by missing teeth. "Come in, come in. I thought I might see you today."

The dog noses ahead. As they pass each other, Anka grabs at Margarita's arm inquiringly. "You didn't tell me you knew her," she whispers. Hurt, shut out.

"You've left me alone too long," the old woman is saying to Yulia, cupping her face and kissing her cheeks.

"Later," Margarita promises. She squeezes Anka's hand. "Come by the shop after. Simeon was going to find Kiril, to talk with him about the wedding."

From inside the house, Yulia calls Anka's name. "The Captain wanted the girl looked at," she's explaining. "Anka, come and introduce yourself to Minka."

Anka mumbles hello as she adjusts her shawl, and Minka seems to sense that she does not want to be embraced. She gestures them towards the table and shuts the door.

The stilted cottage is just one room. The dog walks three times around a small rug by the fireplace and settles down to sleep. The opposite wall is dominated by a cabinet with glass doors. Inside, a hundred glass vials stand neatly arranged on deep shelves. Where there is space on the walls, drying herbs hang from wooden pegs. It looks remarkably like the apothecary, except for the bed pushed into the far corner and the curious chair set beside it, whose seat is a half smile, hardly enough room for a woman to perch. *For birthing*, Anka realizes, and feels a little faint. Beside the birthing chair, on top of an old trunk, sits a cloth model of a nude woman's torso, with two stumps of thigh and a painted pink hole between them. Arrayed beside the practice body are a range of cloth dolls, practice babies in different sizes.

Neck hot, wool itchy, Anka turns to the midwife. "What's the smallest you've seen survive?"

Minka points to the second doll. "He lived well until the war. He left with your uncle and father but didn't have the good luck to come back. They said his lungs gave out climbing a mountain."

"You knew my father?" Anka asks. The Captain never speaks of him. What little she knows of him comes from the baker's wife: that he shaped and fired her favorite earthenware guvech, that he had a fondness for the cats she kept to chase mice from the sacks of grain.

"Not terribly well," Minka says. "He was quiet, and dedicated to his craft. Skilled. He made this, as a matter of fact." She points to a mortar and pestle on the table. A pattern of yellow and green waves glaze the sides of the bowl. Anka picks it up and feels the ripples under her fingertips, smooth and cool.

Yulia sheds her coat onto a peg by the door, then takes a seat at the table. It is spread with plants that Anka doesn't know. With deft hands, the housekeeper takes up a spool of thread and starts cutting even lengths with the paring knife from her apron.

"Please," Minka says, "sit down." She carefully takes the bowl from Anka's trembling hands. "Tell me why you've come."

"The Captain started talking of having her examined again last night," Yulia says, measuring a length of twine between her thumb and forefinger. "I thought it best to bring her here."

Minka hmphs. She fishes a pipe from inside her dress and lights it at the grate. "He doesn't know yet that you bleed? Don't worry, I can't tell by sight—" She exhales smoke and gestures to Yulia. "I've known for some time."

"You told her?" Anka asks.

Minka clucks her tongue. "She likes her gossip, that's true

enough." She pats Yulia's hand, and Yulia swats at her with a bundle of weeds. "But she didn't speak of this loosely—she only warned me you might need my help someday. If your uncle doesn't know yet, you must be adept at hiding."

Anka shifts in her chair. A crooked pin presses into her thigh. "Yulia helps me," she says. "She gives me rags to soak it up and takes the dirty ones away. But I'm always afraid that it'll show through, and he'll find out." She feels suddenly very small. "And it *hurts*."

"I can give you something to chew on for the pain," Minka says, going to the glass cabinet. "And maybe—aha." She opens a drawer and lifts out what looks like a pair of large, yellow cherries dangling from strings. "Sponges," she says. "Picked from the sea. A man I know brings them when he passes through."

Anka touches one, testing its stiff, porous edge between her thumb and forefinger. It's big enough to fill her cupped palm.

"They'll soften up when you soak them in water. Wring one out, and—" Minka makes a circle with her fingers and mimes pressing the sponge into a slim canal with the other hand. She makes a popping noise with her mouth. "Up it goes, and let the string hang free. It'll catch whatever you bleed before it gets out of you. Midday, you change it out." She raps the tabletop near the second cherry with a stubby yellow nail. "Careful not to make a mess; they can drip when they're full. Best take off your skirts and do it over a pot."

"It just . . . stays? It won't fall out?"

"It stays. When you need to remove it, use the string." Minka jerks lightly on one string and the sponge dances across the table. "Yulia can tend to them same as she does with your rags."

Anka rolls the sponges into her pocket. She nibbles at her cheek. "Can you make it stop? I've heard of you in the village—they say you're a witch."

"Anka," Yulia says warningly, but Minka only grins around the stem of her pipe.

"Whenever something goes wrong, they come and knock on my door," she agrees. "But now I hear they've found themselves a new witch. Listen, my girl: I can keep a man's seed from quickening. I can purge a womb once it's filled. And our Yulia here, she knows everything there is to know about poison—"

"Poison?" Anka says.

"Oh, yes. But that's medicine, not spellcraft. I can't stop your bleeding."

"Even if you could, he won't wait forever," Yulia says. She sets aside the last bundle of herbs. "We can tell him she needs more time, but someday that won't be enough. He's growing anxious to have her as a wife."

Minka nods. "Then maybe the best thing would be to leave. Steal away in the night."

"No," Anka says.

"It's not easy; I don't mean to say it is. But if you can't stay—"

"I've tried it before."

The first time, she made it barely a mile from home before she got lost in the woods; the searchers found her asleep in a raspberry thicket at dawn. Four months later, she tried again—a whole day and night gone, and this time, she was following a well-worn road down the hillside. When they caught her and brought her back, the Captain sent her away with Yulia to bathe, and the house was quiet for half an hour. Anka was fixing her apron when she heard a scream, and Yulia's footsteps running down the hall. In the parlor, they found Kiril on his knees, his arm hanging loose and wrong from the shoulder. The Captain lowered himself into a chair and opened a book. "The good wine tonight, Yulia," he said, as though Kiril weren't wheezing at his feet. He turned a page. "We should toast Anka's return."

"He always brings me back," Anka says. "I should have gone this summer, while he couldn't leave his bed, but—" *I was afraid of what he'd do, I was afraid of the villagers.* "I was afraid he would die."

Minka sighs and taps the ash from her pipe.

"Tell us what you do want," she says, not unkindly.

Anka imagines the dagger in her hand again, its broken tip pressed to her chest. She couldn't even cut through her bodice. What does she want?

For Kiril to kill me so I don't have to do it myself.

She closes her fist around the yellow sponge in her apron pocket and chews at her lip. "I don't know," she says finally.

The dog huffs a sneeze and tilts his head back to look at her, tongue lolling. The old woman smiles sadly. "Then the best we can do is buy you time," she says. "I hope we can buy you enough."

KIRIL FINDS THE key to his father's shop in the bottom of the Captain's desk. He goes digging while the house is still asleep:

46

the doors all shut, the floors too loud, the books in the study quiet. The drawer is empty but for the key and the bottle-shaped lighter, rolling loose on its side.

He has avoided the shop in the village square since he was a boy, turning his eyes from the green shutters whenever he passed, never looking down the path that branched from the narrow alley to an abandoned cottage in the woods. He remembers the shop as his mother and father ran it: a neat storefront with a large window, where a pretty red dress and a smart blue traveling cloak looked onto the street outside, while his parents spent most of their time at the table in the back, snipping and stitching with mouthfuls of pins, light falling golden across their work. That would be a good place for an examination room, he thinks: a curtain for his patients' privacy, two comfortable chairs, an armoire for his tinctures and tools. The shop is his by right. It does no good sitting empty.

This morning, the paving stones in the village square are puddled with blue-white splashes of clear sky and cloud. Smoke rises from the bakery's thick chimney, but everything else is still. When he turns the key in the lock, the swollen door protests to wake the dead.

Kiril's first step over the threshold is muffled by a carpet of dust. His eyes adjust to the shop's dim insides, and he sees that he isn't the first person to enter since the door was locked: footprints creep under the windows, and scavengers have left scrapes along the sill where they forced their way in. Behind the counter, the bolts of fabric that once filled the wall have dwindled to just a few, and the shelves are occupied instead by cobwebs and the husks of dead insects. The dress and the traveling cloak are long gone. The thieves have left behind a thin roll of uncolored muslin, at least, that he might have Yulia boil and cut for bandages.

He's pleased to find the windows unbroken, though the bottom sash won't stay when he hoists it up; he has to hold it overhead while he pushes the shutters out. They squeal miserably.

He pauses, blinking into the sun. Across the square, he sees the pregnant widow sneaking between the houses. She's wearing a different dress, one not torn and muddied with shit, and she's managed to unknot the tangle of her hair. It's hard to tell how far along she is, given her malnourished frame, but the baby can't be far off. She steps timidly, looking often over her shoulder. She doesn't notice him inside the shop.

A cheerful voice startles him: "So we'll be neighbors soon!"

The window sash slips and knocks Kiril hard on the back of the head. A splinter tears deep into his palm.

"Shit!"

"Sorry." Simeon grins. "I didn't mean to scare you. Good morning."

Eyes watering, Kiril fumbles for the black leather bag he dropped on the counter, with the few supplies he brought from the city. "Morning," he grumbles.

He had expected this. Simeon was bound to come after him before long. He'll want some assurance that they can be like brothers again, that his marriage to Margarita won't change anything, and so on. Kiril just didn't think the bastard would be so quick about it.

"We didn't know when you'd come home," Simeon says, leaning in the doorway. Kiril digs a long needle and a bottle of strong alcohol from the leather bag, then squints at his palm. He wets a clean rag and rubs at the skin; the splinter is rigid and black. "That's interesting," Simeon observes.

"Antiseptic surgery," Kiril mutters, wiping the needle down. "It's the latest fashion." He digs in after the splinter and hisses.

Anyone else would have excused themselves, come back at a better time, but Simeon seems content to wait while Kiril digs the vile thing out of his flesh, a whole minute of dusty silence punctuated by frustrated cursing. His gaze travels the run-down shop front.

"Not quite ready for customers yet, is it," he says. "You should oil those hinges. I heard you come in all the way back by the ovens."

"It needs work," Kiril agrees. He shucks the splinter onto the floor and wipes his hands down again. There's no blood, but the back of his skull smarts. He rubs his head bitterly, then reluctantly extends a hand for Simeon to shake.

Simeon ignores it, of course. He steps forward and wraps Kiril in a warm embrace instead, kissing him on both cheeks. He's still no taller than Anka, but like Kiril, he's grown broader in the chest. His pale head smells of leaven, flour, and smoke.

"You never did say goodbye," Simeon says. His smile is soft, boyish, so different from the leering grin Kiril has imagined over and over again in his time away. Sadness pinches his brows. "Did you think we wouldn't want to see you? Margarita was terribly upset. We're both so glad you're back." He claps Kiril on the arm, then holds out a warm loaf in a white napkin. "Here," he says. "Have you eaten?"

Kiril hadn't wanted to trouble Yulia so early. "Not much," he admits.

He'd hoped they would miss him. A guilty thrill goes up his spine at the thought of Margarita weeping in his absence.

He sets the bread on the dusty countertop. "I'm afraid you're right—I'm not ready for company just yet."

Simeon holds up his hands. "I won't keep you long. Try the bread—I've been experimenting with a different process. Lena and Iliya have been giving me the leavings from their beer."

"I look forward to it."

"My father is skeptical, but my mother and Katia like it much better than the old way. Listen, though, that's not the only reason I came by. Margarita and I—"

"You're hurt," Kiril interrupts. There's a gray bandage wrapped around Simeon's left forearm. "What happened?"

"What? Oh—just a burn. It's on the mend now."

"Let me take a look," Kiril says, going to his bag again, eager for a different topic, for a patient, but Simeon pulls his sleeve down over the bandage.

"Really, it's not necessary. Margarita's father fixed it up last week. The next time, though—" He looks around the dismal shop front. "Well, I'm sure you'll have a proper salon by then, and I'll come right to you." He smiles ruefully. "There is always a next time. It's good you've decided to do this, Kiril. I think your practice here will be a great help to the village."

He is always so insufferably kind. Irritated, Kiril unwraps the bread.

"You came to tell me something," he says. "I suppose it's about your wedding? Anka let the news slip last night."

Anka—has she woken yet? Left her room? The door was still shut tight when he left, turned to him like an unfriendly back. The anger he felt last night has soured in his throat; he had to stop himself from knocking to wake her on his way out.

"We thought she might. I suppose she told you she's to be Margarita's maid as well?"

"I assumed. Who else would it be?" Kiril's stomach rumbles and he tears a chunk of bread off the loaf. "This is good," he says through a beery mouthful, and Simeon beams.

"It couldn't be anyone but Anka," he agrees. He hesitates. "Would you join us, Kiril? Be my best man?"

A few days before he left for the city, Kiril went to the apothecary late in the evening. He was to deliver some herbs that Yulia had promised Margarita's father. The shop windows were shuttered, but the door had been left unlatched. In his memory, Kiril didn't even touch the handle: the door opened as though beckoning him into a trap, the bell a distant shimmer overhead. A single candle guttered in its holder. Margarita balanced on the counter, head thrown back, her skirts pulled up to her knees and her stockings sliding down her calves. He saw the bare skin of her thigh, legs bending wide towards the tabletop, one of Simeon's hands pressing her open like the cover of a book. Behind them, glass bottles glittered like jewels on the shelves. Dried roots hung from the ceiling, near enough to pull her hair.

On the crowded floor of his boardinghouse in the city, the memory grew more rotten with every sleepless night, filling the cramped apothecary with wet smells and throaty grunts. Once, with his head full of Margarita's laughter (had he even heard her laughing?), and driven half mad by the endless, labored snores of a boy on the floor to his left, Kiril lunged across the room and beat the sleeper bloody, breaking his nose. It was good to silence them both for a few moments.

He swallows a dry mouthful of bread with difficulty. Simeon has never been one for cruel jokes, and yet—"You want me?"

Simeon looks at him like a foolish pet. "Who else?" he repeats. "Hasn't it always been the four of us?"

But we were children then, Kiril wants to say, *and now*—what are they now? Not children anymore.

"There won't be much to do," Simeon assures him. "You and Anka will walk with us, you'll dance with her at the party. We'll need a wedding banner, too, but apart from that—"

"Fine," Kiril says. "I mean, of course. Of course."

Simeon and Margarita are both well-liked, despite their closeness with Anka. And he'll need support from the villagers if his salon is to succeed. This is what he tells himself as Simeon cheers and embraces him again, as he begins telling Kiril of plans for a supper together soon, to discuss the work to be done. There's a guilty knot inside him that he isn't ready to unravel. The town, his reputation—that's enough to agree, he thinks. Well reasoned—his uncle would be proud.

"We really have missed you very badly," Simeon says on his way out. The door squeaks pitifully behind him.

KIRIL AND THE Captain are almost done with their dinner when the witch arrives. Anka is away, dining with Margarita and her family. The Captain doesn't have much to say tonight; they talk a little about the season's meager harvest and then drink their wine in silence, listening to the crackle of the fire.

The jug is almost empty when she knocks. There's a moment's muffled conversation in the hall, and then Yulia comes in with a coat over her arm and announces, "The blacksmith's widow to see you, Captain."

Kiril goes outside and takes a seat on the front steps. He can see Hasan's comet tonight, very clear overhead. Hasan told him these things move at tremendous speeds, far faster than any modern train, but it's hard to believe when the comet stays so perfectly still above the peak of the church tower. Kiril folds his hands under his arms. He's considering going in for his coat when Anka appears at the end of the path.

"It's dangerous to go alone at night," he teases.

Her laugh is a warm drop of honey in his chest. "Shouldn't you be in bed, Doctor? You were up early today."

Kiril nods to the house. "He has a visitor. The witch they had locked up. She's been in there awhile."

Anka sits beside him. "Her name is Nina. I don't think she's really a witch." She balances her elbows on her knees, and the shawl around her shoulders peeks open. Kiril can see the marks he left, dimly visible in the moonlight. It feels like looking into the windows of someone else's house. How strange to think of his own hands holding her down, a past version of himself barely a day removed and yet already as remote as the student in the anatomy theater, already as far from him as the child up to his knees in the muddy yard under summer rain.

He thinks, *I feel like I remember this place more clearly from my dreams*. When he could sleep, he must have come home every night: walked the stairs and the corridors, sat at the dining table, stood watching Anka and Yulia in the kitchen. But to say it would bring them back to the subject of his leaving, so he says nothing, letting the silence pool between them.

When he looks at her again, Anka is staring intently at a glass bottle between her palms. It is filled with a thick tonic whose color he can't quite discern in the dark. It clings to the walls of the flask, and he imagines its foul taste sticking inside Anka's throat as she tries to swallow it down.

"For your menarche?" he asks, and Anka purses her lips.

He looks away, up: moon, comet, stars scattered like a loose handful of salt. At weddings, people give bread and salt to the newlyweds, a prayer that they'll never go hungry. Simeon's father, the baker, will do excellent business the day his son marries.

Behind them, the door opens. Nina stumbles out onto the steps and freezes when she sees them. Kiril stands to let her pass, and she darts towards the path, quick like a rabbit.

"Wait," Kiril calls. She flinches to a stop, hunches instinctively smaller.

"He told me to go," she says.

Kiril reaches into his pocket and closes his hand around a fistful of coins. He holds them out to her. Nina's eyes go from him to the money. She hesitates only a moment before she takes it, and then she's gone.

Anka watches him curiously as he returns to the stoop. "You stood up for her in the village, too."

"It was senseless, the way they attacked her. I didn't know you saw it."

"Margarita told me."

"Of course." Kiril runs a hand through his hair, then nods up the winding path. "He never pays them enough."

He met whores in the city, plenty of them. Women with simpering, rouged lips. They were a different breed than the frightened, penniless wives and widows the Captain summons to the house. Kiril senses their shame like a wafting stench whenever he sees them in the square. It will get better once Anka can marry—the Captain has only ever wanted her. The other women are mere distractions.

Anka turns the glass bottle over in her hands. "It's only fruit syrup," she says, holding it up for him to see. "The old woman doesn't think there's anything wrong with me. It'll sort itself out on its own. But we knew he would want to hear that something was—was being done."

She holds out the bottle, and Kiril takes it. He uncorks it and turns it over with his finger to its lip, then tastes. It's sour cherry syrup, mixed with something bitter. He pictures them standing together over a bowl, the old woman's wrinkled fingers grinding together a useless mush of fruits and fireplace ash.

"The Captain will be furious," he says, and hands the bottle back.

"Will you tell him?"

"No. It would only put him in a foul mood, and it wouldn't solve the problem."

Anka studies him closely. "Do you promise?"

"I promise."

She smiles and scoots closer to him on the steps. She leans her head against his shoulder and points up. "Tell me again what your friend said about comets."

She is a warm weight against his side, her woolen shawl tickling his neck. He puts his arm around her and tells her everything he can remember.

three

T HIS IS HOW the stories go. First, the body empties.

A loved one succumbs to fever after days abed, the heat only leaving her cheeks when she grows stiff against her pillows.

A man whose arms have torn at the earth to bury a dozen children digs his wife's grave, then sets down his shovel, hangs a rope from a rafter, and steps off a stool.

A boy playing in the lake on a hot summer's day loses his footing on a moss-slicked rock. His head hits something on the way down—a slimy, creeping tree root or a sunbaked stone—and he never takes another breath.

Dying is noise and movement, but what follows is silence. The bed frame no longer creaks. The rope spins to a slow halt. The lake does not ripple, except for the faintest push of the wind across its skin. And in that most quiet moment, in that airless corner of the world, there is a flicker. A cat jumps over the body. A human shadow falls across the corpse in the orange light of the setting sun. And in the strange, other place, whose creatures live in the creases and folds of the world—in the reflections on still water, between the fingers of flame in cook fires—something stirs. A spirit peels itself like a hangnail from the dark and rises up, ravenous, to lay its claim.

Night falls. The sawtooth reach of the treetops grows longer as the sun dips, burning hot at the edge of the earth and then slipping down, down, down below. Gloom tumbles in while the body is set on a slab, or is interred. Wrapped in old linen, in sackcloth, or nailed into a half-sized coffin made of soft pine. The earth is moved and resettled, patted down with the flat ends of spades. A cross is built to mark the place, but it means nothing to the old spirits.

A shadow chooses the body. The body is its womb, its vessel while the demon grows. It threads its veins with the dead woman, man, child; they become one, and the shadow learns to bleed, sharpens its hunger. It stalks the earth for food, slipping from one gnarled tree or ragged rock to the next. It's weak while it's young, but it can be anywhere in the dark. The vessel waits for blood. The shadow captures a mouse, a rat, and it feeds, sinking needle teeth into fur and meat. It grows stronger.

The important thing to remember is, it's easier to destroy a vessel before the demon outgrows it, just as it's easier to crack an egg than to kill a rooster once he's crowned.

With time, with blood, flesh carves away from the corpse. The demon knits itself a shape. This half body, formless, hunts at night. It can cover more ground now. It rips and suckles at its prey: it has teeth, a stomach. It bites old hounds, piglets, and the teeth leave raw wounds.

The vessel waits, and the vampire grows. Slowly the misshapen sack of flesh distinguishes its limbs. Its mouth unfolds human lips. Teeth calcify into firm rows. Its digits separate and hinge human fingers. The vessel becomes the model: as God made man in His image, so the vampire makes itself in the image of a man. Little by little, night by night, it grows, until it is fully formed. It can go among the living. It can even speak.

The slayers, sabotnici, share these stories. They teach them to ordinary people, pass them from mouth to mouth, because you must be able to see a monster before you can fight it.

The change takes forty nights. Then, the dead appear to walk again. They can slip into the world that the vessel knew and hide in plain sight.

AT DAYBREAK, THE villagers peek into the square, looking for new signs, but nothing is out of place. They won't admit it, but most of them are disappointed. They are looking for calamity: a coming famine, the mortal sweep of a plague. They get no satisfaction from an isolated omen. Little tragedies are like hiccups: a spasm, and then they wait, afraid to breathe. There is horrible helplessness in waiting.

In the neighboring towns, people tell Yana that the village Koprivci is cursed, if you believe in such things. The children of Koprivci all wither in infancy, they say. The brides of Koprivci bring bad fortune. The workingmen are doomed to harvest little more than dead rocks each and every year.

To prepare, Yana combs the periphery of the town, learning the landscape. She knows how to pass invisibly, silently through the crowns of trees and along rooftops. To manifest spirits, she works unseen. She has never been discovered before—the girl raiding her camp was a surprise. Yana almost left town then, watching the girl dart away with her dagger.

Mama's ghost wanted her to, told her to abandon this place and disappear—*but I've already started, Mama.* She's caused these people panic and fear. She can't leave before she finishes the spell. Her worry about the girl in the woods lingers, but today, Yana wants to be seen. She arrives when the sun is at its highest point. She steers Magaro in a great arc around the village so she can approach by the best-traveled road.

She passes a man and a woman threshing their field. The man has stripped to a sweat-stained tunic, perspiring freely as he swings his scythe. The woman ducks methodically between the blows to collect armfuls of wheat and shed the berries into a bucket. She looks up when the man stops cutting and straightens. His hair is just beginning to thin, and he breathes hard as he leans to rest on the weathered pole of his instrument. The woman has a sunburnt face and a scarf over her head, and her shoulders curve from a lifetime spent hunched over fires and elbow-deep in washing. Yana sees their curiosity, and she sees the apprehension that comes with it.

What do they see? A young woman sitting tall and proud astride an old donkey as it trots down the road, her posture and her trousers like a man's. Her hair is thick and curls about her head, and dramatic shadows fall across her face, like the dappling of light through trees—but when she draws nearer, they realize it is not the shade but her very skin. Her hands are pale on the reins, but her cheek and throat are brown. When she turns her head to look on them, they see her two faces. The man sets down his scythe and rubs his eyes with a red fist. The woman clenches her jaw and hugs her bundle of wheat.

Yana's first real memory is of her own reflection. She saw herself in a silver mirror in a shop window. Her mother was delivering cleaned laundry, and Yana was frightened, clinging to her mother's skirts as she ventured out of sight of their door for the first time. "Stand right here," Mama had instructed, and left Yana in front of a large window.

A beautiful woman in a lush green dress was peering at something in the shop's display: a tall, black object, the size of a full-grown man, cut into a long oval and polished to shine. It looked like a puddle standing on its side. The woman examined her dark double in the mirror, her shape moving inside the stone. And then Yana saw that around the black slab, the display glimmered with smaller panes showing fragments of sky and street and busy people as they passed. There was the woman's green dress, and there was Yana's brown sleeve beside it. As she moved, the picture shifted, and suddenly one of the fragments showed her face in the full colors of the world, not like a rain puddle at all. Yana blinked, and the girl in the glass blinked back.

When he drank, her father would grow angry and call her a cow. He shouted at her mother but pointed at Yana. Her mother would tell Yana not to listen, covering her ears with her hands and kissing the top of her head. In the mirror in the shop window, Yana saw what her father did. For the first time, she recognized her own face, the twoness of it.

The woman in the green dress had seen her then. Her mouth twisted in disgust, and she lifted the hem of her skirts and bustled away. The shopkeeper came out, slinging a rag about his neck, and his eyes narrowed.

"What are you doing?" he demanded. Her mother's hand closed on Yana's shoulder and the man said angrily, "She yours?" He sucked his teeth. "I don't want lepers in my shop. She's frightening my customers."

They left. After, when Yana asked why mama hadn't told the man she wasn't a leper, her mother had simply said he didn't deserve their answers. "What business is it of his?"

By the road to Koprivci, a man with a black patch over his eye stops loading his hay cart to watch Yana pass.

"Are you lost?" he calls to her. A breeze flutters his patch, and he covers it with one hand. She doesn't respond. She guides Magaro down the path at a slow, steady pace and keeps her back straight.

When she reaches the village square, she finds it empty. No mob waits to drive away the fraud. A girl of six or seven stands alone in front of the stout stone bakery, scratching a broom across the dirt. She's more than a head shorter than her broom-stick, and she stares openly as Yana dismounts.

"Hello," Yana says. The girl clutches her broom and squints into the high sun. "Is anyone else here?" The girl says nothing, but lifts her fingers to the apple of her cheek. "Your father, perhaps?" Yana suggests, taking a step forward.

The girl bolts like a startled fawn, dashing through the bakery door, knocking at the walls with her broom as she goes. She calls for someone inside. A moment later, a young man comes out, brushing flour from his hands onto his apron. He can hardly be older than Yana herself.

"Hello," he says uncertainly.

Yana and Magaro stand tall, ringed by their tight midday shadows. She greets him and gives her name. "I followed your troubles here," she says.

Faces begin to appear in windows around them. A woman chooses this moment to walk to the well with her bucket, and then stands there without drawing water, watching.

"Our troubles," the young baker says.

An older man, perhaps his father, comes to the doorway behind him. "How slow is your mule, girl?" he asks. He stretches his arms behind him to crack the crescent moon of his back.

Yana doesn't laugh, and she doesn't falter. Magaro sneezes and scratches at the ground with one hoof. She pats his neck, keeping her eyes on the men.

"Who is your authority here?" she asks. "A priest? A judge? I have a message for him."

"We have a priest," says the old baker, nodding to the church. "And we have a katepan."

"Perhaps I should speak to them both." Yana unbuckles Magaro's saddlebag and lifts out a heavy book with a leather cover. "I can see myself to your church. It would be wise to send for your Captain."

The baker and his son exchange glances, and the older man nods. The boy unties his apron and hangs it on a nail by the door.

"You can hitch your mule there," he says, and points.

Yana secures Magaro to the hitching post, pinching the book between her elbow and ribs. Then she crosses the square, sensing a dozen eyes still watching through finger-gapped curtains, and pulls open the heavy door of the church.

"I FOLLOWED A darkness to your village," she says solemnly, when the priest and the Captain have assembled.

The two of them make an odd pair. The Captain is an unscalable wall, broad and thick. His hands are each as wide as both of Yana's own, and his eyes are quick and alert under the skeptical ridge of his brow. His nose is a predator's beak. Beside him, the priest is in danger of drowning in his black robes. The rope cinched around his waist suggests he's scarcely wider than Yana herself, but if he's any shorter than the Captain, there can only be a hair or two between them. He folds and refolds his long-fingered hands; they scuttle nervously. He's terrified already, just being in her presence. If the girl in the woods warned anyone of Yana's charade, the news hasn't reached this man. She relaxes a little.

"You've had great misfortune here," she says. "I sensed it from far away. But I fear something far worse is now circling above you. The world of the shadows is trembling with it—I could feel it even before the night sky drew fire to this spot."

"Pull yourself together," the Captain mutters to the priest, whose face has gone gray.

Yana takes the book from under her arm. It makes a pleasing, heavy sound when she drops it on the lectern. She takes her time finding the correct page, letting them watch. The book is a spectacle. The cover is stamped with a hungry, knife-jawed demon, the leather cracked right between its wild eyes.

The vellum pages are stiff and shiver like moth wings as she turns them.

She has no idea where her mother found the book, only that it appeared one day, long after they had left the city. The pages were half empty then. Many nights, by their campfires or in cheap, cramped taverns, Yana watched her mother add new pages, new illustrations. She had no inkwell but dipped a pen in a crystalline bottle that might once have held perfume, though Yana does not remember her ever wearing a scent. She drew ferocious monsters and taught Yana to read certain passages. There were half a dozen languages in the book, and they'd never met anyone who knew them all. "I have no idea," her mother laughed when Yana asked one day what was on a particular page. "It might as well be a recipe for soup." She sketched venomous fangs the length of Yana's palm in a hairy, horned face beside the soup recipe.

The priest fumbles in his robes and finds a pair of leather-framed spectacles, which he wiggles onto the bony slope of his nose. They make him look like a malnourished owl.

Yana pauses, her fingers on the ink-spotted edge of the page she wants. "Here," she says, and smooths it open. The priest's eyes bulge behind the glass lenses. The Captain folds his arms.

The illustration shows a lamb, painted as though from above. Its wool is whitened with chalk, and its four limbs look broken, splayed away from its bloody trunk. A gash runs all along the animal's soft underbelly. Its heart is a red lump at the bottom of the page. The priest leans so close to the book that his thin beard scratches against the vellum.

"This means something to you," Yana suggests.

His eyes twitch past his shoulder to the Captain. "Just two days ago," he mumbles, removing his pince-nez. "A hen, killed. Just like this. Just outside this church."

When Yana crept up to the coop, the chickens were calm, clucking softly in their sleep. It was slow, but simple: a handful of breadcrumbs, patient and steady. Eventually a bird lifted its head and pecked. She stroked the bony ridge of its skull with one finger, and when it didn't flap or squawk, she lifted it out of the nest. She bled it in the woods, sitting on a fallen log while she waited for the drip to stop. Then she took it to the square.

"Just like this," the priest repeats, tapping the book with the rim of his spectacles.

Yana nods. "I was warned," she says, dropping her voice. "The world of the spirits is difficult to describe to men who have never seen it and never can." She resumes turning pages. "I was born at the coldest hour of a Saturday night, in the dead days of the first month. I was half wraith, half alive—with one foot in this world and one in the world below. The midwife pulled me back. Ah."

She gestures for them to look. The text here is dense, a black iron gate in her mother's spiky script. Above it, a series of small pictures: a feline shape caught mid-leap, a shade looming over a bed. A misshapen ball rolls across a grassy field, with a dark circle of mouth etched into its fleshy side.

"Because of the conditions of my birth," Yana says, "I walk in both worlds, even now. I see your world and theirs, always."

"Here?" the priest whispers.

Yana smiles. "No invisible satan lounges in your pews, Father. Your church is as holy as it has ever been. The screen between one world and the next is not so thin as that. I perceive both worlds at once, just as you see the walls of your church with your eyes but hear the sound of its bells with your ears. One world may press against the other, the wind may move the trees, and the spirits may show me their designs, but the connections are more subtle than you imagine."

She lays a hand on the book. "When I seek a vampire—"

"A vampire?" says the Captain. He sounds like he's just caught on to a joke they're both playing on the priest, and he finds it charming.

Yana holds his gaze. "When I seek a vampire, I seek shadows. I follow burning lights. A strange omen has lit your skies these past nights—have you not seen it? An evil descends over this village. Even before I came here, and saw your empty houses and blighted fields, I heard whispers that the village Koprivci was cursed. A village of the damned."

She's met men like this Captain before. Not a believer in folk spirits, but an adherent to practical things. Men like him see most clearly the value of a public cleansing. They understand that wealth and prosperity come with trade, with people, and people want assurances. People want to be safe.

"Everywhere," Yana says, "they talk. You must know this."

Even a fake seer is of use, as long as she is convincing.

Outside, there's a sudden commotion. Indistinct shouting. The doors fly open, and two women come running through the nave.

"I told her to wait!" the older one cries, tugging at the woman's sleeve. "I told her you were not to be disturbed!"

The second woman is undeterred. She skids to a stop by

the lectern, panting heavily, and holds out a bloody, crumpled eggshell. "First my hen is slaughtered, and now *this*!"

"Woman, keep your voice down," the Captain says. "What's the matter with you?"

"Blood! That's the matter! I sent my girl to the henhouse today for the eggs and every single one, *every last egg* I cracked for my husband's breakfast, I find it filled with *blood*! It's the witch who's done it, I'm sure of it."

"Preposterous," the priest says, shaking a large crucifix free of his robes and bringing it to his pale lips. The older woman clings to his cassock.

"*Preposterous*," the farmer's wife repeats. She reaches a trembling hand into her apron and takes out another egg, this one intact. "You see here—"

She throws the egg to the floor. It breaks in a dark mess on the gray stone. The priest and his wife both scream. The farmer's wife slumps against the lectern, sobbing. Yana and the Captain kneel and bend close to look.

Gingerly, the Captain picks up a piece of shattered eggshell. He touches one finger to the red spill and brings it to his tongue, then grimaces. "Blood," he affirms.

Yana nods curtly in agreement. The Captain studies her for a moment, rubbing his face with his hand. Maybe he smiles, just a little. He gets to his feet.

"Danika," he says to the farmer's wife, "I will come with you to see your husband and get a full report. I will question the widow myself, though I am sure she knows nothing of this." He holds up his palm before she can protest, and then turns to Yana.

"My garden cottage is unoccupied," he says, and Yana feels as though he has shaken her hand under the table. "I will have my housekeeper prepare it for you. You may stay until this— this darkness has been purged from our village. We don't have much to offer as payment, but I'm sure the people will find ways to show their gratitude if you can, indeed, help."

She bows her head in assent. The priest crosses himself violently.

The Captain bids them good day and ushers the sobbing woman out of the church with a huge hand on her back. She's still sniffling as the doors shut behind them. The priest's wife scurries off for a rag and a dustpan.

"Now, Father," Yana says, once he's kissed his crucifix and closed his prayer. "I would like to meet your dead."

four

I N BLUE TWILIGHT, Anka goes looking for the chicken. Not long ago, the nights were heavy with fireflies, but now a dry chill has swept back into the hills. The hairs on her arms and thighs stand up as she makes her way to the pit.

She should be home, working on Margarita's veil. *You don't get involved*—yes, yes, she knows—but usually when the people here talk about omens, they mean ambiguous things. Bad luck, the business of living. A healthy animal that dies quietly, all of a sudden, a strange pattern in the weather choking new buds with frost. To the villagers, Anka is the very worst omen.

On the night of her birth, a spark from her father's kiln set fire to the house. By the time the villagers arrived with buckets of water, it was too late to save the potter. The Captain pulled Anka's mother from the flames, but she never woke. The midwife delivered Anka by blade on the dirt in front of the house. After that, when babies died, the villagers pointed to Anka. When the orchards failed to fruit, they gritted their teeth at her. If there's something else so plainly wrong here—even if it isn't real, even if the stranger in the woods made it happen—she wants to see it for herself.

Margarita saw the priest's wife carrying the chicken carcass at arm's length to the burning pit, near the smithy, so that's where Anka goes after the streets quiet and the windows light. There are white tufts of feather caught in the bushes nearby and a day's worth of rubbish on top—small bones, worn rags, broken glass—but it doesn't take long to find the animal.

There's no sign of the bird's head. Anka fishes the body out with a stick hooked through its broken chest, and the chicken lands at her feet in a damp clump, feathers dusted gray with fireplace ash. No blood, Anka notices as she bends closer. She rolls it over.

After two days in the rain and sun, the animal's exposed flesh is slimy, and it smells like spoiled wine. There's nothing impressive about it: just a rotting piece of meat. She wrinkles her nose, and her eyes water. In the dim crevice of the bird's open breast, she sees the white wriggling of maggots.

"Eugh!" She bats the bird back into the pit and throws the stick after it, scrubbing her hands on her skirt.

"If you're looking for more filth to paint over my walls, I've had enough."

Anka whips around. Nina has come from the smithy with a bucket. She holds a kitchen knife loosely in hand.

"Snakes nailed to my door. Shit on the counter inside. I've had enough of it—you can tell the rest of them that. I just want to be left alone."

Anka takes a small step back. The pit yawns between them. "I didn't come here for that."

Nina squints at her, and the bucket creaks by her side. "The Captain's ward isn't out at night throwing away household trash."

"I—" Who would she tell, and who would believe her? If it

71

were a contest between them, Anka isn't sure who the villagers would rather hear. "I wanted to see the chicken," she admits.

"I thought everyone got an eyeful the other day," Nina mutters, and dumps her bucket. Dirt, dead leaves, a glossy flash of snakeskins.

Anka shivers in the wind, thinking of the dagger hidden at the back of her closet. "You didn't put it there."

Nina grimaces, sets down the bucket, and presses a hand to her belly. The comet hangs right over her head. For a moment, Anka really sees her: still a young, pretty woman, worn down by a bad year—the loss of her husband, imprisonment, and now the Captain. Anka's chest gets hot and tight. The sounds that carry from her uncle's bedroom to the parlor— low grunts, pained cries—she could ask—

"I didn't touch that bird," Nina says. "Not with my hand, not with my fiendish spirit."

"Are they really rubbing shit on your walls?" Anka asks, willing her flush to recede.

Nina laughs like a knife scratching a plate. "Can you imagine. They'd never touch your house, no matter what they think you are."

"His house," Anka says.

"His house."

Anka looks down into the garbage pit, the loose snake- skins coiled in the dust—in the rising moonlight, she's sure they're moving. The chicken has landed chest up, crawling with white worms. She breathes through her nose, cold air on her hot cheeks. She feels clammy, claustrophobic in the midst of decay. During the summer, the Captain spent more than a month in his bed, too weak to lift his head, the room stinking and stuffy with fever and the promise of death. Yulia climbed the stairs three times a day with bowls of thin yellow broth and brought them back mostly full, and Anka was afraid to enter, afraid of what she'd see, afraid he'd get better and afraid that he wouldn't.

"Do you wish they'd killed you?" she asks. "While they still had you locked up?"

Nina surveys her across the garbage pit. "They're right about one thing," she says finally. "You're a bit odd."

"Yulia says that after the sun goes down, that's when people show who they really are."

Nina sniffs. "I didn't want to die. I just wanted to get out. Maybe sometimes they felt like the same thing." She slides her kitchen knife out of sight and pinches the narrow bridge of her nose. In that moment, Anka sees the years between them, all the life that Nina has lived until now. She had been popular in the village, perhaps even said derisive things about the Captain's ward herself before she was alone, before her husband was eight months gone and her friends all turned their backs. Anka knows how vicious the villagers can be—anything from a sick cow to a man's indigestion has cast blame on her. All it takes is their anger. All she's ever done is pass by the wrong place at the wrong time.

"You should go home, Anka."

It's dark now, and her mind is full of rotting birds, naked flesh, snakes and maggots. *Maybe sometimes they felt like the same thing.* A cautious, frightened excitement starts to rise in her as she hurries up the path, her hands pinched beneath her arms, her head down against the wind.

At home, she finds Yulia in the kitchen scrubbing the cook pots. The housekeeper's pale hands are bloodless and white even swimming out of hot water. A shelf behind her is lined with jars of her homemade remedies—for an upset stomach, for a bad rash. How much distance is there between medicine and poison?

"I think I know," Anka whispers, slamming the door shut against a heavy gust of wind. "Minka asked me what I wanted—I think I know. I need your help."

Yulia's gaze sweeps from Anka to the open cellar door, the stairs up to the hall. She presses her thin lips together. Her hands hover over the soap-marbled washtub. "Not here," she says. "Tomorrow—Minka's, in the morning. Before it's light."

She nods to the stairs. "They're waiting for you. Go." And her hands disappear noiselessly back into the water, like fish.

"I'VE HEARD OF surgeons like this," Kiril says, swirling the brandy in his glass. The Captain bends out of his chair to throw another log on the parlor fire. The light in the room dims, then flares. Anka hisses over her embroidery—she's jabbed herself with the needle. "In places where people worry about revenants—they only operate on the dead, cut the tendons in their legs to keep them immobile in their graves. Charlatans, of course."

The Captain pours himself another drink and corks the

bottle. He's in a good mood tonight. "But don't you understand that it doesn't matter? You should have seen Danika with her eggs. Our seer may be a charlatan, but she knows her business."

"How do you think she did it?" Kiril asks. "Maybe a syringe, first to empty the shells and then to fill them again?"

"Whatever she did, it worked. I tried to take Danika home peacefully, but she was in hysterics—put on quite a show."

Kiril heard the commotion himself while he was wiping the grime from the wall of shelves in the shop. From the window, held open now by a large tin of rusting needles he'd found under the counter, he saw the Captain leading the sobbing farmer's wife away. She reached into her apron pockets again and again, pulling out eggs, smashing them in wet red splatters against the stones. With every one, she cried harder, and some passerby shrieked or swooned.

"You'd think she was carrying the whole henhouse in her skirts," Kiril says. "I tried to discuss my salon with some of the neighbors, but those damned eggs were all anyone would talk about." Just that day he'd met a woman with a horrible toothache, another with an unlanced blister the size of an apple on her arm, and an old man with no teeth at all, who cheerfully admitted that he'd felt his loins burning whenever he peed for the past two weeks. But none of them were interested in medical advice; they only wanted to know if he still thought the witch was innocent.

He sighs into his cup. "It's amazing how easily people will believe an obvious ruse."

"Most of them have never been anywhere but here—

they've never seen the rational world. It's easy when they want to believe. And you'd do well to let them keep on believing— leave the girl to run her show. I don't want the people coming down on the widow again—or Anka, God forbid."

Anka doesn't look up at the mention of her name. She's squinting at her embroidery hoop, needle hand motionless. The Captain sets aside his glass and reaches out to stroke her chin.

"How is your work, little bird?"

"It's difficult." She holds up the hoop. By the light of the fire, her roses float in midair. "This fabric Margarita gave me is impossible. There's nowhere to hide any mistakes."

Kiril leans closer. There's sheer tulle netting stretched across the hoop. The cobwebs he cleared today looked more substantial. "Where did she even get this?" he asks, thinking of the empty shelves behind his counter.

"Her father bought it, the last time he went looking to find her a husband. She said it was his way of apologizing. For making her wait so long for Simeon. But, Uncle, the seer— she must have been here longer than she admits. Watching the town."

"Almost certainly," the Captain says, scratching the back of his neck. "I'm glad for your friend, but I hope this Yana can help with that sort of problem, fraud though she may be. Margarita's poor father was beside himself. Whenever he so much as mentioned the name Koprivci, they slammed their doors in his face. Nobody wants to wed their son to the village where no child survives."

There had been times in the city, when Kiril felt his loneliest, when he fell into a certain fantasy: himself, an established physician, writing (easily, flawlessly) to Margarita's family with an offer of marriage, a chance for her to escape. He sometimes got as far as their well-kept apartments overlooking the river, the fresh silks of a modern wedding gown, but the dream always dissolved before he could see under her veil. And then he came home—back to the dusty village, to wrestle a dirty shop front into something clean and useful. He touches the place in his palm where the splinter had been; it's a little pink and tender still, but nothing worrisome.

I can help, he thinks. It won't be the seer's tricks and grotesqueries that save the village; it will be clearheaded science and the medicine he's brought home in his black leather bag.

But all he says is, "It will be a very pretty veil."

The Captain pats Anka's knee. "Yes, I'm sure Margarita will be thrilled with whatever you make for her. What about you, boy? What are your marching orders?"

"There isn't much for now. I'll accompany Simeon the day of the ceremony. Anka and I will dance together. There's the matter of the wedding banner, but his mother is preparing all of the baubles. All I have to do is cut the post."

The Captain smiles into his brandy. "You'll want to practice that. I've done it myself, for your mother and father."

"Cutting down a sapling?"

"In a single stroke, with the whole town watching? It's harder than you might think. Especially for a soft-palmed boy like you."

Kiril's neck prickles. He wants to protest that his hands aren't so soft, not anymore, but the calluses he earned shoveling for the surgeon have already begun to recede. He clears his throat. "This seer—you're sure she won't point the finger at Nina? Or at Anka? She could be dangerous."

"Ivo questioned her some in that regard. He says corpses are her specialty. And I don't believe anyone in this village would be so stupid as to attack your cousin—not after the last time."

The last time. Anka was only nine years old when a man in the village decided she was responsible for his wife's barren womb. She was a knock-kneed lamb, and he was bigger even than the Captain, a beast with arms as thick as her waist. He cornered her in the bakery and began to yell, already drunk by midmorning. The day after a stern talk with the Captain failed to convince him otherwise, the man was found at the end of a rope in the woods, not far from the old burning point for offerings. *Ashamed. Clearly unstable.* They buried him outside the churchyard with the other suicides.

Kiril digs a thumb into his bad shoulder with a grunt. "Corpses," he says. "That's a strange specialty for a young woman."

Anka yelps and throws down her embroidery. She sucks a finger into her mouth.

The Captain pets her hair. "Calmly, little bird. It will be beautiful."

"What does that mean?" Anka asks around her bloody finger. "That 'corpses are her specialty'?"

"Ivo said she was disdainful when he asked about witch hunters. Apparently she prefers to lay blame on subjects who are already dead. Similar to your revenant surgeons."

"Corpse desecration and animal sacrifice," Kiril says. "It's less efficient than witch burning."

"But perhaps more traditional."

His brandy run dry, the Captain rises from his chair, and Kiril follows suit. His uncle takes a book from the table and wishes them both good night.

"Don't stay working too late," he warns Anka.

She picks up her embroidery from the floor. "Good night, Uncle."

Upstairs in his room, Kiril lays awake thinking about Margarita, and about bodies in operating theaters and on sacrificial tables. He falls asleep before he hears Anka go up to bed herself.

ONCE YANA HAS finished at the church, the Captain's pale housekeeper arrives to show her to the garden cottage. She leaves Yana to settle in, then comes back a while later with bread, cold mutton, and a pitcher of water.

"Your donkey is with the Captain's horses," the housekeeper assures her. "In excellent care." She lingers by the door and frowns, but says nothing more. Perhaps she disapproves of the grisly nature of Yana's work. Going, she leaves Yana with a faint whiff of bergamot and the strange, absent feeling that she's forgotten something important.

Think carefully, Mama whispers. In a few days it will have been a year since her mother died, but at times like these, Yana still sees her. Tonight, Mama stands by the window and looks out. She watches the housekeeper's retreat.

The cottage has a bed with fresh linens, and a large fire-place that Yana lights when the sun sets and the windowpanes start to rattle. There's a table with a chair as well, and it's here that she sets out her supplies to prepare for the coming weeks. Small and large knives, thick and thin ropes, a shallow pan made of tin.

The priest balked at taking her to the church cellar after the Captain was gone, but in the end, he covered his mouth and nose with his handkerchief and led her down the spiraling stairs. The oldest body had been waiting on its slab longer than any corpse Yana had ever seen, and the cold underground did nothing for the smell. When she pulled back his shroud, the man's face was purple. He looked like he'd begun to deflate, and the slab was wet beneath him.

"Why has he been left so long?"

"He was our gravedigger," the priest said, words muffled by the handkerchief. "The other men have been occupied with the harvest."

Too far gone, Yana had decided on the spot, too grotesque even for her. No magic left in him. So she turned to the second body, the smallest of the three. She lifted the pall and there was a boy there, no older than six or seven. A strip of cloth had been laid lovingly across his eyes.

"They kept opening," the priest said miserably, when Yana gently lifted the edge of the blindfold. The boy's gaze was cloudy under the priest's lantern. "His poor mother, she was terrified he'd let a demon in." He nodded to the third slab. The woman sleeping there had been very thin when she died, as though grief had eaten her from inside. Deep wounds trailed up each of her arms. "Some of the villagers are outraged I allowed her to rest here, even just for a while. But all she wanted was to be with her boy." The priest's lantern trembled. "Is it her?"

And before Yana could stop herself, she said, "No."

You're too tender, her mother whispered, frustrated. A body is just an object. It would have been easy to pick any one of them, perform the burial, and leave Koprivci before the leaves finished turning. Especially here, where Yana knows she's exposed, she should get away as quickly as possible.

But it's done. Next, she will wait a few days if she can, to let the apprehension mount. She can question the villagers in the meantime. It makes them feel important to be heard. She may even learn something useful. After her mistake in the church, she'll have to investigate the most recent graves—exhumations are more difficult, but they can cause the right kind of stir. The priest had mentioned a summer fever.

Too tender. "Yes, Mama, I know," she mutters. "What we do is hopeful. There was no hope in that cellar." Yana picks up a knife and whetstone from the table and sets about sharpening the blade. "I'll find another way."

There's a knock at the cottage door. The housekeeper returning to take her plates in the dead of night? The Captain coming to make some demand? But when Yana opens it, the girl from the woods stands in the overgrown path. The wind whips at her edges.

There are a hundred monsters in her mother's book, but Yana's favorite were always the samodivi. Beautiful maidens with hair like moonlight who danced in woodland clearings to lure unsuspecting men. Travelers who fell for them would dance to death before the dawn. When she was a child, Yana hoped she might see them between the tree trunks while she and her mother camped away from the road; she wanted a glimpse of the feathered gowns that let them fly. They were said to know great secrets of healing, and sometimes shared them with young women of pure heart.

The girl in the doorway is just a girl, short and thin and wearing a shawl over her white nightclothes. An embroidered bag hangs from her bony elbow. She looks Yana over from head to toe, lingering on the knife in her hand, then stamps her unstockinged feet in the cold. She looks like she's been standing there a long time, mustering the courage to knock.

"Were you just talking to somebody?" the girl asks, and tries to see into the room.

Yana squeezes her knife's handle. "My dead mother."

The girl's eyes widen. Then she smiles. "Can I come in?"

She goes straight to the fire and stands there rubbing the tops of her thighs to warm them. In silhouette, her features disappear, and the firelight carves out her shape: her bramble of shawl, a braided rope of hair falling over one shoulder, the lines of her skinny legs through the scrim of her skirt. Yana sits back down at the table with her knife.

"I used to come here all the time," the girl says, when her teeth have stopped chattering. She examines the tools spread across the table. "It was a secret hiding place for my cousin and me. It looks different with your things in it."

Yana rests her elbows on her knees. "You're the Captain's daughter?" She sees no resemblance between the mountainous katepan and this skinny girl, but perhaps she takes after her mother.

"His niece. His ward. My name is Anka."

"Anka. What are you doing here? Shouldn't the Captain's household all be asleep at this hour?"

"I couldn't sleep." Anka makes to sit down on the bed, then pauses. "May I?" she asks, and Yana nods. Anka pulls her feet up and folds herself into a ball, her arms around her shins. "Are you really a seer? My uncle says it doesn't matter if you're a fraud, as long as you're good at it."

Careful. Yana slides the whetstone across the blade with a singing slip, and she sees Anka prickle. Mama smiles, and steps closer, tilting her head at the girl. Slowly, Yana says, "It depends on your purpose."

Anka takes the end of her braid and begins to pick at it between her fingers. "What's *your* purpose?"

Anxious, Yana realizes—the girl is blustery, but afraid. Nervous in a way that doesn't match the reckless curiosity that raided her tent.

"I help people," Yana says. That's what Mama told her, when she taught her to trick and lie. *We help people—they just don't see how we do it.* Speaking her mother's refrain aloud, Yana feels the hollow beat of grief in her chest. It's been such a long year on her own.

"I saw you," she says. "At my camp. You know more than you're saying."

Anka's jaw moves like she's chewing something. The skin around her fingernails has been picked away, Yana sees, pink wounds stretching up as far as the second knuckle. "I won't expose you," Anka says at last. "You say you help people. Will you help me?"

"Why would the Captain's ward need my help? Doesn't he provide everything you need?"

Anka unties her braid and begins to separate the strands with her pink fingers. Her hair falls into a frizzy curtain. "You went down into the cellar," she says. "At the church? So you saw little Mitko."

With his milky, frozen eyes. Yana nods.

"The people here loved Mitko. He was such a sweet boy." Anka smiles. "He wasn't afraid of me. Once, he gave me some wildflowers he'd picked down by the river. He loved the river. Then he drowned." She meets Yana's eye. "You've been watching us, haven't you? For at least a few days? Have you noticed anything strange about this village?"

"Every place is strange," says Yana. "In one way or another."

"There's no school here," Anka says. "There aren't really any children here—Mitko was the youngest we had. They say babies can't survive in Koprivci. Now it's Simeon's little sister, Katia—she's the youngest."

"The girl at the bakery," Yana remembers.

"The people here think it's because of me."

"That there are no children?"

"They think I brought a curse with me, when I was born, that made the women sterile, and those who aren't . . . a lot of babies die here their very first night. They say the night air gets into them." She rips at a cuticle. "It doesn't matter that there are a few kids who live—they decided it was because of me."

"What people believe, it's . . . flexible. The strongest beliefs have to be." Yana frowns. "Why you?"

"Because of the way I was born." Anka starts combing her hair out with her fingers. "The night of the harvest festival, there was a fire. My parents died. The midwife had to cut me out."

Yana can picture it: a baby shrieking over the fire's roar, a woman bleeding onto the grass. Spectacle and shock—isn't that how she herself makes her living?

"That's terrible," she says.

Anka shrugs, and her scarf slips. "It's not important. What matters is, the Captain took me in after that, even though I'm not his blood. I call him Uncle, but he's been like a father to me, all my life."

Yana nods to the bruises on her neck. "Did he do that to you?"

Startled, Anka tugs her shawl back up. "No," she says. She begins separating her hair for a new braid. "It's not that. He wants to marry me. He decided it years ago—he loved my mother, but she's gone. He's been waiting for me to start bleeding so that I'll be old enough. He says I look more like her every day. I've heard how he treats the women he takes to bed. He *raised* me. I can't marry him."

Yana frowns. "Surely your priest would forbid it?"

"They're old friends, the priest and my uncle. They were in the war together. You met him, didn't you? He's not a bold man. If I'm unmarried, a woman, and *cursed* . . ." Her fingers work. "If the easiest way to solve a problem is to let the Captain do what he wants, there's nobody in this village who will stop him."

Yana picks up her knife again. She liked the Captain when she met him today—a pragmatic man, quick, and comforting to his neighbors. He's given her the cottage to use. Often, the best she's offered is a free spot in the stables.

But she hesitates. The walls of a house can hide more than rooms. Her father was popular in their neighborhood, too, an endless rotation of men at their table in the evenings. Once, when Yana was very small and starting to lose her milk teeth, she sat giggling and clicking a loose incisor back and forth. Her father was talking with a friend, each of them with a fan of playing cards in hand. Without warning, he grabbed her chin in a vise and forced his fingers into her mouth. He ripped the tooth from her gums and dropped it into her mother's glass. The friends kept drinking. Even so young, Yana was too shocked to cry. She sat prodding the new wound with her tongue.

You misremember, Mama says grimly. *They were shooting dice that night.*

"I don't have money," Anka says, abandoning her hair and reaching into her embroidered purse. "But the Captain brings me things when he travels. You can have them—I think they'd fetch a price." She lays them on the bed: a tangle of golden jewelry, silk gloves in spring colors, jars of fragrant rose wax. Yana could sell these treasures and easily last the winter, but the thought of touching them repels her. They are the gifts a man gives to a mistress, not a daughter.

Anka hesitates, the purse in her lap. "There's also this," she says, and produces Mama's broken dagger. Blushing, she holds out the hilt. "I'm sorry. I didn't mean to take it."

A lump hardens in Yana's throat, and it takes her two tries

to swallow it. The girl she observed in her camp was rash. Now Yana sees something else in her, outshining that dangerous abandon. It's hope. Anka wears it like an unfamiliar coat. Maybe she hasn't felt it in a long time. *I want to help her, Mama. Is that lunacy?*

Mama's ghost looks from Anka to Yana and smiles.

Yana takes the dagger.

"I still don't understand," she says at last. "What I do—it's just illusion. If your neighbors believe me, I can bring them some comfort, something to carry them through winter, but I can't work magic—you understand that, don't you? I can't change your uncle's mind. How do you think I can help you?"

Anka secures her new braid and pushes it over her shoulder. "I've run away before. He always brings me back. I think the only way he'd let me go—" She bites her little fingernail, already ragged at the quick. "He said you do your work with corpses. So what if we make me a corpse?"

five

THEY WORKED AT night in the city—Kiril and another trusted student or two, one on lookout, the others digging. Sometimes there were execution wagons parked in the alleys, but most often they had to dig. They knew when the watchmen took their rounds, when the shifts changed, when the late-night man would knock off for a smoke. After filling the graves back over empty coffins, they walked their specimens to the surgeon's house as drunken friends, weaving and singing, smelling of dirt instead of liquor. The university anatomy theater was permitted only one subject every three months—how else could they learn? Some of the boys relied on books. Kiril and his companions crowded into the surgeon's cellar, still muddy, and drank whole wine bottles of water while their teacher cut and showed and talked.

All night now, Kiril dreams of chopping trees. He feels the heft of the axe in his hands, the gravity-pull on his arms as he lifts it, the spin of his torso as he swings. In his dream, it feels just like a shovel. He hears the *thunk* of the thick, metal tooth biting the flesh of a sapling—a wet, bodily sound. Laughter hides in the trees behind him—he turns to see a shape retreating, and wakes with his arms aching. It's rained again overnight; he can smell the damp earth even through the windows.

He washes his face, dresses, and then takes an axe two dozen paces into the woods behind his uncle's house. He finds a tree, tall enough to carry a wedding banner and the width of a woman's wrist. One good blow—how hard can breaking such a thing be?

He knows how to chop wood. For years, he sat in the Captain's study, struggling with his letters, while outside the window a gangly village boy halved winter logs in exchange for a few pennies. When Kiril turned thirteen and still could not fluidly read a verse, even as little Anka had read most of the Captain's library herself, his uncle threw up his hands and ordered Kiril out. *Go do something useful instead.*

Once, he overheard the priest and the Captain talking while he split firewood thirty paces away. "Surely he could be bred for something more dignified," the priest said, sounding doubtful.

"It seems the more dignified work won't have him," the Captain replied, raising his voice—or had it carried on the wind?

But nobody cares if it takes more than one swing to fell a tree for a fire. The first sapling he strikes springs back against his blow in protest and almost takes out his eye with its smallest branches. He finds another, but it's too thick—the axe sticks in its meat. Another, another—he practices swinging as hard as he can, leaving behind white bites in the bark until his arms start to tremble and sweat runs down his back. While he works, the sun comes up.

"You should try it at an angle," says a voice. Nina has appeared without a sound. *Like she just flew here*, Kiril thinks wildly. "I didn't mean to scare you."

"You didn't," he lies. He wipes his face with his sleeve. She looks more composed than she did the night she fled the house, though her skin is thin and blue, and her baby weighs on her like a stone. The surgeon told him once of a woman he'd seen whose child became a statue in her womb; his own teacher had cut the lithopedion out after she died of great pox. By then, she had been pregnant for almost six years. "What are you doing here?"

Nina holds open her apron, showing the small mound of berries and nuts she's collected in the canopy of her skirt. "I've missed most of the gathering time, but the bushes here haven't been picked clean just yet. You should try swinging like this." She takes both corners of her apron in one hand and shows the path of the axe with the other, angling her palm sharply down against the tree's stalk. "Not dead across."

He should know this already—shouldn't he know this already? Kiril's glad he's flushed with work, or she'd see the embarrassment creeping up on him. The axe handle pulls uncomfortably on his skin; he'll have blisters on his soft palms.

He realizes that he doesn't want her to see him fail again. It will be worse, though, if he just stands with the axe at his side, too afraid to try. "At an angle," he repeats.

He chooses a new sapling, mimes the blow once, twice, imagining where it will land, before—*crack*. The blade slides deep, and this time the tree doesn't jump back at him. As he tugs the axe free, the slim trunk yawns open and falls to the ground, held to its stump by a skin of pulp and papery bark. Kiril laughs in triumph. A bead of sweat slips over his temple and down his neck.

"Beautiful. Thank you, Nina."

She doesn't answer. He turns around and scans the trees, but the sun is against him now, and she's disappeared. He was so caught up in the task that he hadn't heard her going.

WHEN ASKING FAVORS of witches in the woods, you bring a gift. That's what Anka knows.

Before leaving the house, she slips into the cellar and finds a jar of honey. It's heavy and warm in her hand. The door to Yulia's quarters is open, and the bed is empty. Outside, Yana is waiting at the end of the path. She steps out of the fog when Anka draws close.

The fever of summer has finally, truly broken. The trees bare their bones, discarded leaves fanned out at their feet. Yana is wearing a long coat made of brown hide.

"Which way?"

"We have to go by the village first. There's someone else I need."

"I'm not used to working with so many assistants," Yana says, adjusting the leather bag on her shoulder.

They stop at the apothecary and creep to the back of the building. A blue band of light bleeds over the horizon.

Scarcely two weeks ago, Margarita appeared below Anka's window in the dead of night. She tossed a pebble against the pane. They hadn't seen much of each other in the summer. Anka had kept to the house, nervous of venturing into the village while the Captain was sick, and Margarita had been busy with her father's shop and, secretly, with Simeon. That night, her engagement was a precious new thing, and she was giddy and desperate to share it. They hugged and giggled, nose to nose, and Anka was happy, mostly happy. The sky was black with new moon, but then all of a sudden the clouds cleared and they saw the white light of the comet for the first time. "A good omen for a happy marriage," Anka had promised, squeezing her arms around Margarita's waist, all the while thinking, *Please, please don't leave me alone.* She wonders now if maybe the comet means something for her, too.

Margarita comes to her window almost as soon as Anka's first pebble taps the glass. She doesn't take long to dress. When she comes down, she throws her arms around Anka and squeezes tightly, holding her for a long beat. They travel most of the way up the hill in silence, the morning hushed over them like the high ceiling of the church. Twice, Anka turns to make sure Yana is still following. She moves silently, even over dead leaves.

When they reach Minka's cabin, the midwife and Yulia are both waiting for them. Minka is still in her nightclothes, sitting at the table while Yulia pours cups of boza. The dog is lazing by the fire, tail idly thumping the floor. "Always in the way," Yulia mutters, trying to get past him to the cook pot.

"How is your young man?" Minka asks Margarita, rising to kiss her jaw.

"Very well, Baba Minka, thank you."

"And you I haven't met," Minka says to Yana. "You must be the seer."

Yana bows her head. "Very good to meet you, Baba Minka."

"I brought you something," Anka says, and holds out the jar of honey.

Minka holds it to the light and smiles. "How kind. Sit, my girls, sit—"

Yulia sets down wooden bowls and ladles out porridge for each of them. Anka feels wiry and vacant. Her insides are too knotted to eat. When Yulia finally takes her place, and Margarita and Yana pick up their spoons, four sets of eyes turn to her.

She's never sat with Yulia like this, to a meal, though they've lived under the same roof as long as Anka can remember. They're an odd company all around the table, she realizes. Young, and old, and ageless. Women from far away, and girls who have never been anywhere. The others are skilled with herbs, with cookery, with birth and death. What does Anka offer but a problem?

She picks at a hangnail on her left thumb and focuses on Minka, her kind old face, her silver hair as long as a horse's tail over her hunched shoulders. "The last time I was here, you asked me what I wanted. But I didn't have a good answer for you."

Minka cracks open the jar of honey and fishes out a dripping piece of comb with her yellowed fingers. She drops it into her porridge, then slides the jar past Yulia, to Yana. "And do you know now?"

Margarita reaches over and takes Anka's hand in hers, interrupting her picking. Such a familiar gesture—how many times have they grasped hands? At festivals, joyful with the music. At church, bored and wrestling with their thumbs. On stormy nights, when rain stranded Anka after supper and they shared Margarita's bed, squealing as thunder shook dust from the rafters. *I've been so lonely*, Anka wants to cry. All year, all alone, not even Kiril's snores through the wall, worrying into the night that Margarita and Simeon didn't care for her anymore, that without Kiril, there was no reason for them to visit the Captain's house at all. When they did come, she was often too ashamed to greet them. How many times had she asked Yulia to send them away?

Yulia hasn't served any porridge for herself. Anka wishes they'd take her bowl away. "Baba Minka, last time you said that Yulia knows everything there is to know about poison. Is it true?"

Minka lifts her bushy eyebrows at Yulia. The housekeeper rests her chin on her folded hands. "There are things that I know," she says finally, and Minka lets out a snort.

Anka is digging purple moons into Margarita's palm. She pries her fingers away and grips her cup instead, not drinking. "I've read stories about . . . about false deaths. People who are so deeply asleep they could be mistaken for dead—who might even be buried while they're still alive. Do you know a poison for that?"

Margarita grabs her sleeve. "Anka, what is this?"

Minka looks grimly aware. Yana stands and begins to circle the cabin, pausing before the limbless torso, the glass cabinet with its rows of secret bottles. Yulia watches Anka in her ghostly, distant way.

"There are things I know," she says again, more softly. "It would be dangerous."

"How dangerous?"

"Anka—"

"Margarita," she whispers, "I'm not like you. I can't marry the man who wants to marry me." The Captain, who taught her to read, who played with her dolls, who hurts the women he summons to his rooms for the crime of not being her mother.

"You know he won't let me go. He'll hurt Kiril again, or Yulia, or you. But Yana can use me—I'll be a victim to her demons. She'll tell everyone that I need to be buried far from the village to protect you from harm. It's what they've always believed, anyway—that I'm a danger to them. And then she can take me away."

"Anka, you're talking about poisoning yourself! You could *die*." Margarita grabs Yulia's thin wrist, pinning her to the table. "Yulia, tell her—it's too risky. You can't let her do this."

"And if I stay?" Anka says. "What will happen to me then?"

Would it be like drowning? Anka has imagined the desolate nothing that follows water closing overhead or Kiril's hands tightening around her throat. But she's also imagined the simple peace of disappearing: passing behind an old tree, stepping into some fold in the air, ceasing to be. That's what she wants—for Yulia to bottle her a vanishing act.

Margarita's cheeks are wet. "But where will you go?"

"Anywhere she likes," says Yana. She resumes her seat and takes her cup. "Yes, this world is hard. But there are cities with life in them. Smaller towns, too. I wouldn't just leave her to starve in the wild. I can help her find a way to get by."

Suddenly Anka feels the enormity of beyond, everything waiting just out of sight, over the rocky shoulder of the mountains. Places she's seen in stories—the empty spans of deserts, the fearsome beauty of the sea. She read once that nothing in nature is truly ugly; the only ugly things are made by men.

"Won't the Captain suspect?" Margarita demands. "He's no fool. He might—" She looks to Yana. "What if he suspects you?"

"He already knows I'm a fraud," Yana admits. "And we can use that. I'll say nothing about Anka yet. Once her death is announced, I'll just exploit it—that's what charlatans do."

"But—"

"She'll fall ill by degrees," Yulia says. "Little by little. It will appear natural."

The dog shakes himself awake, then, and trots over to the table, looking for scraps. Anka dangles a crust of milky bread over his jaws. "I'll be here for your wedding," she says, avoiding Margarita's eyes. The dog licks her fingers. "I would never miss that. And after that, you won't need me."

"Need?" Margarita repeats. "You have to go, Anka, I know it. But don't—don't pretend it doesn't matter." She blows her nose into her apron. Miserably, she reaches out to scratch the mutt behind his ears. He barks once, happy.

Yulia goes to Minka's cabinet and starts handling the bottles, examining their yellowed labels. "We'll want belladonna, maybe bryony. Margarita, you'll check your father's stores. Some things we'll have to harvest."

Yana takes a sip from her glass and grimaces, but swallows. "How did you learn this? It seems beyond a housekeeper's duties."

Yulia doesn't turn around. "I've been with the Captain's house almost fifteen years," she says. "Before I came here I lived a different life."

Minka produces a roll of paper and a bottle of ink, and Yulia carefully draws the leaves and flowers she'll need. "This your father will have. This is in my garden. These you'll need to find in the woods."

Around them, Minka begins clearing away breakfast, the barely touched bowls and cups. The dog pops onto his rear legs and begins nosing after spilled honey.

"You girls will be missed soon," Yulia says, rolling her drawings into a tight scroll and tucking it into Margarita's apron.

So Minka shoos them out into the morning. They blink in the bright light, Margarita biting back her protests, squinting back tears. Anka leans against her shoulder and breathes. She should be terrified, but it's hard to feel fear under the golden sunrise. She's found a crack in the ice. Maybe she can squeeze through.

"Are you ready?" Yana asks, looking back at the cottage. As the door falls shut, Minka and Yulia are bowing their heads together by the cabinet, sorting through their potions, muttering secrets under their breath.

six

AFTER DINNER, WHILE the Captain is pouring sweet wine, Yulia sets a glass bottle in front of Anka. They use the same flask Minka gave her, hiding the trick in plain sight. That afternoon, they mixed poison together, Yulia's white hands showing exactly how to grind and measure the herbs, explaining each ingredient. When they'd finished, she gave Anka a folded page written in brown ink and said, *Hide it well.*

Her uncle and cousin pay no mind to the bottle; they think they've seen it before. They're laughing about a man Kiril met today, something about boils in unspeakable places. Anka takes the flask and measures out a spoonful.

It looks no different than Minka's first tonic: red and black, fruit tinted with pepper. When she puts the spoon on her tongue, it tastes the same, too, like sour cherries. Yulia told her: *That's how the best poisons work—no color, no taste, no smell.*

How does she know? Yana wondered, but when Anka asked, Yulia's eyes grew distant, the kind of retreat from which she wouldn't soon return.

Anka sits with the tonic on her tongue, waiting to feel something. What if it all happens too quickly, and the Captain uncovers what they've done? What if she slipped as she mixed, too heavy, and she drops dead right at the table? What if Margarita picked the wrong herbs, and there's no effect at all?

Kiril is looking sheepish, uncommonly pleased. He starts telling of his morning practicing with the axe, the trees he failed to cut down and the one he finally did with Nina's guidance. Witches in the woods, sharing sage wisdom—isn't it just like a fairy tale?

Anka sets down her spoon. The Captain's library is crowded with dry histories, accounts of battles detailing precisely the numbers of troops, horses, and barrels of wine. But there are also stories of kings who keep deadly drafts in the hollow handles of daggers, queens who kill with poisoned hairpins. They have a handful of plays and novels on the shelves, purchased for Anka's enjoyment, all with tragic endings: arsenic and henbane, toxic robes, an asp held to a bared breast. In the stories, heroines see spectral shapes and lost loves as they die. The dead beckon.

The Captain is laughing; he slaps his hand once on the table. The silver and glasses rattle. Yulia circles the dining room, clearing dishes. By hearth and candlelight, the evening swims, but it isn't the poison. Anka swallows and waits, heart thumping, but she feels nothing.

Minka, in her creaky voice: *A seed, newly planted, won't disturb the earth for days to come.*

The Captain strokes Anka's wrist fondly, and Yulia takes the bottle away. No ghosts appear, not yet. A little while later, they all go up to bed.

Interlude: Origins

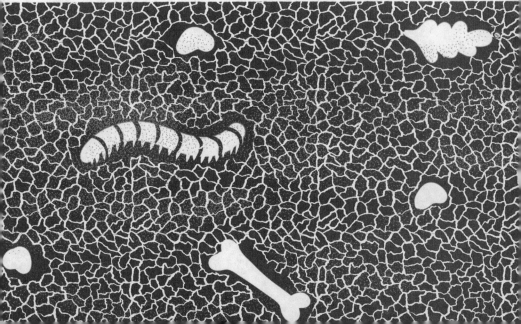

ONCE, LONG AGO, a girl from a small village went to seek an old witch who lived alone. The girl had lost her love in war, and she wanted desperately to bring him back. All the wise elders of her village told her that no such thing was possible, and the girl knew that it was wrong to meddle in the order of life and death, but she missed her beloved too terribly.

She carried with her three gifts from her lover, to help the witch find him among all the spirits of the dead. The first was a blue ribbon, which she kept tied around her wrist, so that she might remember her beloved always, even when he was nowhere nearby. The second was a pebble, as round and white as the moon, which he'd given her as a promise that his love would always be as immutable and solid as stone. The last was a wooden comb that he had carved for her, with a pattern of roses, which he pinned to her hair to hold it out of her eyes, so that she would never be hidden from him.

The girl walked for a long time. In those days, the land was empty, flat and barren in all directions. When she finally found the witch's house, she knew it at once, though she had never been there before. It stood alone, in a murky pool of shadow under the cloudless sky. When the girl knocked, the witch welcomed her in: she was very old and walked with a heavy cane made of a bone. The shadow kept her home as dark as night, lit only by candles and her fire, and inside it smelled of dead things. But the girl was determined. She entered when the witch beckoned. The crone offered her a seat and returned to the large pot she was tending by the fire.

"Why have you come to me, precious girl?" She set aside her bony cane and raised a large wooden spoon.

The girl told the witch of her fallen love and explained that she wanted him returned to her. She produced her lover's gifts. "I brought these tokens of our love, that you might recognize him in the world of the spirits."

"And what have you brought for me in exchange?" the witch asked, stirring her pot with the spoon. "I am very hungry. Have you brought me bread, or meat for my stew, or cool water to drink?"

But the girl had not thought to bring anything, had not even a morsel of food with her, and she said so.

"Then you will give me this ribbon and this stone and this comb," the witch suggested, "which I can trade so that I may eat." But the girl refused to part with her lover's tokens, and pulled them close to her.

The witch was offended. She did not care to return the girl's beloved without proper payment, but she was clever. She hid her anger.

The witch told the girl that she had been right to believe that the spirit world would need proof of their love in order to find and return the boy. But trinkets such as these could never be enough. That proof lived in the bodies of the lovers, and she would have to draw it out.

She asked the girl to tell her about the lost boy, about how much she missed him. As the girl spoke of his goodness and his valor, she began to cry. Tears rolled down her face, and the witch caught them in the wooden spoon.

"Now let us see if the spirits will recognize your love in the salt of your tears," she said, and she stirred the girl's tears into her pot. Instantly, the stew turned the sparkling white of salt.

"You see!" the girl cried, pointing to the pot. "The spirits know us!"

The witch sipped a taste from her wooden spoon, but spat it onto the floor, for the stew had become too salty.

She produced a needle and asked for the girl's hand. She pricked the girl's finger, and a drop of blood bloomed on her skin. The witch caught it with her spoon. "Let us see if the spirits will recognize your love in your blood," she said, and she stirred the girl's blood into her pot. At once, the contents of the pot turned deeply red, and the girl gave another cry.

"See how it changes!" she exclaimed. "The spirits know us."

The witch sipped again from the brew, and again she spat it onto the floor, because now the stew was too thin.

At last, the witch took a knife from her belt. "The spirits don't recognize you," she said. "Give me your little finger, and perhaps they will find proof of your love in the flesh of your body."

At this, the girl balked. She suddenly understood that the crone did not care to help her, because she had brought no tribute. The witch would cook her and eat her instead. But when she refused to give the witch her finger, the old woman grew angry. "If you will not give me your finger, there is no hope that your lover will return to you," she said.

The girl wanted to run, but the witch stood between her and the door, and witches are often much stronger than they appear. Her only hope was to trick the old woman. She held out her hand.

The witch raised the knife and cut off the girl's little finger. The girl wound her bleeding hand in her blue ribbon. "Let us see if the spirits will recognize you now," the witch said, and dropped the finger into the pot. At once, the contents turned thickly brown, a stew bubbling with meat. But this time, when the witch bent to taste with her spoon, the girl was ready: she shoved the old woman forward into the enormous pot, and she fled.

Out the door, out of the shadow, through the tall grass she ran, pursued by the old woman's screams. But the witch was not so easily beaten. Her cries did not fade, and it was with horror that the girl realized that she was being followed. When she turned, she saw the witch sailing across the empty landscape in her stewpot, rowing through the air with her spoon.

"Beloved, protect me," the girl prayed, unwinding the blue ribbon from her bleeding hand. She threw it over her shoulder. Instantly, the ribbon turned into a wide, flowing river, splitting the land into two banks. This is the river that flows so close to us now, that gives us fish and fills our buckets when there is no rain. "Thank you, my love," the girl cried, thinking that she had escaped.

But the witch was not stopped by the river. Her pot slid

over the water as smoothly as a boat. She swept easily across the current, using her wooden spoon as her oar. Soon, she had reached the other bank. The girl ran faster, hearing the old woman's triumphant cackle behind her.

"Beloved, protect me," the girl prayed again, and threw the round white pebble over her shoulder. Where the pebble fell, the ground shook and cracked. Instantly, mountains grew out of the earth and towards the sky. These are the mountains we live in, that our houses now cling to, home to wild climbing creatures and highland flora. "Thank you, my love," the girl cried, thinking that she had escaped, but again, she was wrong. The witch's stewpot rose into the air, flying higher than the mountains. By the light of the setting sun, she cast a long shadow across the girl's path. Her laughter reached the girl's ears as she ran.

Now night was falling, and distantly, the girl could see chimney smoke. She was almost home.

"Beloved, protect me," she prayed a third time, and plucked the wooden comb from her hair. She threw it over her shoulder, and where it fell, tall trees sprouted at once. Hundreds of them, thousands—they say that in its thickest parts, the Witch's Wood is so tightly overgrown that you cannot see the sun even on a bright summer's day. These are the woods where we hunt for game, where we harvest berries and timber, where so many children have lost their way.

At last, the witch's cauldron was no match for the girl and her love. As the old crone flew her stewpot into the trees, she became hopelessly tangled in the branches, and the forest consumed her. She never emerged.

A short while later, the girl safely reached her own village. Her lover never returned to her, but she could see him forever in the sway of the trees in the wind, in the glitter of the water tumbling down the mountain's face.

The girl never strayed far from home again.

seven

Befre leaving for his salon in the mornings, Kiril goes to the woods. *Cut at an angle, not dead across.* He has the motion of it now: the axe slices through a sapling, and the tree slips from its trunk like snow melting off a ceramic roof. He winds through the forest and leaves a trail of sharp stumps in his wake.

It's peaceful in the woods, but lonely. A few days pass before he realizes that he's waiting for Nina to appear, as silently as she did before. Sometimes he thinks he feels her breath on his neck, the rustle of her dress against his back, but when he turns, the air is empty behind him. He looks for her in the village square, too—scanning the shadows one day while Simeon helps him fix the broken window sash. But when he finally does see her again, it isn't in the village or in the woods. She walks right up to him in the middle of the road.

The path is slick with wet red leaves, and she walks haltingly, grimacing as she goes. She's wrapped herself in a brown coat that must have been her husband's: it's too wide and too long, but she's nearly managed to close it in the front. He thinks she smiles when she sees him. "How's the cutting?" she asks, pausing to catch her breath.

"Fine, now that you've told me how. I've been practicing.

Yulia asked me to stop—she says we have enough wood for three winters and nowhere to store a single stick more." In his dreams, he reduces the whole forest floor to a bed of short, thick spikes. "Are you—is it still a gathering time?"

"Your friend at the bakery has been very generous with bread. I might last the winter after all." Her cheeks have filled a little. Today her skin is bright with exertion. She nods up the road, towards the house, and touches a too-long sleeve to her forehead. "I have an appointment with your uncle."

"Of course," Kiril says. Is that safe, for her and the baby? He's embarrassed even wondering. He has a sudden urge to offer his arm and help her up the slippery walk, to—to deliver her to his uncle? At their wedding, Margarita's father will walk with her in the church and present her to Simeon, and Kiril will stand beside him, giving his tacit consent.

Just a week before he left for the city, the night he saw her with Simeon in the apothecary, Margarita came to his window. Kiril's heart leapt at the sight of her, pulsed in his throat as he slipped down the stairs. She waited under the cover of the garden trellis, hiding among climbing geraniums.

"I know it hurt you to see that," she said. She had come to pity him. His grand declaration of love soured on his tongue. "We thought it would be easier if you didn't know."

"You talked about me?" Heads together, laughing.

Margarita didn't answer. He wanted to shake her. He gripped the trellis behind her and leaned in to kiss her, but she turned her head and slid under his arm. Only a strand of hair caught his wet lips as she fled.

Standing in the road, Nina buckles. She grabs at Kiril's

shirtfront to steady herself. A noise escapes her—a single note, a pinched *ah* that snags him like a fishhook. He catches her about the waist.

"Are you all right?"

"Fine, I—" Her body bows; she crumples like paper. "I should go—I'll be late."

"Your baby," Kiril realizes. A gust of wind rips down the road and under his coat. "Nina, how long—"

"Yesterday. It hasn't been bad, so I thought—my mother had false labors, and I—"

"Right. I understand." Panic rises hard and fast, but he cuts it down. There's no time. She's dead weight clinging to his arm. She'll never make it back to his salon.

Kiril clears his throat and tries to sound like the Captain, deep and calm. "We're going to my uncle's house, all right? I'm going to take care of you, Nina."

Her face is turning a mottled red. She looks ready to cry. "I don't think—" she begins, and falters. Kiril hoists her arm over his shoulders and starts to guide her. They weave clumsily up the road.

Who's left at home? Anka went to Margarita's early after breakfast, and Yulia disappeared about her errands in the village as soon as the plates were cleared. The Captain, waiting on Nina—

She stumbles. Overhead, the sky is growing grim and heavy, and he has a wild vision, a tableau: three of them huddled in a dry hutch among the trees while a storm descends, a new child in her mother's arms, the physician glowing saintly nearby.

They round a bend, and the house comes into view. "Almost there, almost there," he murmurs. Her fingernails dig through his sleeve. Just this morning, he noticed that the cuts Anka left on his neck had healed and faded away.

Nina slips on the leaves again. This time, she screams. Somewhere behind the house, he hears a door slam open—the seer comes running. She seems to understand at once. "I can go for help," she says. "Your midwife—"

"I can handle this. Help me get her inside."

Yana takes Nina's left arm, and together, they move. Two dozen painful paces to the house, Nina panting. Then the front steps, one at a time. They crash through the door and stumble down the hall.

"Up this way," Kiril says. "My cousin's room—we'll need the space to move around."

The Captain appears as they're rounding the banister. "The baby?" he says, and turns on Kiril. "Do you want her to die in your care?"

But if the baby lives—

"You'll be all right," Yana whispers over Nina's hunched shoulders. "We're almost there."

"She won't die," Kiril says loudly.

The Captain curses indifferently. He brushes Kiril and Yana aside like dust, then lifts Nina easily up the stairs. Her arms circle his neck, hands white-knuckled in his collar.

"To Anka's room," Kiril calls after.

Yana clears her throat. "Is there anyone I should get for her?" she asks. "Any family?"

"No," Kiril says. Upstairs, the Captain says something

low that Kiril can't hear. *I have an appointment with your uncle.* "She's alone."

They climb the stairs. Yana slips into the room without prompting and goes straight to Nina's bedside. In the hall, the Captain shuts the door.

"Yulia went into town. She should be back soon." He speaks with his back turned. "You made a mistake, bringing her here like this."

You brought her here, Kiril thinks, irritation flaring. "She'll be fine."

"You know what they say about children in this town."

"You don't believe any of that."

"No—*but the people here do believe it.* How often do I have to tell you? That matters more than what's real."

"I can take care of her."

His uncle rubs his knuckles over the banister, mulling over the thought. He considers Kiril in the dim light of the hall. "Whatever comes of this, they'll talk about you. They won't care much about her. If she dies, you'll only be a witch killer—they may even celebrate you. But pray that her child lives. You could make your name here today."

Usually it grounds Kiril, to know he's thinking like his uncle, but this feels like opening the larder and finding something inside has spoiled.

"They'll both live," he says, raising his chin.

He goes in. Yana is walking Nina gently around the room, letting gravity work. "Don't worry," she's saying, in a voice like a lullaby. "The doctor knows what he's doing."

Nina squeezes her eyes shut. "Do you?" she asks.

"Yes," Kiril says. Twice in the city, he'd sat by and watched as the surgeon's wife took care of women becoming mothers— poor women who offered themselves as subjects in exchange for a small purse. The surgeon was an endlessly curious man, fascinated even by women's problems. He encouraged the same of his students, though many of them bristled. But Kiril wanted to learn. He wanted to help the mothers back home, wanted to pull the villagers out of the grave where they'd buried themselves in grief and delusion.

"I'll take care of you, Nina. I promise."

He directs Yana to the washtub to scrub her hands, and then turns his back and tells her how to examine Nina under her skirts. "Then there's a while to go still," he says, when she reports back, and he hopes that he sounds gentle, reassuring, firm.

Yana supports Nina in her small circuit around the room. Kiril fluffs the pillows. He remembers suddenly that he used to sleep in this bed every night. He and Anka would fall asleep curled together like frightened kittens. Outside, the rain begins. He hears a gurgle of thunder in the distance.

Something dislodges from the pillowcase and falls to the floor: a piece of gray felted wool, a few inches wide and as long as his palm. He's never seen it before. He picks it up and turns it over, unsure, and then he realizes: it's intended for a woman's bleeding. There's a pale stain across it, rust that's been diligently scrubbed.

"I need to lie down," Nina says, unsteady arm stretched into the air for balance.

Kiril shoves the felt back into the pillowcase and punches the pillow into place. "Easy there."

They settle her into the bed. She takes his hand and doesn't let go. She clings, her breath punctured and ragged on a rocky shore.

HOURS PASS. YANA lets herself peek around Anka's room. The walls are clean and white, the ceiling crosshatched with stained wooden beams. A red rug spreads between the bed and the wardrobe, and a gilded icon and a bouquet of dried flowers hang from nails by the window. Shelves line the wall facing the bed. They house an old cloth doll, some dozen books, and a row of clay pots for rouge and perfumed wax— gifts from the Captain's travels. A silver mirror perches at eye level.

Yana stays by Nina's bedside even as Kiril anxiously paces the room in her stead. In the early afternoon, when the rain stops and he goes to his salon to gather supplies, Nina turns her head to look Yana right in the eye.

"I've wanted to say something to you." Her hair frizzes around her flushed neck. "It's been a wretched time. And your dead chicken didn't help matters at all."

Yana bows her head. "I am sorry for that. I never want my work to hurt anyone. If I'd known about you—"

Nina smiles faintly. "You know, I believe you." She clenches her jaw through another spasm. Her teeth have worried her lower lip raw.

"Breathe," Yana reminds her gently. She strokes the back of Nina's sweaty hand, the red-cracked ridge of her knuckles.

The moment passes. Nina shakes her head. "It's strange—your work, it seems like it should have died away a long time ago."

Yana considers this. "In small villages like this, time moves differently. But sometimes I find work in cities, too. Humans have always needed people like me—as long as we've needed monsters."

Nina looks skeptical. "Do people need monsters?"

"A person can't fight a plague, but they can fight the beast that cursed them with it. If not vampire or varkolak, it's the Devil, or it's witches. My way doesn't end in witch burnings."

"If you're careful," Nina says.

"I will be. You're not from this village, are you?"

"I married into it."

"You could leave," Yana suggests. "Go find your family, wherever they are."

"Dead," Nina says. "At least here I have a house."

It hadn't even occurred to her. Yana hasn't lived in a house since her father was alive.

"Tell me about your husband. What was he like?"

Nina's face softens, then breaks. She turns away for a while. The rain is starting again, a gentle patter against the windowpanes. Kiril will get caught in it, but there's time, Yana assures herself—he'll get back in time. "Kind," Nina says finally. "His name was Luka."

In Yana's imagination, Luka borrows the young baker's

smile. She can picture Nina as happy as Anka's friend, a joyful young bride with a whole loving life ahead.

"How did you meet?"

"My father's horse threw a shoe on the road—he never meant to stop here, but he did. Luka repaired it, and his father invited Papa to stay the night." She squeezes her eyes shut. "My father didn't believe in curses. He thought this would be a good place for me."

"And it was, for a while?"

"It was. We had friends. We were healthy. He made me laugh every day I knew him."

Yana tries to remember her father making her mother laugh, but all she can conjure are dimly lit murmurs from across the room, when she was small and out of sight.

"He sounds like he would have made a wonderful father," she says.

Nina lets go of Yana's hand and wipes her face on the bed linens. Her body curls with another spasm, or maybe she cries awhile. Yana brushes her hair gently with her fingers.

"He never even knew," Nina says at last, unbending herself. "I never told anyone about the baby until after he died."

The rain grows heavier. She tells the story: a startled horse, a hard kick to the head. She came home to the smithy and found him surrounded by people doing nothing, the apothecary on his knees on the slate floor, helpless against the blood that spread from Luka's cracked skull like a corona.

"They said they found a snake hiding in a feedbag. It was the Captain's horse that did it—he didn't need the new shoes for another week, but Luka wanted the job done. He'd only had the shop a year then, since his father died. He wanted to make a good impression." She pauses, eyes closed. "I heard the Captain shot the horse himself that same day."

"The Captain," Yana says, conscious of the open bedroom door. "What do you think of him?"

Nina hesitates. Before she can respond, Kiril's footsteps clatter up the stairs. He appears in the doorway with his black leather bag in hand, his hair and shirt damp with rain.

"All right in here?" he asks, out of breath.

"Fine," Nina says, lifting herself gingerly from the pillows. "Yana, I think I'd like to walk again."

THE TIME TO push comes shortly after sundown.

Kiril uncaps a bottle and offers Nina a glass dropper with a rubber bulb. "For the pain," he says. "Open your mouth."

She does. Looking not at the bottle, but at him. She stretches out her tongue, and he dispenses three drops. He clears his throat. "That's it. You can swallow."

Yulia and Anka have returned, hovering in the hallway, waiting to be called. As he puts away the tonic, Kiril locks eyes with Anka, just for a moment. He sees her look from him to Nina, in her bed, and he thinks about the felted rag in the pillows. Anka has looked a little pale for days, but now it might be panic draining her color.

Later. He can't let himself get angry. He has to focus on the task at hand.

Yana signals to him. "Now," he says. Nina screams as she

pushes. He smooths her hair, a strange lightness in the pit of his stomach. "Breathe now," he whispers. "Again—push."

The bed frame, the floorboards, the earth creak and tremble. He sees ripping seams, a flooding river. Anka haunts the crack of the door. Kiril's fingers catch in Nina's hair and skim the sweaty shell of her ear. "Once more—"

Outside, the rain has ended, but the wind wrenches a shutter loose. A last bolt of lightning splits the dark, and the air smells harsh and chemical, like the surgeon's cellar. And then there's a moment, a blank space in the world. Kiril suddenly hears nothing but the ringing bells in his head—and he sees nothing but Nina's face, wrenched and pained and red and beautiful.

A new throat begins to cry.

"A girl," Yana whispers.

Kiril peels himself away from Nina's side. He takes a clean knife from the shelf. His body feels like gelatin, but his hand doesn't shake as he cuts the cord. Yulia slams the door wide and sweeps in with a warm rag to wipe the baby down.

"Please," Nina says, and Yana brings her. Pink-purple, squinted and small. She's barely more than an egg, Kiril thinks. She's stopped crying.

Nina stares. Her eyes are big and dark with the painkiller, like wet ink. "She looks healthy," she whispers. "Does she look healthy?"

"She does," Kiril says. His hand is pockmarked from her fingernails, and his legs are threatening to give out. Yulia takes the knife from him. He'd forgotten he was holding it.

"The afterbirth—" he starts to say, but Yulia shoos him towards the door.

"Go," she says. "Catch your breath."

Anka is waiting in the hall with water for his bloodied hands. She balances the bowl on one arm while she scrubs his fingers with a washcloth. Kiril feels drunk, everything around him too bright. Anka grips his wrist and holds on until he looks her in the eye.

"What did you—" she starts to say. But the Captain comes up the stairs.

"All well?" he asks. His expression is curiously soft. He peers through the cracked door. Inside, Yulia is wrapping the baby in clean linen while Yana blots Nina's brow with a damp cloth. "There are people waiting outside in the rain."

Kiril tugs his hand from Anka's grip and shakes the water off into the basin. "What?"

"Our neighbors have come to witness," the Captain says. He's smiling. He holds something out to Kiril—he's brought two glasses of brandy. "Even a witch's newborn is good news, after so long. They'll want to hear from the doctor."

It's pride in his voice, Kiril realizes. He's actually managed to impress his uncle. Numbly, he takes the glass.

"She's healthy," he whispers. "I mean, both of them are. I think they'll both be fine."

The Captain clinks their glasses together and drains his drink. Kiril swallows without tasting.

"They're at the front door," the Captain says, nudging him down the hall. "Reassure them she has no hooves or horns."

eight

KIRIL INSISTS THAT Anka take his bed, unrolling a rug for himself on the floor by Nina's side, but she sleeps badly under the unfamiliar slope of his bedroom ceiling, where the roof tapers down and rain runs into the barrel by the back door. The baby wakes every few hours, but Anka doesn't dream between the cries or the lullabies. She stares at the tilted roof, her heart loud. The cold look Kiril gave her is printed on the darkness. What did he see?

In the morning, Yulia examines the circles under her eyes by the light of the window. She purses her lips and gives a tight nod. "We can make up a bed in the parlor for you, away from the baby. You should get as much sleep as you can."

"I think Kiril knows," Anka whispers. "I think he saw, while—"

The floorboards creak in the hall, and Yulia covers Anka's mouth with her cool fingers.

All day, she waits for a moment with Kiril alone, but he never leaves Nina's side. The hours are stuffy, self-conscious, the quiet punctured sometimes by the baby's voice, but otherwise hushed with care. In the evening, sipping brandy in the parlor, the Captain tilts his head at Anka and says gently, "You're looking a bit pale, little bird."

She doesn't know if it's poison or fear. She mumbles something about too much excitement.

"Yes," he agrees, smiling. "A new child is very exciting. You'll see for yourself, someday soon."

Yulia calls her to take Yana some dinner. The knife and fork clatter against the plate as Anka carries the tray to the cottage.

"You look terrible," Yana says, not unkindly, when she opens the door.

"Kiril knows I'm hiding something." Anka leans against the wall, the tray still buzzing. "I think he saw one of the pads I use, when he was in my room with Nina. Yulia folds them in the bed linens for me when she cleans. Minka—she gave me these sponges to use instead—and the rag has just been sitting there. I didn't know anyone but us would go in my room, but then Kiril, he gave me this look, like—"

"It's all right," Yana says evenly. "Sit down—you're freezing. Here, let me take that." She tugs the tray away.

Anka sinks onto the floor by the glowing grate. She puts her back to the warm brick and covers her face with her apron. "Did he say anything? While you were with him?"

"No. But we were busy with Nina. What has he told you?"

Anka folds her hands under her arms. "Nothing. He's been with her all day." She takes a long breath and pushes it out until she feels like a shell. "Your dinner will get cold."

Yana picks up her fork but doesn't eat. She starts pacing. Anka watches her wearily from the floor.

"Has he been acting strangely?" Yana asks.

"Everything is strange today—a witch and her baby

are sleeping in my bed. The Captain is proud of Kiril. This tonic—I'm afraid I'll start seeing ghosts at any moment." She digs her palms into her eyelids. "I thought at least I'd be able to catch Kiril alone after everyone went to bed, but he slept on the floor to be with Nina. He won't leave her." She pauses to bite at a hangnail, an unsatisfying crunch that leaves behind a small, painful weed at the edge of her nail bed. "I think he likes her." After the desperate, heartrending years Kiril spent in love with Margarita, it feels odd to phrase it so simply, but Yana nods.

"I think you're right," she says, tapping the tines of the fork against her bottom lip. "And that's to our advantage. She's all he'll think about for a while. Will he go to your uncle while she's in the house? I doubt it."

Anka chews her finger. "No," she says at last. A dim hallway, hands at her throat. "He'll come to me first."

Satisfied, Yana sits and spears a bite of stewed carrot with her fork. "As far as he knows, the tonic you're taking is nothing but fruit juice. There's no reason for him to connect it to your health. So our plan doesn't change."

Anka's fingernail starts to bleed. She squeezes her hand into a fist.

"What is our plan now?" Not much has happened since the eggs. Yana has been questioning the villagers, Anka knows—she says they like to feel involved, that they're all chasing the stories they will tell decades from now on long winter nights—but no new horrors have manifested. The town is holding its breath.

"Terror is built from waiting," Yana says simply, and takes another bite of dinner. "We'll feel it when it's time for the next strike. A few days more, I think—Nina's baby shifted the balance. I'll act before your friend's wedding."

The wedding, not even two weeks away. The veil is ready, and the dress. Anka had almost forgotten. All that's left now is the cooking, days of preparation for the feast. Soon, Margarita's mother will begin kneading a wedding loaf for the guests. Simeon has been painting wooden bottles of brandy with bright colors to give as gifts.

"There are lots of opportunities for bad omens at a wedding," Anka says.

"No. I don't want Margarita and Simeon under suspicion. I'll perform public rituals in the days before, to protect them. But I think I've picked a target."

"Your vampire?"

Yana wipes her hands on her trousers and pushes her tray aside. "Have a look," she says, smoothing a piece of paper on the table. It's a black lead rubbing of a grave marker—a wooden grave, not stone. A name, a date, nothing more. "We might use your old midwife. The one who died over the summer."

Anka sniffs. "I wouldn't mind seeing her impaled."

Yana smiles grimly. "Of the newer graves, hers was most overgrown. The marker was crooked, but nobody had fixed it. She wasn't well-liked?"

"Not by me." Anka tips her head back against the wall, considering the question against the black beams of the ceiling. She feels the old woman's cold pincers on her body. "Margarita told me she went to her for help once, when she and Simeon—

you know. She was afraid she'd get pregnant. That hag chased her away and threatened to tell her father."

"I was thinking of the newborns who didn't survive. She would have tended to them and the mothers?"

"She lost their trust," Anka remembers. "It probably wasn't her fault, but they started calling Yulia to attend to births—I guess she must have taken Minka with her. It didn't make a difference, in the end."

"Yulia has a broad skill set for a housekeeper. Where did she come from, before this?"

"She never says. Only that she's *lived many lives*." Anka's voice is lilting, distant.

Yana laughs. She traces the dates on the grave rubbing. "Have you been into town today? Your cousin is very popular all of a sudden. I thought they might resent him for helping Nina, but they're much too excited about the baby. All day I heard women asking why he wasn't at his salon."

"What about you?"

Yana's smile is beautiful, Anka thinks. The way her face glows like a cut jewel. "They don't seem to know I was there for the birth, and that suits me just fine."

She studies the rubbing for another moment, then flips the page over. On the back, she's drawn a neat map of the village and the closest farms. The woods are marked with a sea of small X's for trees.

"I've been thinking about the story you told me," Yana says. "About the girl and the witch. It's all a matter of perspective, isn't it? The girl isn't really the hero. The witch, all she wants is something to eat, but there's nothing where she is."

Yana gestures to the knot of woody X's, the smooth gray slide of the river across the page. "She tricks the girl into building the landscape for her, so she can gather and hunt."

"I've never gone hunting," Anka says.

"Sometimes I have to, when I'm traveling, but I don't like it."

"Don't you kill animals all the time? For your work?"

"It's different. But I don't much care for that, either."

Near the edge of the map, two squares indicate the Captain's house and the garden cottage. Yana's drawn a five-pointed star over the room where they sit. Anka touches the main house, the corner where her room is, and the line blurs to smoke, leaving a black mark on her finger.

"What's it like?" she asks. "Killing something?"

"Making a sacrifice," Yana corrects. "It's horrible. Bloody, loud. They want to live. If they didn't, it wouldn't be a sacrifice."

"I thought you didn't believe in magic."

"No. But I believe that death matters."

Anka leans closer to the map. Yana's attention to detail is remarkable; in the rows of boxes, she can easily identify the apothecary, the bakery, Kiril's salon. Across the east meadow, she sees a slash where an earthquake split the land when she was younger, leaving behind a deep ravine. She and Kiril were forbidden to play near it as children, but of course they did, dropping in pebbles to listen for the bottom. When they were caught, the Captain set Anka writing lines and then beat Kiril so that he winced every time he sat for the next week.

Following the road from the square, Anka finds an empty spot on the map. She points to it. "My parents' house was here, before it burned down." Her blackened fingertip leaves a gray smudge on the paper. "There's not much left there now. You can still see the kiln and some of the foundations."

"I've seen it," Yana says. "I didn't know it was their home."

"When will you go out again? To make your next sacrifice?"

"A few nights from now, I think." She indicates the far edge of the map, where she's shaded a pasture in thin diagonals. It's a farm, owned by a couple with no living children.

"I know that place," Anka says. Margarita likes to stand at the collapsing fence to watch the newborn lambs. Her heart starts to beat faster.

"I would think you know every place here," Yana says. Gently, she tugs the map out from under Anka's hand and gathers it into a scroll. Anka's finger has stopped bleeding now, though the nail is lined in red where it meets her skin.

"Can I come with you?" she asks. "The next time you go out?"

Yana pauses, tucking the scroll away in her leather bag. "I'm not sure that's a good idea," she says. "You're already weak from this tonic."

"Please." Anka isn't sure how to explain. The making of a sacrifice—suddenly she's desperate to see it. By the time she saw the chicken, there was almost nothing left.

Yana kneels by the fire and stays for a long time, longer than she needs to. Finally, she rises and replaces the poker in its iron stand. "If you're strong enough when the time comes," she says. "I'll tell you when."

Anka remembers the glint of Yana's knives in the firelight,

the hiss of the whetstone the first time she came to the cottage, the weight of the broken dagger on her palm. She feels that shiver again, cool down her back.

"I won't get in the way," she promises.

Yana's smile is weary and thin.

THEY MOVE THE baby before dark, to satisfy Nina's superstitions. A newborn younger than forty days can't be touched by night, she insists. Sofia is only three days old, and Nina isn't interested in anything Kiril has to tell her about the medical facts of the matter.

Yana offers to go ahead, to scout the road. Even with the sun still burning the treetops, they meet no one on the way, and the windows they pass are all shut tight against demons.

Nina is wary of her own home, afraid someone might come for her baby in the night. There are families here desperate for a healthy child—what might they do to have hers? So, Kiril takes her to his mother's cottage.

The house in the woods has stood empty since he was a boy. When his mother went cold in her bed, his father squeezed Kiril's shoulder so hard it could crack and said, "Wait here. I'll be back." Two days later, Simeon's mother found Kiril dry-lipped with thirst and woozy with hunger, still sitting on the floor by his mother's bedside. He'd realized by then that his mother wouldn't wake, but he'd been told to wait, so he waited. Later, he learned that his father's horse had disappeared in the night, leaving behind only hoofprints in the mud.

"This way," he murmurs to Nina, and they turn down the

overgrown path. He came here sometimes as a boy, to hide, but he hasn't dared go inside since he came back from the city. He wanted to come and clean today, but Nina held him off, afraid he would be seen.

The door opens easily. Dying sunlight slips through the broken shutters, painting the corners of the room red. When the baker's wife called the Captain to the house that day, he filled the doorway with his grief. Morning bled onto the floor-boards around his long shadow. He spoke rough, adult words, and his hands drew a cross like armor. He grabbed his sister's wrist for a moment, long enough to find her cold and stiff, and then he dropped to his knees and said his nephew's name maybe a dozen times before Kiril turned his head.

"It isn't much," Kiril says to Nina apologetically. The room has long been stripped of its furniture—he remembers a bed and chairs and a table, but all have been taken by shrewd neighbors in the night. The kettle and cooking pot have vanished from their hooks by the fire, and even the grate is missing a few bricks. All that's left are a lumpy mattress folded over itself and the bones of a dead mouse on the floor. "We can bring some things from my uncle's house tomorrow. I'll light the fire for you now, if you like."

"No. Someone might see the smoke." Nina runs a hand softly over her baby's back, a prayer for silence.

"Then take this," Kiril says, slipping out of his coat. "There used to be some blankets here, but—"

"You'll freeze on your way back," Nina says. Her voice is a frayed cloth starting to unravel. She wants him to go, Kiril thinks. Is she tired of him? Afraid of him?

He folds the coat fluidly over one arm and kneels to straighten the mattress on the floor. He's pleased to find it dry, apparently free of vermin, though it's hard to tell in the unlit room. Nina wraps her daughter in her own oversized coat, making her a woolen nest in the mattress.

She looks smaller without the baby in her arms, without the pregnant bulge under her dress. Kiril tries to remember her from before, but the images in his mind—Nina at the market, Nina in the church—feel so posed and thin that he's sure he's inventing them. Did he think she was pretty, when he was still a boy and she was already someone else's wife? He must have—there were so few women in the village to admire—but then, as long as he could remember, he had eyes only for Margarita.

In the city, there were women everywhere. Wealthy ladies with their maids and escorts, washerwomen carrying baskets of linens, fortune tellers sitting cross-legged on faded carpets on the street. It seemed any of them would sell a piece of her time in the confidence of an alleyway or a sweaty bed, one often used but rarely slept in. It was all so vain, so trivial. He found a strange homesickness in the shape of the village women, the certainty of where he stood in relation to each of them. Now, in his own house, his head swims and his ears ring. His throat runs dry; he wants so badly to touch her. He felt like this in the city: unmoored, tossed about in the unknown.

Nina goes to the window and peeks out. The sun has fully set now, and the moon is rising. The comet glows above the church steeple, visible over the trees.

"I think it's safe for you to go now," she says. "I don't see anyone."

He means to. He means to give a short bow from across the room, walk through the door, and leave her at peace. Instead, his feet carry him towards her. "At least take this," he says, holding out his coat. "I'm used to the cold, and my uncle must have a dozen more at home."

A shadow passes over her face. The moment hangs like a wet sheet between them. When Nina doesn't move, he swings the coat over her shoulders—carefully, so as not to touch her skin, so as not to make her nervous. She runs her fingertips over the wool. It's a little road-worn, but clean and thick. Her thumb traces a button, the small silver-worked head of a lion.

"Thank you," she says. "I'll give it back."

She gathers her hair from under the collar and sweeps it off her neck. A leather cord hangs from her throat, where she's kept her wedding band since she gave birth. The golden ring rises and sets behind the horizon of her dress. Kiril bites his tongue. He doesn't just want to touch her. He wants to taste the hollow of her throat and snap the leather cord with his teeth. He leans in.

It isn't like kissing Margarita—Nina doesn't turn away. He slides his fingers into the warm weight of her hair, and she tilts her head back. He tastes blood from a cut where she bit down bringing Sofia into the world, or maybe where his uncle hit her. Ghosts of other men haunt every room in her body. Before she was jailed, a farmer had sworn that three times in one week, he woke terrified in the night, pinned to his bed by Nina's wanton spirit, helpless to stop her as she coaxed flesh and devoured weakness. When she sighs against his lips, Kiril knows he would let her fill him with whatever black spellwork she desired, if only she'd let him stay.

On the mattress, the baby stirs. The overture to a cry burbles into the still air. The moment fractures. Nina slides easily from Kiril's arms and goes to her daughter, scooping her up, already whispering to comfort her. *Hush, darling, or the devil will hear.*

"I'll go," Kiril says. A fever blooms up his chest and neck. "Good night."

She says his name as he crosses the threshold, but she doesn't come after him when he shuts the door. He's shaking as he hurries away from the house.

Three months after his arrival in the city, on a frigid winter night in January, Kiril wandered the streets. He often did. The boardinghouse was stuffy with sniffling, flatulent bodies, but outside was too cold and empty, shaped from slick cobbles and curls of smoke. The houses were painted in bright colors, like the candies sold in shops by the river, so sweet they hurt his teeth. There was no good place to be. His loneliness ground him down.

It had snowed the night before. The streets were trampled flat, but great drifts still pressed doors shut and filled the throats of uncovered wells. In one courtyard, an old fig tree had buckled under the weight, a branch lying like a broken arm across the square, the tree's soft flesh exposed from its wound. It was quiet for the first time since he'd set foot here. The snow swallowed the city's voice, and he could hear the frozen lake in his ears, feel it under his clothes.

He rounded a corner and there was one door bleeding

music: a flute, a harp, interrupted by peals of laughter. Kiril stood by the window listening for a melody, but it seemed a pointless tune, one plucked from the air as the musicians went along. Incidental music, languid, in service of something else.

The door crashed open, and a woman and a man swung out with it, locked in an embrace, scattering snow beneath their feet. The man stumbled drunkenly into the night, throwing soft, moony looks over his shoulder. The woman blew kisses as he went. When he was gone, she turned her smile on Kiril. She invited him in from the cold. He gave her one of his uncle's coins.

Inside was warm, and he left shades of snowy footprints on the stairs as he climbed, following her up three full flights to a room with a window cut into the ceiling to let the sun and the moonlight through. There was a bubbled pane of glass across it, covered by a scrim of blue snow.

"How do you like it?" the woman asked, standing very close to him, and it took a moment to realize she wasn't talking about the room. He didn't know the answer, wasn't quite sure he wasn't dreaming. He could smell the rose oil she'd dabbed behind her ears and on her throat. Her hair was sleek and wavy, her figure generous like Margarita's.

"I see," she said gently, after a long silence. "I can show you."

She did. In her bed, looking up at the snow-frosted window, he felt warm for the first time in months. She uncovered noises that he didn't know were locked inside him. How strange that human bodies could do this to each other, that flesh could be so powerful. He'd known, but he hadn't known. He understood now why the priests feared it.

He cried out when he finished, as if she'd struck him. His

body jerked like a fly caught in a spiderweb. Suddenly her weight on him hurt, the feeling of her too much, too heavy. She lay down beside him, resting her palm on his chest, which rose and fell in a panic. He covered his face with his hands.

A grotesque memory tugged at him, a time he'd been about eleven years old: he'd woken from a beastly dream with his nightshirt damp, a shameful cooling against his belly. Anka breathed beside him, but he was sure from the slant of her shoulders that she wasn't sleeping. It wasn't long before the Captain gave them separate rooms, and Kiril was always certain he'd somehow known.

"Are you all right?" the whore asked. He'd gone rigid. Her voice had lost its smoothness. By the blue light, he could make out the pits and pimples in her complexion, starting to show through her layers of paint and powder. He seized her wrist. Had she laughed at him? He could have sworn he saw her mouth split, her mocking teeth. He tightened his grip, and she tried to pull away.

"You're hurting me," she whined. "Please—just go."

Pop and grind of cartilage and bone. She whimpered, and he opened his fingers. Fumbling for his clothes, he ran down the stairs before she could yell for help. Later, he stared at drawings of human musculature, bodies beneath their skins, gripping his own wrist and squeezing to feel the slip and crunch of the joints, and wondered how badly he'd hurt her, poorly comforted to know he could have done worse but hadn't. Shame and rage bubble up whenever he thinks of her now, when he thinks about the wide smiles of women. Anka has grown such a smile, and Margarita, too. Bile, like ink, bubbles over.

His hands are numb with wind by the time he makes it back to his uncle's house. He folds them under his arms as he walks, his body bent against the gusts. The cold is a pale phantom reaching through the water to grab at his ankles, teeth bared in a covetous grin.

Nina's smile is different, he thinks, as he fumbles the door open and the warmth of the parlor washes over him. Frightened, but pure. Somehow clean. In this moment, he believes that with all his heart.

nine

SHOULDN'T THINGS ALWAYS get worse?" Yana had asked, thinking of fairy tales. Bigger and more tragic victims, one after the other, until at last the culprit was named and beaten.

Her mother was bent over the book, drawing a vampire's burial, the unhinged jaws. She shook her head. "Our way is better," she said. "It puts their own fear to work. Remember how it was at home?"

A broken plate, a blackened eye. Then a stretch of gentle nights, interrupted only by huffing, stubbled breath over glass, the scrape of a chair that froze Yana where she stood. When Mama talked about Yana's father, things happened all on their own: *when your finger broke, when my arm was hurt, when your doll fell in the fire.* He existed only as a disembodied fist swinging out of the shadows, right up until *when your father died.* Yana was young, but old enough. Inside the quiet, anything could happen.

In the village Koprivci, she manifests a string of small horrors.

A plot of healthy wheat shrivels black in the field overnight. When the farmer digs to see what has infested the roots, he finds the decaying heart of an animal.

On a cold morning, a woman runs screaming into the vestry, holding a loaf of steaming bread at arm's length: baked inside, the priest finds four human teeth. Simeon looks as alarmed as anyone, wringing his apron in his hands.

"But it's all about blood," Anka says. "Right?"

Blood, to feed the shadow. Blood, to strengthen the flesh. Blood that runs faster in fright, whose pulse draws the line between life and death like a row of Anka's light, quick stitches on a muslin skin.

"Yes," Yana agrees. "It's all about blood."

Soon after, the village roses are destroyed. The last wrinkled blooms of the season are slashed from their stalks by sharp claws. Upon waking, the villagers find sprays of red petals beneath the flower boxes and outside their front doors. "The vampire has very delicate skin," Yana explains to a throng outside the tavern. "It is easily threatened by thorns. One rip, and it could lose all its strength." Her brows draw tightly together. "This one seems particularly aggressive."

An old man has been talking loudly in the square about one year when he was a boy, a winter so cold that rocks cracked and fires refused to catch—only a handful of families survived, none of them intact. The villagers worry aloud about their winter stores, about tainted grains and bread that sprouts teeth in the rise. The comet is glowing brighter, and the witch and her baby have vanished. At night, the villagers are afraid to dream. Yana tells Anka that it's time.

Anka arrives at the cottage while Yana is taking stock of her supplies. Her bag is heavy and her pockets are full of clover.

"You won't be afraid?" she asks, eying Anka at a slant.

She's unnerved; she's never done this work with anyone but her mother, and this girl is still unknown to her. Desperation is a danger they can't afford.

And what are you desperate for, little star? Mama mumbles, running her finger along the frowning brim of Yana's hat, upside down on the table.

"Afraid of what?" Anka asks.

"Ghosts."

Anka laughs. "I don't believe in ghosts."

"Everyone believes in ghosts when it's dark enough."

They track close to the tree line and down the road. The wind is restless. Anka looks distinctly ill now, her features grown sharp. She's wearing her heavy shawl again, this time over an unblemished throat, and it threatens to swallow her. Yesterday, she confided that Margarita worries over her constantly—whenever they're alone together, she begs Anka to pour the poison into the dirt, but Anka faithfully measures out her spoonful each night.

True to her word, she doesn't speak or interfere as they steal away from the house, except to ask once for a short break behind a good patch of brush cover so that she can catch her breath. The villagers hide, too, but the scent of burning wood escapes latched shutters and drawn curtains, betraying every tightly buttoned house they pass.

The farm is quiet when they arrive. It was easy for Yana to sneak into the house that afternoon and pour a draft from her flask into the evening beer. Now the always-alert farmhand has fallen asleep at his post, on watch for monsters. The sheepdog is curled at his feet, snoring like a man. Yana has a bloody goat's bone in her bag, but maybe the dog likes beer, too. He doesn't bark or move as they slip over the fence like moonlight and creep towards the flock.

"Which one?" Anka whispers. Her white face glows under a sheen of sweat. Yana's stomach turns over. She points to the smallest lamb.

The sheep's huddle is warmer than the thin night air. Here it smells of hay and earth and manure. The chosen lamb's eyes are open, and it watches them curiously while its mother dozes. Yana reaches into her pocket and holds out a fistful of clover, already treated from the flask. The lamb lifts its head and sniffs the offering. Yana can see the light of the comet reflected in its sweet black eyes. The lamb puts out its tongue and eats.

Yana tries to forget about Anka, hovering behind her, radiating morbid excitement. She strokes the lamb's head and ears until it relaxes into her touch. She backs up a few steps and holds out more clover. The lamb hesitates, then unfolds its sapling legs to follow.

Another handful, another retreat. By the time they're at the fence, the lamb's eyes are drooping and its gait weaves. Carefully, they guide him over the posts and out of the pasture, back into the trees.

"This is the old burning point," Anka whispers, when they come to a stop in the woods.

Yana looks. It's a good spot: hidden on all sides by thick trees, with a flat slab of rock in the clearing. She came here to prepare the chicken, but it hadn't occurred to her that she might not be the first to use the place, that the stone slab might not be natural. Everything is blanketed in fallen leaves, leached of their colors in the dark. The lamb's legs wobble, and it looks at her, waiting for her next move. She sinks to her knees and pets its head again. It shuts its eyes and nuzzles into her lap.

"It trusts you," Anka murmurs, stepping closer.

"Animals are simple," Yana says. "A kind touch. Some food and the right medicine."

Anka reaches to pet the lamb's flank. "Maybe it just likes you."

That sounds much worse. "Open my bag," Yana says, keeping her voice light. She directs Anka to remove a stained wooden bowl and a curved sheet of metal. "These are for the blood," she says, not looking away from the lamb, now peacefully dozing against her thigh. "We're going to cut its throat. We'll use what it sheds later."

She reaches casually into her belt and finds the right knife by its hilt. "Come here with me," she instructs, and Anka kneels beside her on dead leaves. She positions the bowl without Yana needing to ask. The lamb blinks up at her but doesn't move, glassy with drugged clover. "Once we start, it will try to get away. We'll have to hold it tight. Are you ready?"

"Yes."

Yana grips her knife, her free hand still gently stroking the thin fuzz over the lamb's head. There's a shape at the edge of her vision: her mother, watching from the trees. The lamb's ribs rise and fall with unsuspecting breath.

Two truths: A body is just an object. This is not a body yet.

"Thank you," Yana whispers, her lips to the animal's soft ear. "Your sacrifice is a seed of hope."

She tightens her grip around the lamb's head. The knife

moves in a quick flicker of moonlight, and the lamb's bone-ripped cry covers her own. Blood hits the bowl like heavy rain.

WHEN ANKA WAS nine or ten, the Captain hoisted her up so that her eyes were level with her mother's portrait over the mantel. His large hands dug hard into her waist, fingertips meeting where they pressed under her ribs. "You're beginning to look so much like her," he said into her hair. "I loved your mother very much, little bird—I miss her every day." He set her down, feet to solid ground, and pinched her nape. "We just need to be patient."

Soon after that, he hired a man in the village to build another bed and gave Kiril his own room. She was alone, four years later, when she began to bleed. She woke in the night to a hot, slimy wetness under her clothes and pain deep in her body. Margarita had been bleeding for a year by then—Anka knew what it was, and she understood what it meant. She lay awake, rigid with fear, until Yulia came to rouse her in the morning. Anka held up a bloody hand, and her chin trembled. Yulia locked the door behind herself and knelt at the bedside. Her complexion was so pale, Anka worried the blood would stain her, like spilled wine over a white tablecloth.

"What does she do with it?" Margarita had asked, frowning, when Anka told her.

Anka had wondered the same. "She says what she can squeeze out is good for the garden. For watering the plants."

The lamb kicks and tries to pull free. Anka feels Yulia's medicine in her atrophied muscles as she tries to hang on. The animal's back leg wrenches out of her grip and lands a hard blow against her forearm. Long after the lamb is rotting in the garbage pit, crawling with white worms, she'll have this bruise: the split edge of a hoof stamped purple on the white of her arm, sickly blue-greens trailing away like twin comets. She shouts in surprise, but manages to grab hold again.

The wooden bowl fills. The lamb grows weaker, easier to restrain as it dies. The longer it bleeds, the stronger Anka feels. Her arm throbs. She's flushed, even in the cold. She's forgotten where they are, the phantom creaking of ropes. *Yes, it's all about blood.* Yana's eyes are shut tight and her face is wet, her lips moving in a prayer. Maybe it's different, after so many killings—Anka can't tear her gaze away.

The lamb's legs twitch weakly. Its wool shines pearlescent under the stars. The open wound is a fathomless void, and Anka feels better than she has in weeks. Her heart pounds, and she wants to dance, to sing the lamb to sleep. So that's all there is to an omen: blood, and the will to use it. That's all. There's power here she can understand.

At last, the lamb goes still. Yana opens her eyes and lets go of its head, stroking its ear with her fingers. Her hands are blue, white, and blood-black under the moonglow.

"What now?" Anka asks, struggling to keep her voice soft and somber. She's shaking, like she's just survived one of Kiril's attacks. Yana draws her bloody fingertips over the lamb's lids to close them. The bowl has filled almost to the brim.

"In my bag," Yana says. "For collection."

Using the hammered sheet of metal, they funnel lamb's

blood into three large bottles. The glass grows warm. Yana corks each one tightly, then guides the last dregs into a vial and hands it to Anka. "This is for your friend. She may need it on her wedding night."

They wipe the bowl with a rag and scatter leaves to cover their tracks in the clearing. Yana repacks her tools with quick precision, gaze flickering to the woods. Anka wonders what her ghosts are like.

"Now the hard part," Yana says unconvincingly, slinging the leather bag over her shoulder.

Slowly, they carry the lamb's dead weight back to the village square. Yana stops them frequently to rest, but Anka is buzzing. The blood on her hands starts to itch as it dries. Her lungs ache, but she can hardly sit still.

"Are you all right?" Yana asks.

"I feel wonderful," Anka whispers, and laughs.

Yana regards her curiously, but says nothing more. Has Anka frightened her?

In the square, they arrange the lamb on the church steps. Yana keeps looking out to the windows for any twitch of curtain or shutter, but nothing moves. Once, Anka thinks she hears a cry, like an infant's, but it stops as soon as she tries to train her ears on it.

Yana produces a larger knife, sharply toothed near the handle, and slits open the lamb's soft underbelly. She saws through its chest and removes the heart. Anka finds a waxed cloth in the bag and packs the heart away. It's heavy like a baked apple in her hands.

"What will you use it for?" Anka whispers.

"I don't know yet," Yana says. "It's good to leave some things unexplained."

They meet no one on the road back to the Captain's house. Unencumbered, they move faster. Almost without Anka's realizing it, they're home, standing by the rain barrel.

"Here," Yana murmurs. A thin shell of ice covers the surface. She cracks it with the edge of the tin cup and pours frigid water over Anka's hands, washing away the tacky tightness. "It was good, having you there to help," she says abruptly. "I've never—I've never liked doing that. But you weren't afraid."

Anka's heart beats a little faster. When it's her turn to pour, her fingers are thick and clumsy with cold. Watching Yana scrub her hands, digging carefully under her fingernails, she wants to grab her and hold on, to warm their hands together. Where will Yana take her, when they leave the village? How long will they travel together? What will it be like to wake from her long sleep, magically transported to a new place, Yana's face the first thing she sees?

"Oh," Yana says, and points. "Your dress."

Anka startles, but there are no stains on her skirts. It's only a spray of blood across the chest of her apron. She laughs. "That's fine," she says. "It will wash away."

Suddenly she feels so exhausted she can barely stand; her legs wobble. Yana steadies her shoulder, and concern wrinkles her brow. "Can you make it up the stairs?"

"Yes," Anka says, more certain than she feels.

They bid good night. She watches Yana retreat down the cottage path. Halfway up the steps to her room, Anka stops to rest. Her muscles seize and jump. She thinks of the lamb, its reflex to run. She wakes with a start sometime later, leaning against the banister. She can hear Kiril snoring from the far end of the hall.

In her room, she struggles out of her clothes. She unknots her stained apron and hides it away in the pot under the bed. Her bedcovers are warm and heavy, sheets freshly changed.

She imagines the scene in the village at dawn: Light spills around the church spire, pale gold over misty morning. The air smells of last night's fires dying and the morning's newly lit. A sharp, red tang cuts through. What does Yana have planned for the bottles they collected?

In her vision, the lamb's body is warm, and steam bleeds from its cut throat into the cold yellow fog. A pair of slippers approach, then stop, and then a voice shrieks: loud enough to startle the birds nesting in the eaves, loud enough to wake the straggling sleepers, louder even than the bells, which start to ring and ring in the tower overhead.

ten

S UDDENLY, THE SALON is busy. Even with no sign of the baby, news of a healthy child shakes loose the distrust of Kiril's strange new methods. Years of untended aches and pains walk through his door, sit upon the patient's stool, and explain themselves in intimate detail. Rotting gums, stiff backs, badly set bones. Half a dozen women, some older than the Captain, swoon in and describe frightful visions that have descended upon them in the night. On waking, they are sapped of all vitality, and much sighing and batting of eyelashes follow. A widow some thirty years Kiril's senior insists on showing him the spot on her doughy thigh where the village vampire has fed on her, leaving her to wallow in lethargy for days. Kiril diagnoses a spider bite and sends her to the apothecary for calamine.

"They write themselves into the great pageant of the day," the Captain says with a laugh over dinner.

"Yana says people want their piece of the story," Anka says. "She thinks it's so they can tell for the rest of their lives how important they were."

The Captain squints playfully, refilling his wine. "I worry what dangerous thoughts might come into your head spending so much time around our visitor, little bird." Kiril accepts a refreshed cup and says nothing.

One evening, while he is disinfecting his tools for the day's end, the bell over the salon door chimes. He's ready to rip it off the wall. "I'm sorry," he calls, crouched behind the counter for a clean rag. "You'll have to come back tomorrow."

The door closes. "You sound tired," Nina says.

Kiril's skull narrowly misses the countertop on his way up. Hastily, he drops his rag and pliers and wipes his hands on his apron, trailing dull smears of the Madam Goatfarmer's blood and bile (abscessed tooth, dreadful smells).

Nina is wearing his blue coat, the sleeves folded back over her skinny wrists. A woven basket hangs from the crook of her elbow; Sofia lets out a small gurgle from within.

Kiril fumbles with the ties around his neck as he circles the counter. "You shouldn't be here," he says, striding past her to hastily snap the shutters closed. There's no one looking in—but anyone could have seen her, then run for it. He wavers. Would it arouse more suspicion to check outside?

"You've been busy," Nina observes calmly, taking in his rumpled appearance. She sets Sofia's basket on the counter. "Is that why you haven't been to see me?"

Nobody is out at this hour, Kiril tells himself. Nobody knows she's here. He balls the apron in his dirty hands.

Of course he's wanted to see her. Every morning, early, he's filled the basket with food, a bucket with water, and left them on the stoop with a light knock on the door, then vanished swiftly into the trees. At night, the basket and bucket quietly reappear, and Kiril takes them away. This is enough, the extent of the contact she wishes with him. He respects it.

He overstepped, he knows—he never should have touched her. He shut her up in his house, isolated her, took advantage. Is he becoming like the Captain in this, too? The thought sits waxy in his gut.

"Are—are you comfortable enough? I thought I'd bring more soap for the washbasin tomorrow—I imagine you're running out."

"We're very comfortable. It's a fine place to hide." She pauses to adjust the baby's blanket. "It's a little lonely."

"You need your rest," Kiril says truthfully. "I didn't want to intrude. I didn't want to bother you."

Nina studies him like a painting. Was he always so flustered? He knew how to talk to Margarita, even as he pined.

She turns in a tight circle and examines his progress around the shop. Since his arrival, he's defeated the accumulation of cobwebs and grime, and unchoked the chimney of bats and leaves. He's polished the shelves and counter to a warm glow. Where the dusty bolts of fabric rolled, he's arrayed his supplies, meager so far: the metal instruments he brought from the city, the bandages Yulia has helped prepare. On the door to the examination parlor, he hung a large drawing of a human skeleton, each chip of bone meticulously labeled. His handful of books, filled with diagrams, are shelved under the counter. He considered displaying them, but the thought of the Captain's scoff as he inspected the salon for the first time dissuaded him.

"You've done well," Nina says. Sofia examines the ceiling with big eyes. "Is it everything you hoped?"

Kiril laughs. There's pink spittle on his shirtfront and yellow pus spattered on his shoes. Soon, he'll need to see the apothecary about replenishing his remedies. The surgeon sent him home from the city with a dozen precious vials, a tremendous gift—he'd complained often to his students how rare certain ingredients had become in the years since the poisoning scandal. As careful as he's been, Kiril's run through half his supply already.

"It's maybe a bit more than I bargained for. But—yes. I think so. Some of our neighbors have been suffering for a long time. Of course, some of them just want my attention, and many want an excuse to ask about you. It's very mysterious— where you've gone. But Yana's given them plenty to talk about, too."

"A new tableau by the church?"

"A lamb, this time."

Kiril saw it early, almost before anyone else. He was coming from the cottage, had just delivered Nina's basket when he heard the churchwife screaming, and was by her side even as hungry windows and doors flew open. This time, the priest acted more quickly—covering the carcass with a sheet before a crowd could assemble, blocking the path with his own black-cloaked body until one of the men could alert the Captain.

When Kiril's uncle arrived, he grimly surveyed the scene, inspected the lamb by a raised corner of the sheet, and then whipped the shroud away.

"They deserve to see it," he declared, over the priest's plaintive whine. "They should know what it is we face." While nobody else was looking, he winked at Kiril. Behind him, people wailed and prayed.

"They're terrified," Kiril tells Nina truthfully. He's very aware of his grimy hands. He holds his stained apron tightly. "But they're also excited, I think. It's strange."

And Yana has given the excitement no chance to settle. Now, there's the blood. Every morning, a fresh puddle appears where the lamb's body lay. After two nights, Simeon volunteered to stand watch, but the dawn found him mysteriously lethargic, unable to remember the past hours, and the notion of guarding the church was abandoned. The priest's wife has taken to waking with a rag in hand, hoping to soak up the spill before anyone can see, but by now the stains are set in the stones.

"It's all very grim," Kiril says. "Yana performed some ritual today, to protect the newlyweds before their wedding." She'd held a burning branch in one dappled hand and veiled Simeon and Margarita in smoke where they stood, side by side, on the bakery's threshold. Kiril watched from his doorway through the wavering lens of a familiar dream. After, Yana poured handfuls of dried barley over their bowed heads, mumbling incantations under her breath, and gave strict orders to the assembled villagers that the grain be left on the ground where it fell. It would confuse the demons, she said—a vampire would be compelled to collect and count every pearl, and forget his deadly purpose until the morning broke.

To Kiril's surprise, the grain has gone untouched all day. "I think people have grown very concerned for them," he admits. "They seem to be forgetting you and Sofia."

"The wedding is tomorrow?" Nina says, eyes on her daughter. "I lost count of the days. Are you ready to play the woodsman?"

Kiril wonders if she saw the trail of spikes he left in the forest. He hasn't been back since the baby was born, the fervid obsession abruptly buried. "I think I'll manage the wedding banner," he says. "Honestly, I'd forgotten to worry about it."

Nina stops in front of a respiratory diagram near the window, the left lung in cross section to show an exactingly rendered canopy of branches. "Have you had something else to worry about?" she asks.

Kiril tosses the dirty apron over his shoulder. He nods to the little brass bell over the door. "Yes, well—as you said, it's been busy."

Now Nina is very close. The shop is so small, just a few paces end to end—how had it seemed so cavernous while he cleaned it? There's hardly enough room for two grown people to stand here together, a respectful distance apart.

"I'll tell you plainly," she says. "If you do have the time— among your many, many patients—I'd like it if you came to see us."

His insides balloon. *What symptoms, Doctor? Aerophagia, dyspnea—*

He clears his throat. "I haven't wanted to intrude."

"But what if you did?"

His vision twins as he tries to focus on her eyes. His arms, weighed down by his unwashed hands, hang useless at his sides.

He left a small jug of wine in the basket, for her supper, and now he can taste it. The room flickers darker, and his chest goes tight (*angina pectoris*). Her thigh brushes his, the blue coat draping around them. She touches her lips to the apple of his throat.

"Consider paying us a visit," she says. "When you have the time."

She sweeps Sofia from the counter. The brass bell jingles, and the door clicks shut. Kiril stands listening to his breath in the small room, ribs straining. When he stumbles to the washtub, he scrubs his hands until his skin feels pink and new as cherry flowers.

"I'VE NEVER BEEN to a wedding before," Anka says, prodding at her plate with a fork.

"Eat," the Captain orders. He puts a hand to her forehead. "I want your cousin to have a look at you, little bird."

Kiril sets down his knife. "I'm sure she's just tired, Uncle. We should be on our way—they're waiting."

Yulia has laid out festival clothes: a red sash for Kiril and an embroidered apron for Anka. By the white light of the parlor window, she pins a lone surviving rose into Anka's hair. Washed out by that square of morning, Anka reminds Kiril of a glassy waif he once met in the surgeon's parlor, who returned three days later for dissection. His anger softens into a moment of worry, but then Anka catches his eye and smiles a watery smile, and the distaste hardens again in his jaw.

"This, too," Anka says. She hands Yulia the silver comb he brought from the city.

"Doesn't she look beautiful," the Captain says, clapping Kiril on the back. Yulia tilts Anka's face to the light and thumbs rouge across her cheeks. The Captain rattles Kiril's shoulder. "My handsome children. You go on together—I have some work ahead of me. A surprise for tonight."

They walk in silence most of the way into town. Anka hangs from Kiril's arm as they navigate the icy puddles in the road. Less than halfway there, she stops him so she can rest on a fallen log.

"You'll stain your dress," he says. He turns his back and stares down the road.

"Are you nervous?" Anka asks. "Or sad? I know you loved her."

"Of course not. Margarita and Simeon belong together." He squints at the balding tree branches. He realizes that he's telling the truth—the place in him where the pang of Margarita used to live has healed. He can barely feel the scar tissue, its raised edges.

He delivered Nina's basket this morning, before dawn. He lingered by the door but didn't knock, not wanting to wake the baby. After the wedding, he decided, tonight—once the villagers have spilled enough wine, he might disappear from the party, and no one will wonder where he's gone. She might welcome him in. Maybe he can secret away some drink and some wedding bread, and they can share it in the dark. The thought warms him.

He puffs into his hands. "Are you ready?"

They don't speak again until the church steeple breaks the tops of the trees. "You're angry with me," Anka says as they round the bend. Their clothes billow. The wind wraps the tail of her braid around her throat. "But you haven't told him."

Kiril grinds his teeth. He looks at Anka, but he sees their neighbors leaving the Captain's house with their heads bowed and their skirts crooked, Nina scurrying into the night clutching a fistful of coins warm from his pocket. Anka could end their torment with half a word. So could he, now.

Up ahead, people are gathering by the bakery. Little Katia twirls in her festival dress, half dancing with Simeon while he laughs with their father over her head. From this distance, she looks like Anka in miniature: short and slight, her apron blooming with her mother's needlepoint and a late red geranium braided into her plait.

Simeon sees them first. He throws up his arms and gives a yell, and then Kiril is engulfed in their embraces. Hands clap his back, lips stain his cheeks. The women all smell of wind and rosewater, the men like sweat and bread. A trio are playing music: droning gaida, frantic gadulka, and the rhythmic booming of a tupan drum.

Kiril loses Anka in the swell of celebration. He lets himself laugh, returning their greetings. Someone hands him a hatchet. The crowd is full of people who have never smiled at him before, who now hold up bandaged limbs and bob and weave to catch his eye. *Much better today, Doctor—it hurt last night, but not so much this morning—*

Buzzing, they usher him towards the woods in search of a slim, fruit-bearing tree.

The company stumbles to a halt at the edge of the forest, where someone has already marked one trunk with a red bow.

Simeon's mother carries a basket of ribbons, apples, and onions to decorate the staff.

"Is he a proper, worthy man, then," someone crows, "to guide the bridegroom along his way?"

Simeon feigns insult, throwing his arm protectively over Kiril's shoulders. "Well, let him prove it, if he must!"

The fiddler stops playing to stretch his fingers. The bagpiper's bald pate shines with sweat, but he doesn't relax his ruddy chops.

Kiril makes a show of shaking Simeon off. He feels so warmly towards these people—he hadn't realized he could. He hefts the hatchet as though he can barely manage its weight, sucks breath in and out, then glances sidelong at Simeon, affecting a reedy, cowardly voice. "You're *sure* it has to be like this?" he says meekly. The men laugh, and Katia giggles, straining against her mother's arms to get a better look. Kiril shakes his head resignedly and squares off against the tree. "All right," he says, voice still high and pinched. "All right, then. Here we go."

The axe hardly makes a sound as it splits the tree trunk— the sapling hits the earth in a blink. Kiril drops the hatchet and lifts his hands in triumph.

"Worthy enough!" Simeon yells to the crowd, grabbing Kiril's raised arm. The fiddler starts to play again, and the villagers press in. For a while, with the day wide open ahead, they dance.

ANKA CAN'T STAY on her feet for long before her breath runs out and the edges of her vision singe. After the ceremony, she dances with Kiril, the traditional steps, and then with Simeon, whose eyes shine so brightly he might spark a fire. They kick each other's ankles more than once, both too fixated on Kiril and Margarita spinning across the square to pay attention to each other.

"Was there ever a more beautiful bride," Simeon asks, face glowing, his head swiveling to track her progress. No, never, Anka agrees—but she isn't watching Margarita. She keeps coming back to Kiril. He looks different—like the open wound of him has closed. He's laughing, relaxed. He looks at Margarita not like a frightened rabbit, but the way that Simeon looks at Anka—fond but unwanting, like a dear friend.

The dances go on, but Anka stops often, bracing herself on the long tables laden with food. She doesn't eat much. By nightfall, she retreats to a seat inside the bakery, near the fireplace, on a long bench against the wall where it's warm. The windows and door stand open, and she watches the celebration go on without her like a traveling play in the chilly night. She wishes Yana had come today. Outside, line dancers loop past—every few minutes, she catches a glimpse of Margarita and Simeon, hand in hand, in the doorway. They don't see her, sitting alone inside. Their joy snags on her like a hangnail. She hopes that's how they'll always be, even after she's gone.

After a few more dances, Kiril comes in, rubbing his hands. "There you are," he says. "They sent me for more wine."

Anka gestures to the table in front of her, the bottles drawn up in neat formation. "There's plenty."

Kiril weighs one in his palm. "Are you all right in here?" Anka shrugs. He seems to come to a decision, twisting the cork free and snapping up two unused cups. He pours a glass for each of them and sits across from her.

"Have a drink," he says. "Put some color in your cheeks. Have you been sleeping lately?"

Anka accepts the cup. "Is this a medical exam? I thought you were angry with me."

He doesn't deny it. He toasts her and takes a sip, rolling the thought over with his wine. "I care about your well-being," he says. "That's my job."

"As a physician? Or as my cousin?"

"Both, I should think."

Outside, someone yells: "Too bitter! Too bitter!" Framed in the doorway, the bride and groom sweeten the moment with a kiss. The guests cheer, and a new tune begins, new voices start singing. Anka can hear Simeon, warm and clear, and Margarita, as sweet as a bell.

"I could have slept better," Anka concedes. She looks down at her cup, a black well. The wine is sour and woody. "A lot has been happening. With the vampire, and the baby."

Kiril shakes his head. Anka feels a small rush of pride when he says, "Our seer knows how to make a scene."

"Do you think it will work?"

"To fix this town? God knows what that would take. But I don't think it can hurt, not much." He thinks for a moment, swirling his wine. "People in pain, they're grateful when you can take that pain away. More grateful than I realized until recently. Maybe Yana is right—at least she's given them a diagnosis."

Anka pulls her feet up onto the bench and leans her back

against the wall, letting her eyes shut. "How are Nina and the baby?" she asks.

"How could I possibly know that," Kiril says, and she can hear his smile. A warm secret inside him, beaming out. "Wherever they are, I hope they're happy."

Anka takes the tail of her braid between her fingers. Her hair has started to come loose. Carefully, she unpins the silver comb and the wilting rose and lays them on the table, then unbinds her plait. Kiril picks up the comb and studies it up close while she separates and rebraids her hair.

"Here," he says when she's done, and she obediently leans forward so he can pin the bird in place.

A jab and a scrape. "Ow!"

"Christ, that's sharp. Sorry." He looks at his thumb, a pink smear across it. "Does it hurt much?"

"No, it's all right."

"I'm getting very tired of blood," Kiril admits, wiping his thumb on his pants. "Every morning in the square, all over me in the salon."

Anka looks at him over the rim of her cup. The firelight glosses the ugly wounds around her fingernails. She wishes she could stop. Tomorrow morning, after the newlyweds' first night together, the village women will inspect their bed linens, looking for blood, and Yana's gift will come in handy. Her chest hurts, like she's just danced a dozen hora without stopping for breath.

"And me," she says. "Bleeding in secret."

Kiril flexes his fingers. He refills his drink and then holds the bottle out to Anka, but she pulls her cup back. The wine has reached her head. He's angry, but he hasn't told the Captain. When she was drowning, he pulled her back.

"All right," he says at last. "I think it's selfish. Cowardly, even. You see how he is with—with women like Nina. He only wants you."

Icy door at the edge of the world, her knuckles scraped raw against it. She hugs her knees. "You think I should let him hurt me instead."

"But he *won't*." Kiril's fist strikes softly on the table. The bottles ring. Orange light flickers in his unblinking eyes. "All our lives, he's only loved you. He never hurts you."

When they came home that day from the lake, soaked and freezing, the Captain was reading in a chair by the fire. He gave a yell when he saw them, and his papers scattered as he swept Anka off the ground and knelt with her by the grate, tipping her blue lips towards the heat as he held her body to his and rubbed her arms to warm them. The fire glow was too hot on her scalp, but she had no energy to turn her head away. Across the room, Kiril watched and dripped cold water onto the floor. Eventually, Yulia came with blankets and draped one around his shoulders. She hugged him and whispered how brave he was, but he never took his eyes off Anka and the Captain.

Anka's stomach churns. Sweat breaks out over her neck and slides down her back. "You haven't said anything to him."

"I thought you might still do the right thing."

"You can't tell him," she whispers. "Kiril, please, he's like our father. You—"

He's looking at her curiously, clouded and serious, the way Yulia sometimes does. Outside, someone calls their names. Kiril turns to the open door.

Simeon's mother spots them and bustles in. "We've been looking for you!" she cries. "Come along—your uncle's prepared a surprise! Poor girl, you're cold as ice. If you're not careful, your kidneys will freeze. Here, take this." She grabs a brown shawl from a peg on the wall and swiftly wraps Anka like a spindle. Then she ushers them both out the door, Kiril still holding the opened bottle of wine.

Outside, music leads the way towards the Witch's Wood. The path narrows and twists, but up ahead, the trees glow. *What ghosts*, Anka thinks, unnerved. Margarita pushes back through the crowd towards her, eyes bright.

"Your uncle did this?" she whispers. "For us?"

In a clearing, the earth smolders red and black with glowing coals. Anka remembers the earthquake—what they expected to see in the ravine that split the ground. It's beautiful, and frightening.

The Captain speaks briefly with the woodwind. He breaks his lips from his instrument, and the trio falls silent. Then the Captain turns to the villagers—drunk as they are, windmilling and breathless—and raises his hands for silence.

"How better to bless the newlyweds?" he demands. It's been years since Anka saw her uncle fire dance, even on the saints' day, but now he bends and unlaces his boots.

"We've had little to celebrate these past years," he says, barefoot at the edge of the burning field. "But now we have much. May the saints bless this union, and all of the people of this village. And may they bless the brave young woman who will deliver us from the demons that stalk the night."

He turns his back on them. Anka watches her uncle's silhouette, as big as a shadow in the dark.

"We will survive you!" he yells into the forest. A windy echo answers through the thick trees: *you, you, you*. The Captain raises his arms again. He turns to address the eager crowd. "Here is the sun, by our side. Here are our saints, God's chosen. I'll prove it now."

The musicians strike the tune. The priest's wife, dressed in white, parades solemnly around the circle with the two wooden icons over her head. Barefoot, the Captain moves towards the coals. His eyes sweep the watching crowd, and then he darts forward. Little Katia lets loose a squeal, but even the onlookers who have seen the dance before gasp and murmur.

For the first time, Anka notices that Kiril is standing beside her. He's smiling, golden and innocent, that different man again. Embers scatter under the Captain's feet. The wind is cold, but Anka's face is hot. Wine fractures the night into soft, strange pieces. She's aware of Margarita taking her hand, squeezing her fingers. She barely remembers the steps that led her into the red woods. Her uncle dances with his eyes closed, entranced, his arms raised, the saints guiding his feet.

All at once, the music changes. The Captain opens his eyes. "To the newlyweds!" he yells, and the people take one breath all together, and laugh, and begin to clap their hands.

The Captain changes his pace, now something like a lively

horo. He has always been a strong dancer, confident and precise. He moves in time with the clapping, circling the clearing, until he's right in front of Anka.

"Come along," he says, and someone screams as he lifts Anka off her feet. They go spinning over the coals, the shawl trailing behind them. She can feel the heat around them—the earth is burning, and every star is a comet overhead, the whole world a glowing red ember. She hears herself laughing, and realizes she's crying, too. She clings tightly to her uncle's neck. Her hem never even comes close to the ground, but every limb is trembling. *What if he drops me, what if I fall, what if he doesn't?* When she was a little girl, he would dance her around the parlor like this, making her fly like the little bird she was, and she felt safe.

The villagers are a glowing, many-headed beast. Once, she thinks she sees Yana among the trees, but when she turns her head to look, there's nothing in the cool gap beyond.

When the Captain finally sets her down on cold, solid ground and takes his bow, Anka swoons, off-balance. The earth bends underfoot. She can't tear her eyes from the heart of each red coal, the whisper of a dance there, too. Kiril grabs her shoulders to steady her. "You see?" he says in her ear. Then, "Here." A handkerchief appears in her hand, and he guides it towards her wet cheeks. "Why are you crying? It's all right."

From somewhere to Anka's left, a voice shouts, "Too bitter! Too bitter!" and the crowd shuffles until Margarita and Simeon are at its center, bashful and beaming, obliging their neighbors with a kiss. The earth is a burning field of garnets behind them, and the comet is a sun-kissed diamond overhead.

The Captain throws a fond arm over Kiril's shoulders, as if greeting a younger brother. His face is sweating; he beams. "You're an excellent dance partner, little bird," he says. "Did you like it?"

"Wonderful," Kiril answers. "Beautiful idea, Uncle."

The Captain sees the wine bottle hanging from Kiril's hand, and he reaches for it. He toasts them both before drinking right from its throat, then wipes his mouth with his sleeve. "This town needed some celebration," he says, satisfied. Then, lowering his voice, he speaks only to Kiril. "We could all use a celebration. Tell me now—where have you been keeping the charming widow? I'd like to pay her a visit."

Kiril steps away. "I—I haven't a clue."

The Captain laughs indulgently. "Don't play games. I know you're hiding her."

"Uncle, really—it's so soon since she had her baby, she shouldn't—"

A loud crack, as the Captain's palm connects with Kiril's cheek. Heads snap towards them. The Captain grins and waves the onlookers away, raising his bottle to them. He leans in close, a fist tight in Kiril's shirt, and whispers something only Kiril can hear. Anka sees Kiril's breath quicken. He looks out past the woods, towards the village. Then his eyes find Anka in the dark.

Yelling from the drunken crowd again: "Too bitter! Too bitter!"

There's a shift in Kiril—it's the way he looks at her behind a closed door, looming over the stairs. Anka tries to say his name, but she can't hear her own voice over the catcalls and the cheers.

She sees the moment: he squares his shoulders, and turns away. He lifts the bottle from his uncle's hand and drinks. Anka can't speak. If she threw herself on the coals, would she die? But she's grown roots, long teeth, caught in the hard, cold earth. *Make me vanish, make me a tree.* "Kiril—"

His back is to her now, unflinching. He touches the Captain's shoulder, brother to brother.

"Uncle," he says, in a voice she both knows and doesn't. "I have good news."

eleven

BEFORE HE WAS a Captain, he apprenticed to the village butcher. A boy of fourteen, fifteen—old enough to squirm around a kind, beautiful girl. And the butcher had a daughter named Zora. Outside, the wolves howled. Inside, when she watched him work, his palms sweat and the knives slipped. One day, a cleaver slid from his grip as he chopped slabs of pork on the scarred block, and without thinking, he reached out and caught it by the blade.

Zora made a noise: not a scream but a quick, composing breath. Suddenly she was with him on her father's side of the counter, bending close to the blood-welling blade in the meat of his palm. No swooning violet, not his Zora. "Don't move," she commanded, sharp as a lash, and vanished up the stairs. She returned with strips of bandage and a green poultice in a brown jar. She'd been raised by shattered nails and missing fingers; blood drew her like a flame-drunk moth. After she dressed the wound, she ran her fingers over the linen that covered the flat of his hand, watching for a reaction, and she smiled at him, impressed, when he offered none. The truth is, he doesn't remember any pain. Years later, Kiril would speculate about his fire dancing—that the ash coats his feet to protect him, that he moves so quickly he can't be hurt. Saints or science—what he knows is that he can dance on red coals, feel the heat rise in waves as he sweats and moves, and still he will not burn.

"I want to show you something," he tells Anka. They leave the wedding celebration behind, the music growing faint. The earth feels powerfully steady after his dance. This night is so much bigger than he knew—unseen beasts prowl its edges. Anka follows him silently, afraid, disgusted. *I know*, he thinks to assure her. Soon she'll understand.

His faith was a surprise. He came through the war a cynic, but clarity arrived the way Ivo often insisted it would—in a beam of light. One moment Anka was a child, playing a skipping game with Margarita and a length of rope, and the next, her long braid slipped over her shoulder and swung towards the earth, her smile was bright and open, and he could see the pink insides of her throat as she laughed. The setting sun gilded her like the maid who bathed in the golden river. The light carved out her pointed chin, the pinched upward tilt of her nose. She became her mother. Joyful and alive, his Zora—as he'd seen her in the village square from a distance, in the gaps between gossiping women. His feet stepped towards her. He could see through the cage of Anka's ribs to that beating heart. She was waiting to grow, wings folded right inside an egg. He had to protect her until she broke through the shell.

"This way," he says, and they turn between the trees.

Anka trips over a root but refuses his steadying arm. She looks like she could get lost in a shadow. At first he feared the same illness that vanished his sister, Kiril's mother—she wasted away in a matter of months, her color and bulk draining like water through a sieve. She grew so thirsty, her body its own drought-cracked landscape, but no amount of drink could help. He's watched Anka closely these weeks, has seen how she barely touches her wine, barely eats a bite of food. Something else, something else.

"Does it hurt very much?" he asks her kindly. When his sister was young, her monthly pains left her in tears, curled on the fireplace rug by the dog. Anka shivers even under a thick layer of wool. "I've been told a woman's bleeding can be very unpleasant."

Somewhere, far off, an animal howls. Clouds creep over the horizon, but for now the sky is bright with moon and comet. For the first time, the Captain wants to believe in this omen. A sign of good things to come, an assurance: *This is right.*

Anka doesn't look at him when she speaks. "Not so much," she says. They glide forward in a safe pool of orange lantern light. She glances around them, a well rising up on all sides.

He can indulge her. "Are you afraid of demons, little bird?"

Her head rustles the folds of her shawl. He knows she must be lying, trying to seem brave for him. She clicks with chattering teeth. "Where are we going?"

His fist tightens around the lantern's handle, the wire digging at scar tissue. "There's something important I need to tell you, Anka. I have been waiting a long time to say it."

They turn off the path, and the hulking, caved-in shape of the old kiln looms out of the dark. Beneath their feet, the earth turns soft and rich. Anka's eyes widen, and the rest of her shrinks. In all the excitement, she hadn't realized where they were headed.

"I've come here often since you were born," the Captain says. "But until now I've always come alone."

With passing years, moss has conquered the fallen beams of Zora's burned house. Many winters' dead leaves blanket thick decay over the ruin. The Captain touches the nape of Anka's neck.

"You know you were born right here." He gestures to the flat clearing in front of what used to be the house. Her body is rigid, a ceramic shard in the ashes.

"Your mother and I were very close, when we were young. I had known her all my life, but when I went to work for her father, things changed. We fell in love. I thought I would marry her."

They had one summer, soft with secrets. She came to him behind the shop while he was rinsing muscle and blood from the knives, and without a word she kissed his mouth, and he left bloody handprints on her apron, so desperate to hold her close. Later, there were humid evenings under honeyed linden trees, in the tall grasses where they could hide, just the two of them. She would shiver against him, fireflies alighting on her unraveling hair, her slender shoulder.

"But then I was called to war. She saw me off, the night before we marched. It was cold, like tonight. I thought I would never see her again, but I wanted her to wait for me." *Don't bury me yet*, he'd begged. She pulled him by the belt into the storeroom and made her promises among disused carving knives and burlap sacks of salt. "By the time I came home, two years had gone by. She was married."

He woke one day after a battle with a darting pain in his chest. The morning smelled of gun smoke, lingering like fog over a pitted field. The pain was so bad that he went to the surgeon, a white-haired man with cracked glasses and a tarnishing ear trumpet. The tent behind him was full of men and boys who were dying—their bodies open in the cold air, moaning for their wives and mothers, stinking of burnt hair and rot. The surgeon looked for shrapnel in his chest for only a moment before ordering him out—he spat on the ground by the tent flap to show the way.

Walking back across the barren field, he realized it was his birthday. He learned later that it was her wedding day, too.

"Your father left with me for the war, but he came home early with a terrible wound in his leg. He almost lost it below the knee, and he needed a crutch for the rest of his life. The pain made him angry, I think—he had been a happy boy, but he became an ill-tempered man. When I came back, he tried to keep me from Zora. He didn't trust me around her. He was right—I still loved her, and I didn't respect him.

"My mother sent letters to neighboring villages, trying to do the work of a father in finding me a wife, but I didn't care for any of them. Even after I was appointed Captain, and men began coming to me directly, their pretty daughters and good land meant nothing. I still visited your mother almost every day. In spite of your father, we remained good friends." She was so delicate in her rejections, calmly taking his wrist between two fingers and removing his hand from her arm, her back, like she was expelling a small, wayward rodent from her house. Her friendship was almost enough.

"Then one morning I saw her, and she was different. She told me she was pregnant." Shame, like water, closing over his head. He forces himself to look at Anka: her white profile, her nose starting to run in the cold. He owes her the truth. She stares ahead at the ruined house. "You were with her. It's one of my greatest regrets, little bird—I didn't congratulate her, or wish her well. I was revolted. Her happiness was unbearable. I left her house and didn't visit her again."

And what of the witch, heavy with child? He'd wanted to possess her and punish her all at once. They'd struck a bargain in the dim little jail. He twisted a lock of her hair tight between his fingers—she'd done no witchcraft, but adultery, certainly that. When he pulled, she let herself be led. She liked to bleed, a little.

Behind them, drunken revelers trip down the main road, singing. An owl calls from tall branches. Anka turns her head, but her vacant mask doesn't change. The singers pass them by.

"This is—it's still difficult for me to talk about," the Captain admits. "For months, I kept my distance from Zora. I pretended not to see her in the square. I was never home when she called. But I did see her, I always did—the look on her face, waiting at the door, while I hid behind the curtains. One day I watched her walk back to the road, and she turned to look at the house, just for a moment—she gave me a smile, like she knew I was there. It was the saddest thing I'd ever seen. I knew she still loved me, but she was ready to give me up.

"I realized I was going to lose her forever. Maybe I already had. I was sick to my stomach all day, lay in bed with a pot by my side. But that evening, I had business—it was the harvest. I had to attend the festival."

Now is the moment. He raises the lantern high, so she can see. The light falls long and honest over the ruins. He feels a bit stronger in its glow.

"Here was the door of your father's house." He kicks the earth, and his foot finds the stone that marked the threshold. The house unfurls around them, its phantom walls growing up from the dirt, the light of its long-extinguished grate glowing hot from the collapsed spine of the chimney.

"I didn't plan to come here that night. You have to believe me, little bird—I had no intentions. I was going to the square, and then it was like a dream—I found myself here instead. All of a sudden, I was walking to their door, and—"

The knock of his fist on the wood echoes loudly through the night. The door opens, and he steps through. He can smell the smoke from the grate, can still conjure the insides of the room: a table, two chairs. A freshly woven basket lined with a soft mat and a blanket. Leaning on the windowsill: a small portrait of Zora, all but finished, her cheeks rosy with pottery glaze.

"Your father answered. He let me in but he said your mother wasn't home." The potter hobbles forward through the mirage, eyes mean. "He said she had gone ahead to the festival."

The ghost points at the door with his crutch, poisonous triumph in his voice. *She doesn't want to see you—she isn't here. Leave my family alone.*

On the table is a single, silver candlestick. The Captain sees his hand grasp it.

"You," Anka says, like she can see it, too. She knows.

The candle falls to the floor, still lit. It rolls. The silver makes a wet, thick noise when it hits scalp and skull, and the man crumples before him. He stays down. But the candle—

Anka's lips are white with cold. "And the fire caught."

Curtains hanging long, tinder for the box. "The fire caught," the Captain says. There's more. "I wasn't thinking clearly. I saw her portrait, the one he hadn't finished, and I grabbed it, shoved it in my coat. Then I fled. I didn't—I couldn't have known."

He stands with Anka on the grass, half a dozen paces from the house. Smoke in the air. "I made for the festival. Somebody saw the flames go up, and we all ran to help. I met the neighbors on the road."

A dozen men sprint towards the blaze. The door is burning; the walls are aflame. Someone goes for the rain barrel, others run with buckets for the river. "I knew he was dead. I knew I'd done it. I can't describe how it felt—different from killing in battle. But suddenly I breathed easier than I had since I'd left for the war. I was watching her house burn, but I could see the shape our lives would take now—you would come into the world and I would fill the space your father had left, and we would be happy—all three of us. It would take time, of course, but I could wait—I had waited for years already. I could wait longer."

The small, precious fantasy. He swallows hard. "The crowd was getting bigger then, and I kept waiting for her to come to me. I thought she was slow because of her condition—she walked so slowly in those last days—but any moment, I would hear her cry and I would have to hold her back, but . . ."

"But my father lied," Anka whispers. She's seeing the story spin out before them, gold threads of it tangling through the burnt-out bones of her home.

There is a cry—not from the road, but beside him—in his memory, the baker's young wife screams and points at the window on the second floor. The shutters open and fall shut. With effort, Zora pushes them wide a second time, then slumps over on the sill and lets out a desperate howl, one last note that brings all eyes to her. She sees him.

"He lied," the Captain agrees. Tears in his eyes, throat threatening to close. He coughs black smoke. "She must have been asleep upstairs, or she would have heard—maybe he wanted to leave her to rest, or maybe he didn't want me waiting for her return. Maybe he just wanted me out. It only matters that he lied."

He runs for her. The heat meets him, stronger than any enemy's front line. Her body flickers, then collapses out of sight. Someone has a ladder—he climbs without a thought for the flames, without feeling the blisters on his hands or the ash in his throat. One shutter comes away from the wall when he grabs it. Splinters bite his palms when he grips the windowsill. She's on the floor, she doesn't move when he calls her name—

The Captain touches Anka's braid, a cool rope to tether himself. His throat feels raw, singed. "By the time I got to her, her hair had caught fire. I put it out with my sleeve. We made it to the ground."

He lays her down as gently as he can, and all the while he's screaming her name, over and over. Now that the flames are at his back, there are tears on his face. The midwife is coming, pushing him aside, laying her ear to Zora's chest, her mouth, shouting for quiet. Someone hands her a knife, and she checks for breath against the blade. She mutters a curse and shifts her grip on the handle.

More wedding guests on the road now, the sounds of a man and a woman laughing together. The Captain shuts his eyes.

"It took four men to hold me back while she cut your mother open."

He is on the ground, a damp chill seeping through the knees of his trousers. There is blood on the grass, wet and black in the firelight. He presses his mouth to Anka's apron and his shoulders shake. The midwife drops her bloody knife and reaches her big butcher's hands into the wound. She shoves her fingers down the baby's throat, making space for her to cry. A hush over the crowd—horrible, burning, bloody quiet broken by snapping wooden support beams, the sizzle of splashing water, the sick silence as men fall back, give up, and watch the fire burn. The house gives a roar as the roof caves in, and then—

"And then you made a noise. You cried the sweetest note I ever heard. You were alive—a firebird rising from ash." He grabs her cold hands in his own and lifts his gaze. Anka's face is washed in shadow; he can't see her eyes. "My little bird—it was the purest magic I'd ever seen. I promised I would care for you, all my life."

So many times it seemed impossible. A mountain rose up before him and he felt he would have to climb its snow-slicked ridges with his bare feet, carrying his world on his shoulders like a nomad bound for the steppe. There were such grim days, what the villagers called curses—bad crops, disease—and they glowered at Anka and muttered that it all started when she was born, that hellish night that blighted the harvests. Once, he hung a rope by the burning point to protect her. Whenever she sniffled or coughed, he stayed awake in a chair by her bed, listening to her breath, the crumpled-leaf crackle in her chest, his blood pounding in his ears with the fear that she would fall silent completely—and worse, that he might be asleep when she did.

"Caring for you hasn't been easy, Anka—I was never meant to be your father. It was hard in this town, where nobody seemed to want you, and your cousin . . . For a long time I didn't know what to do. And then one day I saw her, inside you." Reborn, waiting to grow. It was like opening a window after a long night's storm to reveal God's garden in wild bloom—so bright it hurt his eyes. "I realized how I would make amends. I couldn't find you a husband, but I could care for you myself. Someday, I'd have to tell you the truth of what I did—to earn her forgiveness. Your mother is gone, but she's still here." He touches the place above Anka's heart lightly with his fingertips. "When we marry, we will complete the grand plan—do you see now? Do you see it?"

Behind them, in the ash-black earth, green things are growing through the quiet and the dark. The fire burns only in his memory. Nothing is lost forever; the shamans and the witches have always understood this roundness of time. The sun, the moon—Kiril says that even comets loop above them, a cosmic circus so wide only God can see the curve of it. Men who know still visit the same rich hollows in the woods, the places where power lives and always will. Creak of a rope, slash of a knife—

they spill blood and make their burnt offerings each year on the ashes of the old, knowing that they will sow new seeds, that life grows from the places where the blood drips.

"This will make it right," he promises. He is still on his knees, every part of him aching with cold. His fists are tight in Anka's apron. She clutches her shawl against the night. *Give her time*, he hears Zora whisper. He feels the emptiness of a poison finally leached away.

"I've waited so long, little bird." He presses his face to her skirt again. Her thighs are cold as stone under the cloth. "But this will finally make it right."

twelve

H E WALKS HER to the bottom of the stairs like a suitor. If he touches her, she'll throw up. Anka climbs, leaving the Captain behind. "Good night, little bird," he calls, his voice strange and foggy. He doesn't follow her up.

She turns the lock. It takes a moment to realize she isn't alone in her bedroom. She lets slip a short yelp—Yana covers her mouth. They wait in loud silence: Anka's breath harsh from climbing, the snapping of firewood into ash. At last, they hear the Captain leaving, fading into the dark of the house.

"I'm sorry I startled you," Yana whispers. "I was worried."

Anka feels herself nod. Inside her is a pit crawling with white worms. "I should have left this summer," she says, and Yana grimaces—too loud. Anka swallows with difficulty. Says, softer, "I should have left while he was sick."

"Have a seat." Yana gestures Anka towards her own bed. She sits, and Yana kneels by her feet. Her hands on Anka's knees are hot and alive. "What happened after you left the woods?"

"You were watching?" She remembers now—Yana's face, a flicker among the trees. What must she think of her, dancing with this man she hates?

"I saw the fire dance. But I didn't see where you went af-ter that." She busies herself removing Anka's shoes. "You're *freezing*," she says, and starts rubbing the dead weights of Anka's feet. The poison has turned her blood to slush. Her wool stockings spark with static under Yana's touch. Anka can barely feel her, can barely think how odd it is to have the seer here, massaging her calves. At length, Yana looks up at her. "You were out there for a long time. Did he—"

"He told me a story. That's all." A story she knew, she realizes now, but never wanted to tell herself before. A burning tickle is coming back to her toes. What does it feel like, to dance with bare feet on hot coals? The silver comb is still tangled in her hair. She tugs it loose and stares at it. The worms seize into a fist.

"Kiril told him." She holds her breath, waiting for her cousin to climb the stairs, summoned by the sound of his name. Nothing comes. He'll be with Nina now, telling her how he's freed her from the Captain's attention. A great day for Kiril, who's gotten everything he wanted. Carefully, Anka sets the comb on the table by her bed, next to her bottle of poison. Yulia has left her a silver spoon and a pitcher of fresh water. Strange collection: bloody bottle, frowning spoon, bird taking flight from the rosebushes. "We went to see my parents."

"At the graveyard?"

"No. He took me to their house." It seems to her now that it's been burning this whole time, sixteen long years, smoke low over the village, blackening every breath she's ever taken. What does that do to a body, a first breath choked with ash? She's heard stories of children who grow up digging in mines or crawling between the monstrous teeth of giant machines, tarring their lungs, sacrificing their tender fingers.

Wet grass, bloody knife, burning walls. She didn't want to see it. Now she tells the story again, the old parts and the new. Now she can feel the seams, the places where her uncle cut pieces away and mended the scraps. Why had she never asked about the portrait over the mantel, where it came from? It simply belonged to him, to the house. It simply was.

"He killed them," Yana says slowly, when Anka's finished. "He's a murderer." He expected her to be stunned, but it's anger that cracks through her. "*He murdered them.*" Somewhere, she had a different life—one where the Captain didn't loom over every day, biding his time. One where she could have just been a child, loved and cared for like all the other children of the village. In that life, maybe there are more children of Koprivci. Maybe there's a school.

Only one picture exists of her father, a rare photograph of all the boys who marched to war. The print hangs in the Captain's study, yellowing in an unremarkable wooden frame. Forty-six boys in three rows, most of them long dead. The Captain is easy to find, tall and broad near the back, but her father is difficult to spot: near the middle, his face hidden by the brim of his cap, obscured by a shouldered gun in the front row. It's hardly enough to imagine him as a father. When Anka does think of him, she sees an undefined profile, a man drawn mostly below the neck, with a crutch under his arm. But one face does come to her now: the man who confronted her at the bakery when she was a child, his beard trembling, yelling that it was her fault no babies in this town could live. Simeon's father threw the bearded man out. Soon after, he'd hanged himself by the burning point. He must have climbed the tree to let himself drop, they said. *He was unwell*, the Captain said. He touched his hat to his heart.

Yana kneads Anka's arms. She's so cold—even a stone would take on blood heat. She licks her chapped lips. "Yana, you have to get me out of here. I have to get away."

Yana squeezes. "Soon," she promises. "Remember, you told me yourself—less than a week until—"

Yes, a week. Each night she shakes the bottle so the poison will be well mixed, and she administers her careful spoonful, no more. Little by little, or she might never wake up. The bottle is full of nights, full of hours. She waits for footsteps on the stairs. She waits for the doorknob to rattle.

The air goes out of her. Her insides turn thick and slippery, and this time she does gag, doubles over. Yana barely gets a chamber pot in front of her before she's sick, foul spirits and wet clumps of bread clawing their way up. What little she's managed to eat, she empties into the pot, a rancid stew. Yana doesn't flinch. When Anka's hollowed out, the seer unfolds a handkerchief and pours water from the pitcher on the night table.

"Here," she says gently. "I have some powder in my bag."

But Anka's shaking too badly to use it; she can't even get the tin open. "I'll make a mess." So she opens her mouth, like a lamb accepting clover. What did it want, think it wanted, other than to feed, a sweet taste?

Carefully, Yana pries the lid off the tin of tooth powder and takes some in her fingers. She reaches into Anka's mouth. Anka shuts her eyes at first, breathing through the strange feeling. Yana's fingers are warm, smooth, the powder gritty and chalky. She draws small circles with her fingertips. It tastes different than what Yulia makes with crushed eggshells and garden herbs in her mortar bowl—there's something lightly sweet and spicy in it that Anka doesn't recognize.

"Tilt your head back," Yana says, and touches Anka's chin. Anka opens her eyes and tries to watch Yana's face as she gently brushes fingers over her tongue. Serious and steady, a furrow between her brows. Anka is conscious of Yana's fingers growing wet. Her chest is tight, her thighs shivering.

When she's done, Yana wipes her fingers on the handkerchief and hands Anka the cup of water. She ducks her head to swish and spit, hiding for a moment behind her unraveling hair. Warmth is coming back to her, bit by bit. Her lips and tongue tingle.

"Yana," she says, after Yana covers the foul pot and pushes it away. Anka sucks at a bitten spot on her lip. Her innards are settling, and her breath comes easier, but something else unspools. The room still spins around them. "Yana, I can't wait a week."

"Listen," Yana says. Anka has a sudden, wild urge to kiss her fingers, to swallow them again, warm herself from the inside. "Do you know why I agreed to help you? The first time I saw you, at my camp, you were reckless—you didn't care what happened to you. But later, when you came to my door, it was different—you had hope. That's everything, Anka."

Anka starts to bite a cuticle, but Yana tugs her hand back.

"I'll get you out of here. I promise."

"Where will we go?" Anka whispers. The unfamiliar spice perfumes both of them, her breath and Yana's skin. "Where will you take me, when we leave here?"

The floorboards wince as Yana resettles herself by Anka's feet. "Wherever you want. I thought . . . I thought maybe you'd like to visit a city. Or go to the sea. Something you've never seen before. We could travel together, for a while. If you want to."

She does. She imagines huddling under a blanket with Yana beside her, stars falling overhead.

Anka opens her eyes, and she's still in the same room where she's always been. But there's softness in Yana's expression that she's never seen before. It isn't pity for the dying. For the first time, she looks vulnerable. The all-knowing seer on her knees, waiting to see what will happen next.

Anka pulls her in by the shoulders. For once, she feels light. She's emptied a lead weight from her stomach. Yana opens her lips.

"I want to," Anka says, bowing her forehead against Yana's. She even laughs. She wants to—there is something she wants. "Does this mean you'll teach me to be like you? To do your work?"

Yana smiles. "If you like. I think you . . . you see a different side of it. When we went together, for the lamb—I think you understood something about it that I never did. I still don't know what it was."

"About the blood," Anka says eagerly. "And power." Then a stormy thought comes, and the cold flows back like water under the door. "But what if—Yana, what if he doesn't let me go? He could insist I be . . . that I be buried here. What then?" Buried alive, dirt piling on her casket, the Captain sleeping by her grave every night. Waking under a pall, or never waking—

crushed by the weight of the earth, straining to scream, to breathe, a different kind of drowning—

Yana sits back. She chews her lip in thought. Anka can see her front teeth clearly, how one is chipped and a little crooked, leaning across its neighbor. "The decision will have to be public," she says. "If the villagers see you as a threat, if they think the vampire's marked you, I can make them insist you be buried far from here. Some secret place, so that even if you rise again, you can't find your way back to torment them." She hesitates. "I don't think it will be very difficult to convince them."

But the Captain? Anka stands, so quickly that Yana falls backwards onto the rug. "We should just go now," she says, making for the door. "While he's asleep." She spins on her heel, and the room keeps spinning. "How far could we get by morning?"

But Yana is shaking her head before Anka can even regain her balance. "Look out the window."

It's hard to see. Anka presses close to the glass and tries not to breathe fog. Outside, snow is falling. A thin layer already frosts the garden, glazing the last defeated flowers of the season.

"We'd leave a trail, or we'd simply freeze. You aren't well, Anka—we have to wait. Listen—this is why you came to me, remember? He'll follow you as long as he knows you're alive. Wait a little longer—a few more days. He'll never know to come after you."

Animals in iron-jawed traps will bite through their own bones to escape. Kept birds sometimes break their bodies on the bars, too desperate to wait for an open door.

"A few more days," Anka repeats. So much could still go

wrong. Snow—quiet dusting the earth. "Will you stay with me tonight? Here? Nobody will know—I don't think Kiril will be home at all."

"I'm sorry," Yana says. "I want to. But there's work I have to do. And quickly, before the snow gets too deep."

"Can I come?"

"Not this time. I need to move fast."

"He'll hear you on the stairs," Anka says feebly. She's sure that Yana can disappear as completely as a ghost if she wishes.

Yana lifts Anka's knuckles to her mouth and kisses them. The vulnerability is gone, her seer's confidence sliding back into place. "I won't need the stairs," she says. "Try to get some sleep—I'll see you tomorrow. I promise."

She raises the window sash noiselessly. Anka can't even remember the last time she opened the window, but she wouldn't be surprised if Yana oiled the rails while the house was empty, just in case. She leans over the sill, snow biting her cheeks, just in time to watch Yana slip down the garden trellis and vanish among the dead leaves.

"HOW HEAVY IS your blood?"

Beyond Kiril's window, the town square is a blank canvas. Anka remembers one simple dream—she was walking under an empty blue sky beside Yana and her donkey. The air was dry and warm. Occasionally the donkey made a low huffing noise and kicked a stone across the path. There was no need to speak.

By morning, Koprivci's sharp edges had disappeared under snowfall. Yulia bundled Anka in extra layers of wool before they left the house. As they walked towards Kiril's salon, the window above the bakery opened, dislodging a spray of powder, and Simeon's mother unfurled a bedsheet from the cornice to show off the proud, red blot at the center of the banner. Kiril, coming to meet them at the door, laughed when he saw it. There was no trace of jealousy left in him.

"Anka? Your monthly bleeding—how heavy is it?"

She shifts on the patient's stool. She can't look at him, so she looks at her raw and ragged nail beds. "I don't know," she says at last. "I don't know what's normal."

Kiril sighs and looks to Yulia. At last, he says, "It could be a deficiency of iron, if you're losing too much blood. It would explain your fatigue and pallor. Yulia, more meat could help— red meat, pork."

"I'm not sure Kosta will sell on a fasting day."

"Tell him it's on my orders. He owes me a trade." Kiril crosses the room and opens a cabinet, then lifts a bottle to eye level, inspecting the label. "We'll try with a change in diet first. If we don't see an improvement in a few weeks, you will need to take iron pills. They're unpleasant for digestion but they should put you right." He sets the bottle down and shuts the cabinet.

Yulia hefts her shopping basket onto her hip. "I'll go to Kosta."

The bell at the front door jingles her out. Kiril leans his back against the cabinet, facing Anka. "You'll have to look at me eventually."

She bites her tongue. When she woke this morning, she could taste a faint trace of Yana's tooth powder in her mouth under a layer of fitful sleep and sour wine. There was smoke caught in her hair.

"You can't spend the rest of your life avoiding me."

"I won't be here that long."

"Don't be so dramatic, Anka. You're a little anemic—you aren't going to die. On the contrary, you're finally going to find your place in this world."

This satisfied, self-assured man—she hardly recognizes him. "You never came home last night," she says.

"The party went on for a long time."

"You look well rested for someone who spent the whole night celebrating."

Kiril rolls his eyes. "I have a house nearby, Anka. You know that. It was easier than coming home. In fact, I intend to move there once you're married. Leave you to run your household without me in the way."

Anka nibbles at a hangnail. "A good night's sleep," she says. "Maybe Nina just doesn't like you as much as she likes the Captain."

He kicks lightly at the leg of her stool. "You don't know what you're talking about."

Anka glances out the back window. "Do you really think it's clever, keeping her hidden there? You really think he won't figure out where she is?"

"He doesn't want Nina anymore. He has you."

She shows him her teeth. "He wants my mother, Kiril. Soon he'll realize I'm not her."

The shop bell rings again. Yulia opens the exam parlor door.

"Did Kosta sell you the meat?" Kiril asks, still looking at Anka.

"There's no meat," Yulia says. Her voice is flat as always, but her pale eyes are wide and glinting. "Something else has happened."

Yana. Yana has happened.

It unfolds like this:

The tavern keeper discovers the first bloody rag peeking out from a barrel of beer shortly after the church bells toll eleven. When she pries up the lid, she finds the barrel spoiled, a red-brown cloth soaked in blood and ale slung over the mouth like a dish towel at a washtub. She raises the alarm by knocking glasses from her customers' lips, throwing herself to her knees outside the tavern door in prayer just as Yulia walks by.

Almost at once, they find another rag in the well bucket, crumpled in a pool of blood an inch deep. The Captain arrives and orders the well closed immediately, chaining the lid shut himself. They are lucky, he says, that they have snow to melt. But before he can leave the square, another breathless arrival: a farmer brandishing a cloth that stained his fist as he ran to the village—the man doubles over as he tries to explain that he came straight to the Captain after he ripped the vile thing from his best goat's neck, and does the Captain think the goat is likely to die?

"Why would the vampire do this?" Anka hears a woman pleading with Yana in the square. "What does it gain?"

"Fear," Yana says grimly, her eyes on the sealed well. "But monsters don't *do* these things in the same way that they kill to feed. It's more . . . a manifestation. The same way weather grows too thick and must break to a storm."

More: a rag found discreetly folded under an unbothered chicken in a coop, painting her eggs Easter red. Another twisted through the cemetery gates in place of the broken padlock and chain, blood frozen to the wrought iron in red slicks. One hangs from the top floor of the dead midwife's empty house, a mirror of the newlyweds' bedsheet, which Simeon's mother hastily removes and hides at the very bottom of her laundry basket when the news of the day begins to spread.

Seven signs, the priest reports by the afternoon, his face so white they could lose him in the snow. Seven like the sins, seven like the seals of hell. The last is the most brazen of all: after weeks of defiling his steps, the beast has grown bolder. It's shattered the front locks. He finds the last bloody rag nailed to the very door of the church, on the inside.

THE CHURCH HAS always been full of demons. They leer down from every corner, every parapet. They have blue and red faces, flashing eyes, wet teeth. Demons with curling claws and long black tongues lashing at cherubim, crouched on spindly pillars of ash and sooty clouds, emerging from fires painted into the ground. When Anka was small, she was afraid of them: she would cry at the threshold every time they went for services, and the villagers looked askance and muttered as she passed. Kiril would try to calm her and point out the others: the angelic bodies spilling gold light from their fingertips. The holy Mother, the Son, the apostles and saints—wise and battle-ready, poised at the edge of the skirmish. She only liked the outsiders: from their perch above the door to the parish house, three human men in red fez caps watch the story unfold. The priest told Anka and Kiril once that these were the traveling artists who painted the murals long before they were born.

In the years since, the churchwife has become fastidious about cleaning—when she isn't scrubbing blood out of stone, she gently wipes soot from the walls, a daily chore that marks the passage of time like a year-round clock, one chapter of the story always brighter and more vibrant than the rest. In springtime, she restores man's Fall. In winter, Judgment emerges from the cinders and shines with righteous conviction. Today, she's polished the left half of Christ's face. He's all but rosy, flushed with revelation.

The Captain gathers everyone in the early evening to quell the herd. At dusk, the snow returns, bringing with it the vicious wind that chased Kiril from the city into the hills. He's already grateful that he won't have to walk back to the Captain's house, that he need only duck through the trees to his cottage. Last night, Nina consented to let him light the grate, satisfied that the neighbors were all too drunk to notice. Tonight, he'll make sure they see him taking the path and leave no doubts about who has kindled the fire.

The church is so full it creaks. Even those who neglect regular services have come to hear what is to be done. The shuttering of the well especially worries them. Kiril stands behind the last row of pews, leaning against a pillar wrapped in roses and ripe fruits. Ahead of him rolls a sea of tense shoulders and damp hats, surrounded by blazing lights. The villagers have been scrambling to light candles for protection. In the late afternoon, the line of penitents stretched past the church doors and into the square. The tavern keeper circled with cups of hot wine, accepting coins and condolences in exchange for refreshments and the story of her brush with the beast—*I knew there was something off because of a terrible stench that hit me, and you know I keep my cellar clean, very neat. That, and I had odd dreams last night, a whole flock of sheep walking backwards past my window, dead in the eyes and bloody at the throats. It was terrible, terrible, and then that smell—*

The Captain takes the lectern, and the villagers hush to whispering. Kiril watches him through the arms of the candelabras. The wind howls, outside and in. The church is oddly built; on cold winter nights, the gale finds cracks underground, whistling in the cellar where the bodies are kept. Sometimes, the candles flicker.

"My friends," the Captain begins. He knows—it's been a trying day, it's been very difficult. Blood in the beer, among the livestock. He lists the seven omens, and Kiril watches the crowd flinch after each one. The beast even broke the lock on the church doors when it forced its way in. Yana stands behind the Captain, looking very serious.

"The seer has been working diligently. She and the father have done tremendous work today." So many blessings Yana and the priest have performed: cleansing, protective rituals for the ale, for the chickens, for the people. They have spent whole sacks of barley pearls. They have emptied full jugs of holy water anointing the brows of men and the beards of goats. And soon, he says, urging Yana forward, soon the seer will know the demon. Its form grows clearer by the hour.

"Yes," Yana agrees, bowing. She sees a silhouette at the end of the tunnel, a shape thrashing with grim hunger, with anguish. The monster is still obscured, but not for long. "The shadows are thick," she says, "but my course is set. My lantern is bright. I will not fail you."

A gusty, boreal voice moans underground. The beast is growing nervous, Yana tells them. Soon they will all find peace.

The pews are so crowded that even in the cold, Kiril finds it hard to breathe. He sheds his coat, an old one of the Captain's, and drapes it over his shoulder. Others loosen the scarves that armored them against the wind.

"Yana will patrol the village tonight," the Captain announces loudly. "She will watch for any signs of trouble—soon this evil will be purged. There is no threat to your families. Soon, this will be put right. I promise you."

Then he pauses. A strange tenderness crosses his features. Kiril recognizes it even from far away. Framed in candlelight, the Captain looks softly at Anka.

"I have one more piece of news," he says. "Happy news. I hadn't planned to do this tonight—I planned to wait. But I see now that this is the time."

His deep-set eyes sweep the room. He must remind them: many years ago, a terrible thing happened here. Many believe it was the start of their troubles. Some of them bear the scars of it still—that horrible fire that took Zora and Emil away.

"Anka, come here." She is trying to hide in the front pew,

trying to vanish into the grain of the wood. The Captain steps forward and pulls her up by the wrist.

"There are those among you," he says, over their murmurs, "who believe this girl has cursed you and this village. *There is no curse*. We have had ill fortune—our seer tells us why. Something evil took root here long ago, but we are now very close to driving it out. My Anka is not its cause—she was its first victim."

He puts his arm around her. She stares at the ground, but Kiril knows she's listening closely to the Captain's every word. Her shoulders are hunched to her ears. Is she really anemic? Suddenly he isn't so sure. She doesn't look well. She's whispering something, or her lips are moving. The Captain ignores her. "My dear friends," he says. "Many years ago now, I had a sort of vision."

Anka's eyes are unfocused, far away, like Yulia's. Kiril watches her chest rise and fall rapidly. *She isn't well.*

"God gave me a difficult task—caring for two children who were not my own, who had come to me by terrible chance. And I have done a poor job."

Was it this, the Captain asks, was it his folly that left them all open to such grim attack? He humbles himself before them. He would drop to his knees and beg their forgiveness if he believed there were any point.

Not now, Kiril can read on Anka's lips. *Not yet.*

"I was never meant to be her father," says the Captain. "That I've tried has brought no end of trouble. I understand that now. God had a different plan for us. We will right this wrong in just a few weeks' time. When we marry, we will help push out this darkness, counter it with light."

Whispers flicker the candlelight around them. The thousand demon eyes painted into the walls glitter. The Captain takes Anka's hands in his and beams at the crowd. "My friends," he cries, "this is joyful news. Celebrate with us."

Is it their dislike of Anka? The strangeness of the announcement, of the moment? They hesitate. There are some soft mumbles of felicitation. Only a few hands come together in halting applause. But it cannot cover the wind from below, the confusion in the pews. And so, it's quiet when Anka finally finds her footing, steps away, and raises her arm to point.

"Monster," she says.

All of her trembles: her voice, her arm, her ragged finger. But it's loud enough to hear.

The weak applause evaporates into candle smoke.

"Monster, demon, murderer—"

Yana moves in, but Anka throws out an arm to block her. The Captain, perhaps for the first time, is stunned to silence. In the light of five hundred candles, it all feels like a dream, like a parade of sheep will backstep down the aisle at any moment. The Captain tries to laugh, but abruptly, the crowd belongs to Anka. Her lips are thin, her hair is flat—but her eyes are wildly alive. Her voice shakes at first but grows stronger as she speaks.

"He—he killed Svetan the farmer at the burning point all those years ago. He laughs at you all in private—how foolish you are. He thinks you're dim-witted, like cows, that you'll believe whatever he has to say. He forces women into his bed—so many of you, I've seen you running from his house in the night. Bruised in places you keep hidden."

She finds Kiril where he hides at the back of the crowd,

and hundreds of eyes follow hers. "He broke my cousin's arm when we were children, because I tried to run away. He beats Kiril horribly—he always has. And—and he started the fire that killed my parents. The night I was born, he knocked my father unconscious and burned the house. He told me so himself."

It's the same ferocity she saves for Kiril in back hallways, the fingernails and teeth. He wants to get closer, to intervene, but the villagers are too tightly packed together. Nobody will move to let him through.

"Enough," the Captain says, trying still to smile, grabbing for her wrist. "You've all seen her, she's not well. It's too much excitement, Anka—let's take you home now."

She wrenches her arm free. A wail from the cellars, the wind rising to a pitch.

"All summer he was ill! I was trapped in that house with him. Forty days and nights when none of you saw him—not a hair of him! Isn't that what the seer told us?" She whirls around to Yana. "The body dies, and the vampire rises. Forty nights— that's how long it takes. *Isn't that right?*"

From the pews, a voice on the verge of tears calls for the Captain to explain. Someone else wants Anka to say more—to tell what she knows—did she see him destroy the roses? Did she see him kill the lamb? And others still are crying out for Yana: *Seer, seer, what do you see? Is it true? What does it mean?*

Yana moves slowly. Looking from Anka to the Captain and back. The Captain hisses something at her. Anka holds her gaze, her chest rising and falling, her arm still outstretched. She shivers, shimmers, candlelight smearing the scene.

"That is what I told you," Yana says. "That's how long it takes. But—"

"This is nonsense," the Captain says loudly. "A very funny joke, girls, but it's gone too far—you're frightening our neighbors."

The church doors slam open. The loose latch gives way in a mighty gust of wind and the door knocks a candelabra to the ground, a deafening crash of iron on stone. People shriek, and three dozen thin, yellow prayer candles roll across the floor. Men jump from their seats to stomp out the flames. The candles left standing go out in the roar of wind and snow. Outside, the village square glows ghastly in clouded moonlight.

"Stay calm!" the Captain booms. Simeon and his father have leapt to their feet and are forcing the doors closed—Kiril runs to help them. The wind pushes back like a solid, living thing. Out of the corner of his eye, he spies Margarita forcing her way up the aisle towards Anka.

Anka is screaming: "Monster! Monster!"

When the door slams shut and he throws his back against it, Kiril sees her. The dim light through the windows finds her where she stands by the altar: a pale blue otherworldly wisp, her hair flying loose, spit bubbling on her lips. Wild girl-spirit pulled from the deepest part of the woods.

She manages it once more—"*Monster!*" And then she collapses to the ground.

Three Interludes: Lovers

SHOPS CLUNG TO the bridge like barnacles. They crusted over its sides, leaning on stilts out over the canal. On one wooden sign, a rose bloomed from a crystalline bottle. Inside, a white-faced shopkeeper stood behind the narrow counter, packing her things for the night. Hair, brows, lashes so light they were like part of her skin.

Night rippled over the water. The lamplighter wove his way to each iron post along the banks, painting the wet cobblestones with green gas glow. Merchants latched their doors and made for dry land. Against the swell, a woman entered the perfumery. A girl clung to her thigh, hiding between mother's rough linen skirt and her curly hair. The air inside was thick with wood polish, rose oil, and bergamot peels.

"I'm closing," the shopkeeper said over her shoulder. She raised the candle douter like a sorcerer's wand.

"I couldn't come sooner."

"Mama," whispered the child, "I'm scared."

The woman put a hand on her head. "It's all right." She smiled for the shopkeeper. Her cheekbone was dotted with purple pinpricks. "She doesn't like the dark. She's never been away from home after sunset. I'm sorry we've come so late, but—someone said you could help me. A friend."

"Help you," the shopkeeper repeated. Most of what she sold were personal fragrances to women and men who dressed in bright silks.

The woman knelt by her daughter. "Darling," she said, "little star. Show her what happened." It took some coaxing, the girl unwilling to leave the safe haven of her mother's dress. Finally she held out her thin arm, her little hand, where two fingers were splinted tight to a piece of wood. Flesh swollen, purpled with bruises that crept up towards her elbow.

"That must have hurt," the shopkeeper said. The girl showed her brave face for the first time. Her complexion split light and dark down the center line of her nose. She nodded.

"If it's medicines you're looking for, the apothecary is across the street. But he closes early—you'll have to try him tomorrow."

The woman rolled her daughter's sleeve back down. "No. My friend—she said you could help me. I can pay." She looked over her shoulder, as if for eavesdroppers. "He can't hurt her again."

After a long pause, the pale woman snuffed out the candle, leaving the shop dim but for outside light, just streetlamps and sickle moon. She reached beneath the counter and took out a plain wooden box, then a key from around her neck. Inside, nestled in crushed velvet, were three glass vials. They looked just like the perfumes on the shelf.

"No scent," the shopkeeper said, lifting one from the box, "and no taste. Two drops at every meal. It will be slow."

The woman hugged her daughter close with one arm. "It's been slow already. It would have been easier if he changed all at once. I loved him so much." A life like a long summer night, when the streets of the city opened and branched, never ending, just for them. She thought it would last forever.

The pale woman locked the wooden box and returned it to the shelf under the counter. She slid the key back under her dress.

"Love does that," she said, handing over a vial cocooned in old newspaper. "Love ends."

"YOU'RE TIRING OF me," Nina said. She had been drinking with Lena and Iliya every night. Lately Lena went to bed earlier and earlier, leaving her husband to support Nina's wretched sobbing body down the alley to her empty home. Luka had been dead for a month, and she hadn't bled for two. She was thinking of going to the old woman up the hill.

Iliya arranged her in the doorframe so she wouldn't fall and fumbled in her pockets for the key. It had been Luka's coat, but it didn't smell like him anymore. "Help me, Nina, where did you put it this time?"

It was a cold night, death to the early spring flowers, and her head was full of yellow fog.

"You and Lena, you—you've already forgotten him. You wish I would, too." Luka had grown with them through childhood, into real life, was theirs long before he was hers—how could they leave him behind so quickly? It must be easier when you could hide your grief in another person.

"That's not true," Iliya said.

Nina groped for the key and held it up. "You wish I would just stay home and—and leave you alone. So you won't have to think of him. You want—to get on with your life. I can't do that. I'm not sorry—I can't."

He grabbed for the key and crushed her fingers around it. "That's not true," he said again. He was taller than Luka. The warm scents of yeast and roasting meat clung to his clothes. She wanted that warmth, wanted to be nourished. Later, she would find the shadow of the key printed on her palm. He kept squeezing until her hand hurt and her eyes watered. He was crying. It was a thin-moon reflection of her own insides, but she could see it. It was real.

She tried to take him to her bed with her. Pulled at the front of his shirt, put her hand low. His shoulders shook when he kissed her. But then he reached past her, turned the key in the lock, and pushed her over the threshold alone.

The room was a drink, sloshing as she made her way across. She threw up on the undulating deck. By the next morning, bile had sunk into the floorboards; at night she could still smell the sour stink from her bed. This time, Iliya followed her. He held her wrists to the mattress so she wouldn't leave marks. When Luka was still alive, Lena liked to tease him about Nina's pink fingernail tracks growing like weeds up over his collar. Iliya wasn't hurt enough, broken enough. He still had the sense to be discreet.

"I heard the old woman on the hill can stop quickening," Nina said one night, looking down at her bare stomach. Nothing looked different yet. She wanted Iliya to tell her that it was nonsense, that he and Lena would help her with the baby. That they would arrange themselves again into a group of four, as steady and solid as the walls of a house. Instead he said, "We can't do this again."

He said it many times, scrubbing himself with a rag from her washtub, his unmarked back turned to her. He said it enough that one night, when he blocked her path to the tavern and told her Lena didn't want to see her, that neither of them wanted to see her, it took her by surprise. She hadn't expected him to ever mean it.

Two days later, the priest came while she was tying her boots for the long walk. Enchantment, he explained gravely. Witchcraft. Serious charges. And she'd laughed, righteous in her shame and innocence.

Then two other men blamed her for their love affairs. She'd come in the night, slithered through their windows and in under their sheets, all sinew and slick hunger. She didn't know them, but what of it? Maybe she had found them in the dark, maybe her grief was too big, her sick spirit boiling over the bounds of her known life. She had never spoken to them, but she was a lost cause—at least they could save themselves.

Her third night in jail, wrists bitten raw by iron shackles, she felt the twitch of movement in her belly. She was alone, and not alone. It was too late for the old woman on the hill.

THEY SAT IN bed together, two old women. She dragged a worn comb through her lover's long hair.

"Think of a dream," she said, covering

wrinkled, soft eyes with wax-smooth hands. She let the comb fall to her lap, strung with silver. The labyrinth of a dream, where time stretches around dim corners, where future and past twine and explode, where the sleeper lives years and walks miles without leaving her bed, waking bone-weary and sore to discover it's been mere hours, all one sly trick of night.

"That's how my lives feel sometimes—like a series of long dreams."

"You talk as though they're beads on a string," Minka said. "But are you reborn? Is there ceremony? No, you continue on. It's all one necklace."

That wasn't right, Yulia thought. Lives were not just birth and death. More important were the things in between. The faces and hearts of the people she'd known: her men, her women, her lovers whose bodies alone could not describe them.

"Imagine," she tried again, "if your whole life fit in one summer afternoon, chasing fireflies into twilight as a child." Children—there were children, too. Three times over she was a mother. Three beads, buried so long now they'd crumbled into the sand. A daughter with apple cheeks and gapped teeth. A son who liked nothing better than to help her with the sewing, whose stitch was finer than her own. A baby she never got to know.

"Come back to me," the midwife said, gentle thumb tracing the curve of her ear.

"You—I love you more than I've ever loved anyone."

"Don't say that. You love me as you love me now. That's enough."

Minka began to ready herself for bed. She hung her dress

neatly over the back of a chair, rolled a second pair of socks over her feet for the cold night. She'd lost weight these past few months. She moved with unoiled gait and bone, struggled to lift the next log into the fire.

"I've been so many things. Farmer, mother, priestess. Now housekeeper, nanny."

"My shape-shifter. Aren't you all those things still?"

She wasn't sure. Was winter the same as springtime? Didn't summer die once it yielded to harvest?

They crawled into bed. Under the covers, the midwife played with the laces of her nightdress. Winding and unwinding. "How long will you remember me, after I've gone? When will I slide out of mind, get lost among your other pearls?"

"If you stayed with me, I wouldn't have to remember. I can show you how."

Minka's sweet eyes were folded deep into her spotted skin, the whites gummy and yellow. "You're still like a child sometimes. You ask questions you already know the answers to." The comb had wedged between the bedcovers and the wall; she pried it free and set it on the night table. "Here is what will happen: you will remember me for some time, you will mourn a little while. And then you will find yourself another beloved."

"I don't want another. I've found you."

"Next time you should choose a younger woman. Then she won't know better when you say such things."

Time wrinkled in her memory. It wasn't easy—it broke her heart to doubt. They shuffled together like the folded bodies of the paper dolls that Anka had abandoned in a hatbox under her bed long ago.

Minka blew out the candle.

"I lived my life in a language I will never hear again," she said. "Your many lives—I have just this one." A cracked basin, drained empty and dry—one wild, thunderous rainstorm couldn't fill it all alone. Yulia would be a great flood if she could. But there was music in her head that nobody else could play, Minka said. On the hill, every house was haunted but hers. "My last neighbor and I didn't speak for a decade, can you imagine? An old family grudge, I can't even remember why. But when he died, I buried him—a man I hadn't said a word to in more than ten years."

Sour, dismissive, pickled in his grievances. "I remember him."

"But you will forget him soon enough. Everyone living will. You choose to keep your memory here, in you, on this earth. But I want to take mine with me to the next place."

"The next place. I have walked this earth for so many years, and—"

Minka pressed a finger to the button of her lips. "No one is less ready to tell me that death ends all things. Hush now. It's late."

They burrowed closer together. Minka told her once that she was so long and thin as to be a knife, a blade to go to bed with. *And I am squat and lumpy*, she said cheerfully, *like a potato*. The quilt slipped, and they rearranged it.

"Listen," Yulia said. Inside her was the infinite space of a dream. On Minka's shoulder, she tapped a rhythm. "I think it's starting to snow."

thirteen

P ERHAPS SHE'S SIMPLY gone mad," the priest murmurs. They assemble in the parlor, a company of serious men: Captain, Father, Doctor. The fire is slow to light, room haze-gray with smoke and breath. Yulia pours brandy and disappears into mist down the hall. "Hysteria," says the priest. "It's not uncommon, is it? In young women like her."

"Is it madness?" the Captain asks. He rests his arm on the mantel, staring blankly at the wall. "Or is it cruelty? What has she said to you?"

"To me?" Kiril asks.

"You could give her more time," the priest suggests. "True, she's known for years you would someday marry, but the reality of it—she has a delicate constitution."

Delicate. Delicate speaks of spider lace, of withered orchids. Anka has never been delicate. Even now—faded, easily bruised—she cuts. A quiet weapon with sharp teeth.

Kiril wanders to the window and looks out. His own face swims out of the rippled glass. His first week in the city, en route to his first dissection, he took a wrong turn into a room papered with diagrams of the heavens. A young man with wire glasses pointed him down the stairs with a smile. Six hours later, queasy and hungry as he left the operating theater, his thoughts trapped under the black hood that draped the dead man's eyes in a sackcloth sky pierced by loose stars, Kiril met the young astronomer again. Hasan introduced himself, steadied Kiril with a hand on his shoulder, and steered him towards supper.

They went to a tavern where a large-bellied man called Hasan *nephew* and served them plates of chicken and yellow rice. They talked about their families. Hasan had four brothers. His father was long dead, and he'd lived all his life with his mother in a comfortable apartment not far from the university. Now he was studying with the astronomers, learning the movements of celestial bodies, predicting where light and shadow would intersect.

"I enrolled for medicine," Kiril said when it was his turn. "The people in my village need a healer. They rely too heavily on superstition. My cousin, Anka, she—well, at home, there's only Anka and the Captain." His plate was empty, and Hasan's uncle came to refill it. A man in the corner was playing a lute. Kiril imagined the lonely dining room back home: the Captain painfully coaxing Anka into conversation while she said nothing and picked at her meat. "Anka, she's . . . difficult. She was unhappy when I left." He wanted to say more. He wanted to change the subject. "Did you find your eclipse?"

"I believe I did," Hasan said. "I'll know in about twelve years if I'm right."

Your difficult cousin, he would call Anka after that. *Perhaps your difficult cousin should come to visit; the city might do her some good. Have you written to your difficult cousin lately? She'd be happy to hear from you, I'm sure.*

"She has been ill," the Captain says. "You examined her this morning—what did you find?"

Kiril touches his forehead to the cold glass. "She presents with signs of anemia. Yulia and I discussed an adjustment to her diet. If she doesn't improve, there are other remedies we can try."

"But nothing—nothing in her mind?"

Anka's mind—what can he make of it? A windswept, frightened place made deadly by jagged rocks. He recognizes it; for so long, his own was the same. Years where they had only each other, dragged along by hard-breaking water. What can't he see now? Behind him, the fireplace logs are finally starting to catch. He watches them flicker, paint his breath on the window like sunset.

"She's afraid to marry," he says. "Ivo is right. It's natural to be anxious about such a momentous change."

The Captain sighs into a chair. "Have I done wrong? I replaced her father—I've been punished for it. I understand. How else can I care for her?"

Ghosts in the night, beyond Kiril's foggy reflection: women, girls running from a house in flames. Fleeing with a few coins or less. Nina, shrinking over her belly, afraid to look up. Anka is already halfway to the woods—marriage will bring her closer, give her solid earth to tread.

"No," Kiril says. "This is how it's meant to be. She'll come around."

Yulia knocks softly at the parlor door. "Captain, you wanted the seer."

"Yes," the Captain says, finally taking his brandy. "Send her in. Kiril, go look to your cousin."

Yana is steady and serious as she enters the room. Her expression tells Kiril nothing as they cross paths. He shuts the door.

By the time he returns to the cottage, Nina has lit the hearth.

"It got so cold," she says sheepishly.

"I'm glad you did," Kiril says. He stomps snow off his boots, and it melts rapidly into a rag rug she's laid at the threshold. The warmth of coming home. The warmth of finding her here, at ease. Anka was still unconscious when he went to see her. Even when he touched her sunken cheek, she didn't wake. Last night he was so sure—with wedding music still singing through his blood, he fell into Nina, giddy and light. It was peace, reward. Wine, a single candle, the smell of soap he'd brought behind her ear. He woke with his hand pressed between her thighs, her damp fingers trailing an invitation up his arm. She whispered in his ear, *I'm not broken.* But now he can't banish Anka from his head. *Your difficult cousin.* She swirls with blue light and screams.

He tries to refocus. For the first time since he brought Nina to the cottage, he takes a proper look around, sees it out of shadow. She's cleaned away the cobwebs and dust. She's rearranged the room, too, materialized furniture. It must have come from her own house—there's a little table, two chairs. A cooking pot and kettle, a kitchen knife, fireplace tools. The mattress on the floor is draped with blankets he doesn't recognize. There's even a pad of drawing paper on the table, a charcoal pencil discarded atop a good likeness of baby Sofia smiling.

"I didn't know you could draw," he says. He knows so little about her. He picks up the pad to take a closer look.

"A little," she says. "My mother encouraged me when I was young. It passes the time."

He flips the pages—Sofia staring up from her basket, Sofia asleep, Sofia sucking her tiny fist. He turns another and stops. Not the baby, but a man who he hasn't seen in months. Nina's husband, the way he must have looked working in his shop—eyes focused, sleeves rolled high up his arms, streaks of ash and sweat on his skin. Kiril shuts the book and sets it down.

"You brought all this from your house?" How did she even get the table here, and without anyone noticing? Witchcraft, the villagers would say. He'd thought she was a kept secret, quiet and safe, waiting on his visits, but she's made her own way. "It seems risky."

"Oh," Nina says. She's eying the basket. "Nobody's seen me. I did it a little at a time, you know, at night. I haven't had much else to keep me busy. You don't mind, do you?"

"No, of course not." Kiril hefts the food. "I'm sorry to be so late tonight. You must be starving."

"It's not so bad." But when he hands the basket over, she begins to unpack it at speed. Earthenware plates materialize in a swirl of her apron, and she sets the table for them. "Did something keep you?"

He doesn't want to bring the trouble in. Nina tucks a loose lock of hair behind her ear as she unwraps the bread and a clay pot that Yulia wordlessly handed him when he went scavenging in the kitchen. Gently, she rocks Sofia back and forth with one hand as she spoons stew onto their plates. The baby is enthralled by the firelight reflecting off the plaster ceiling. No, no trouble yet—it's better to sit here in this clean, ignorant space, where Anka won't despise him forever, where he can share a meal with a pretty woman and a sweet child.

"Nothing that should worry you," Kiril says. He finds the wine and uncorks it. As soon as the food is laid out, Nina begins to eat. Kiril breaks off a hunk of cheese, but he hasn't much appetite.

She drags bread across her plate. "You never told me about the wedding."

"It was beautiful." He listens to himself, and finds that he's honest. He's released Margarita like a caged bird, found her even lovelier in flight. "I haven't seen the villagers so happy in a long time. I think it was good for them to celebrate." He hesitates to tell her about the fire dancing. Would mentioning his uncle break the spell?

While Nina eats, his eyes travel the room. She's hung a spare dress from a nail on the wall. Freshly laundered stockings dry by the fire. Just a little more could make it a real home—a wardrobe, a bed.

"I thought I could bring some things," Kiril says. "Make it more comfortable here. The villagers know I sometimes stay now—it wouldn't appear odd, I don't think."

"You don't need to go to the trouble for me," Nina says. "We're comfortable enough."

"It wouldn't just—well, it would be for me, too. When my uncle marries, I think I'll come for good. You—you could stay, of course."

Nina wipes her mouth with a napkin. "When he marries?"

Who else is in her sketchbook, Kiril wonders. How would she draw him, or the Captain? A boy playing doctor, playing house. A twist of charcoaled limbs, writhing on the paper. The tavern keeper swore to the priest that Nina had bewitched him for months, let the devil take control of his body night after night for her pleasure. In a dim room, a figure with glowing red eyes bends her body. Her wet breath draws fog across a counter sticky with beer.

"He's found a bride?" Nina asks. She folds her napkin and sets it aside. There's still food on her plate.

Kiril rises and crouches by the fire. He takes the poker she's brought from her house and rearranges the collapsing logs. Did her husband make this? He can see the hammer strikes that shaped the sharp end.

"My cousin," he says. There's an incomplete split in one log, a delta that grows deeper as the fire licks it, flame driving an invisible wedge through the wood. "The Captain announced his plans today to marry Anka."

"You don't seem surprised."

"No," he admits. "He's wanted this for a very long time. It isn't quite as unseemly as it sounds. She isn't related to us by blood. When she was born, he took her into his house because nobody else would."

"I've heard the story. Are you done eating?"

She clears the dishes. She returns what's left of her stew to the pot, then scrubs the plates clean over a bucket.

"The well was closed today," he says. "More of Yana's work. But I can bring more water tomorrow. There's snow, in the meantime—I hope that's sufficient."

"We have enough for now." Lined up over the mantel, she's collected discarded wine bottles and filled them. She must have snuck out to the village square early, gathered wedding debris while he slept. She and Yana could have been out at the same time, witch and seer both haunting the dawn. He hadn't realized he'd dreamed so deeply. He rolls the throat of a bottle between his fingers, watches a dimple in its body spin. *Put some color in your cheeks, cousin.* She'll never speak to him again.

"Are you all right?" Nina asks.

He sets the bottle down with a *thunk*. The glass rings where it touches its twin, then keeps ringing. "I fear I've done something unforgivable."

Nina hangs her rag on a peg by the fire. "You'd be surprised what most people can forgive. Here." She takes her seat again and tugs him along, folds his hand into hers. The night he came home from the city, Anka bit into the ball of his thumb but didn't break the skin. Nina's fingers rub small circles into the dip of his palm.

He asks, "What's the worst thing you've ever done?"

Nina laughs. An echoing well, an unknown cave, a pit. "I don't get to keep my secrets in this town," she says. "You never did ask if I'm really a witch."

"I don't believe in witches." No spellcraft, no coal-eyed demons burning out of the dark. Just desolation, desperation, flesh to fill what's empty. Three red, shame-faced men admitted humiliating, sublime agony before the whole town—the Captain laughed as he told the tale. *The penance for adultery is greater than the penance for a lie*, he said. Are there pictures of the tavern keeper in her sketchbook? He pushes the thought away.

"Was it worth it?"

She rubs the cuff of his sleeve. The broken barbs of her nails catch in the woolen threads. "I don't know how to answer that." Her hair is coming loose from its knot; she unpins it and lets it unwind over her shoulder, a slippery black river. "I hurt people. I paid for it—more than I think I should have. But did it help? For a while, yes—it helped to be with him, even though he wasn't really there with me. Not in the same way."

Had it helped, when he visited whores in the city? Every so often, his lonely desperation grew to a wild frenzy. When the surgeon had nothing to show them, when Hasan was too absorbed by his spyglass and his calculations to share his time—then, sometimes, Kiril fled the boardinghouse and into the streets. In summer, sex spilled into the alleys. On the hottest nights, people sprawled half out of doorways or slept on their roofs. He remembers once a woman sitting on her windowsill, her dress hiked to her knees, one leg dangling out into the night air. Even from the cobbles below he could see the calluses on her heels, the spread of her bare toes. There were women under archways and in bedrooms with paper walls, their sweat cheaply perfumed, their mouths hot where they touched him. Women out of stories: beautiful by moonlight, pulling him in by a crooked finger under his ribs, whose masks slipped when they grew bored. Gathering clouds revealed pointed fangs and rending claws. And still, sometimes, he would have let them rip his flesh and swallow him down, piece by piece. He would have licked clean the blood staining their teeth. For a while, yes—it helped.

Nina dips her head and kisses the inside of his wrist. Under the table, her palm skates up his thigh. A spark lights in his spine.

"What is it?" she asks. "This unforgivable thing? Is it the worst thing you've ever done?"

Splintered bones, vicious sprains, Margarita running from him in the garden. They're all memories that shame him, but none compares to Anka. Anka in the hallway, Anka with eyes distant and unfocused and falling shut as his grip tightens. He could have killed her, so many times. Sometimes he almost thought she wanted him to. But she's never looked at him like she did last night, like she did today. When he left for the city, she begged him to take her along: on her knees, her arms wrapped around his legs. The next day, she wouldn't come out of the house to see him off. But even then, it wasn't like this. Something has broken. Something he didn't know could crack.

"My uncle always knew how it would look, if he married a girl so long in his care. He tried to find alternatives, wrote a hundred letters, traveled often to meet suitors. Nobody wanted her. No man in Koprivci would have the girl who cursed the village, and no man outside it wanted a bride born here. To leave her unmarried—even worse. As long as she was just a girl, the problem could be ignored—and she was slow to mature. She grew older and older and never bled. Yulia assured the Captain it was normal for a girl of fourteen, fifteen, even sixteen."

Yulia, who has been like a mother. Did she lie as well? The

thought worms through him. She knew what keeping Anka from the Captain cost the women of the village—she saw them in and then straightened their clothes before they fled. In the Captain's house, trouble was always bound up with Anka. Kiril's failures were all bigger beside her, the shadows growing longer and deeper by her flame. *Anka can read and you can't. Anka is loved and you aren't.* But the light is changing; he scrambles for its warmth. The Captain toasting him with brandy, the Captain's arm over his shoulders, a twinkle of pride in his smile. He's always wanted Anka alone—let him have her. It will be better for all of them when he does.

"I found something when you were staying in her room. For absorbing the blood, for hiding it. It took me a while to understand." Anka with him on the front steps, asking about comets, a vial of useless tonic in her lap. He'd thought she trusted him, that she meant to forgive him for leaving, but she was only playing with him. It was a game.

"I don't know how long she hid it, how long she lied. Maybe years. Last night, he—the Captain had a lot of wine. He wanted to know where you were. He insisted I tell him where I'd been *keeping you*. I wouldn't—I couldn't. Not after I watched you leave his house, after the way he's treated the women here for so long. I knew I could end it. So I did—I told him about Anka."

Nina's gently circling fingers go still. "You decided to keep me for yourself instead."

Startled, he pulls away. "No," he says. "Of course not."

"What, then?"

"It's nothing to do with— I didn't want him to hurt you

again. You, and—and all of the others here. Anka's been self-ish. I did it to protect you."

Nina stands, so quickly her chair tips back onto the floor. Sofia releases a bleating sound. "I spent four months chained to a wall so some men could feel safer. Do you know what it's like to be sacrificed?"

"He's never raised a hand against her!" The walls are shift-ing; Kiril's head spins. He should have forced himself to eat. "Please, look—" Desperate, he fumbles with the buttons on his shirt, tugs shoulder and sleeve down to the bend of his el-bow. There's a crooked, calcified ridge he can feel under his skin; it bruises if he presses too hard. "Anka ran away when we were younger—more than once. He always brought her back, but he never punished her. He punished me instead—do you understand?" He grabs her hand and grinds it into his bone, lets her feel the crackling grit. "Nina, please."

"And when you move here, into this house, who will he punish instead? There are plenty of us. If he doesn't break her bones, you'll never know. Do you want to know? Do you want to see?"

The baby begins to sniffle, but Nina doesn't look at her. She starts unbuttoning her dress, nimble with anger.

"Stop it," Kiril says, but she ignores him. She's sliding the dress from her arms onto the floor. Gray shift, the sketch of her body underneath. A spray of freckles across her shoulder, marks like fingerprints. She rips at the shift, and he throws an arm over his eyes. "For the love of God, Nina—"

Sofia is unbinding a mighty wail that could pierce every ear in the village. Blindly, he turns on his heel and goes to her.

His back to Nina, he offers the baby his little finger. "Hush," he says. "Hush, it's all right." A miracle—she quiets, gurgles, suckles at his pinky. Kiril feels his neck burning. Nina stands behind him, her nakedness like a brand hovering by his cheek. He rocks the basket back and forth, back and forth. His ears ring with glass bottles.

"Get dressed," he says. "Please."

No rustling cloth, no creak of floorboards. "You won't even *look*," Nina says.

No, he won't. He won't stalk the Captain over her skin like a tracker through the woods. Here, a contusion left by slow knuckles or the protruding root of a tree. There, a stubbled abrasion, a rash from stinging nettles, the ring of a bite that plucked her breath from her lungs. He won't seek the places where her anger winked out and she let herself shiver, mouth open.

"Get out," Nina says.

He yanks his finger from Sofia's gums and rips his blue coat from a hook near the door. He stumbles out onto the path without looking back. As the door swings shut, the baby begins to howl.

fourteen

THE DARKNESS IS big, absolute. Far away, Anka hears voices. Cold tangle of bedsheets winding about her neck, threatening to drag her under. Sometimes, a presence: big and melancholy by her side, taking the hand she can't retract. Sometimes cool white fish swim over her cheeks, angle her head back. A painful rattle of metal between her teeth, something thin and warm dribbling down her throat.

Bodies need sustenance. A body is just an object, Yana said. Objects exist to be claimed and owned and used. All living things, just bodies: meat and bone and blood. Meant to be cut, broken, spilled.

More than once, she feels Kiril folding back her covers. Even darkdrunk, she knows it's him. Too heavy to shrink. He unlaces her nightdress, presses a cold coin to her chest, her back. Leans close. His pinched breath tight over her neck.

Weak, he says into an arch of light, retreating. *But getting stronger.*

Fingers in her mouth press a hard round bead down her throat. White fish make her drink water. A wall sits by her bed and prays. Finally, a cold wind startles the firelight. A girl like a jeweled cat dropping through the window, uncurling by her bedside, frozen starlight caught in her hair.

"I had to," Anka whispers. Her voice is lost deep within her; she pulls heavy ropes to lift it out. Throat like tinder, lips flint-cracked. "I need them to see him." Say more, say sorry, beg forgiveness, beg forgiveness, beg not to be alone. But the window opens. Snow blows across her face, melts on her hot eyelids, then stops. All gone.

When she does wake, the light is yellow, the curtains askew. Kiril sleeps in the chair by her bed, a blanket crumpling off his shoulders. He jerks up when he hears the bed creak. Anka has legs, has lungs. She pushes herself to sit with trembling arms.

"Slowly," Kiril says. Voice stern and eyes red, underslept. "How do you feel?"

Empty as a room with the window sliding shut. She puts her face in the pillow. "What happened?"

"You frightened the whole village half to death." He retrieves a small black horn from her bedside. "Lean forward. Breathe deep." A cold round mouth between her shoulders. Her breath gets lost in a thicket. She feels it struggle through the underbrush. In the story, the witch got caught in the woods and never pulled free.

"Have they said anything? About him?"

"What should they say? Open your mouth—towards the window." He pulls back the curtains and squints down her throat.

"Anything," she says. "Can't they see?"

"Anka, you accused him of . . . What should they *see*? What did you think would happen? Now sit back. Tilt your head up." Fingertips press under her jaw, drawing circles.

"Is the seer still here?"

Kiril bends to the leather medicine bag by his chair and begins to dig. "She's still here. Trying to undo the damage you did."

Anka blinks up at the ceiling. Thick gray clouds blind her. She's violated Yana's most important rule—*I don't hurt people.* The seer won't return to her now; she said her goodbye as she slipped over the sill.

Kiril takes out a bottle of round pills. "I need you to swallow one of these. And the Captain will want to know you're awake."

"I don't want to see him."

He considers her for a moment. "I'll tell him you need your rest. But take this." He sets the pill in her hand and gives her a cup of tepid water, then watches closely as she swallows. The metallic pearl catches painfully above her ribs. Anka grimaces.

"You'll be all right," Kiril says. The pill bottle rattles as he sets it on the table. "You're going to get better. Everything will be fine."

Anka lies down and curls her back to him. Bones tight, heartbeat an echo. If only she could be a knife. If only she could be a lamb, drunk on clover, slipping away into dead leaves. Kiril sighs. The bedroom door opens and closes after him.

She sits up and takes the cup from her bedside. It feels strange to drink, water carving through drought lines inside her. She examines the pills on the nightstand, turns the bottle over and watches little silver moons tumble past each other. She sets it down beside the hair comb and the flask of Yulia's medicine. There are two fingers of red tonic still left. Careful weeks spent measuring, fretting, planning, all for nothing.

She's still here. Tending to the mess you've made.

How many spoonfuls at the bottom of the flask? Six? Seven? It could be enough, if Yana will still take her away. It might be too much, and she'll never wake.

But the alternative—a wedding ceremony, a marriage bed. Large hands that kept her safe when she was a child now prying her open. A crack like chicken bones coming loose at the joints, cartilage popping free. *It's my favorite part, too,* the Captain said conspiratorially, watching young Anka bite the white caps off gray bones at the dinner table. She liked the rubbery bite of them but not the grainy marrow underneath. After Kiril's dislocated shoulder, she could hardly even stomach the meat.

Kiss of the bottle's cold lip. *What if.* She drinks. Sour cherry and black pepper stick on her tongue. Will the dead come? Mother and Father walking out of the fire, a painting and a brown photograph ready at last to claim her. She swallows. She swallows. *Bury me far.* She swallows.

The bottle is empty.

She fumbles to cap the flask, and the cork rolls away. Yulia will know what to do. Yana will take her, just as they planned. She should have said goodbye to Margarita and Simeon, but they don't need her anymore. They'll understand.

The room bends, light splitting into shooting stars. Her unsteady lamb's body can't stay upright. She collapses into the grasping linens. Kiril's pills tasted like blood going down, but what more can blood do to her? What else could she lose? What else?

fifteen

YEARS AGO, KIRIL woke to find his father sitting on the floor. He was curled around his knee like a child skinned by the hard earth. Late morning cut unforgiving lines across the room, but Kiril's mother still hadn't moved from her bed. When he spoke, his father jumped so sharply that he cut his tongue on his teeth. He'd forgotten he had a son. He no longer had a wife.

Wait here, his father said, blood staining his upper lip.

When Kiril finds Anka, she's breathing, but he needs a mirror to see it. He knocks her shelf of trinkets to the floor with a crash. He grabs an oval glass, holds it by her red-touched mouth. There's a drop on the front of her nightdress. *Consumption*, he thinks, fear seizing him—how did he miss this? what could it mean?—but then he spies the empty bottle, hidden in a wedge of shadow between the nightstand and the bed.

It's only fruit syrup. Tell me again about comets.

Some people think they're ill omens, Hasan explained. *But they're no more supernatural than the weather.*

Anka's eyes stay closed when he shakes her. He must be shouting—he hears footsteps, and then Yulia's white face slices through the unlit square of the doorway. Her distant gaze snaps into tight focus.

"We have to make her vomit," she commands. "Empty her stomach. Now."

He forces his fingers into Anka's mouth and down her throat, but nothing happens. She's as pliant as a fresh corpse. Just an hour ago, she was breathing for him, faint but getting stronger. Kiril pulls his fingers free, wipes them on the sheets. She's warm—at least she's still warm.

"Another way," he says. Sweat breaks across his back. He gropes for his medicine bag.

There was a night when a man came pounding at the surgeon's door in the middle of a dissection. He was dripping with sweat, carrying a limp child, stammering about a bottle of sleeping draft. The students hurried to cover the body on the worktable. The surgeon led them swiftly to the kitchen. He ordered his wife to heat a pan of salt water on the stove and produced a length of rubber hose. Kiril, tasked with extinguishing the lamps and bolting the cellar door, was the last to join them. He stood on a heavy trunk filled with old beakers to watch the surgeon feed the tube down the child's throat. The boy's head was a ball at the end of his neck, threatening to roll away.

"We'll need warm water," he says to Yulia. "And a tub."

It's harder than he expects, getting the tube in. It wants to coil, snakelike, wants to wander. Yulia used to tell them the story of the good maiden who bathed in the golden river, who became golden. Did her skin become hard like metal? Kiril wanted to know. Would she soften in the hot sun? Could she sweat? But Anka wasn't interested in the golden girl, was eager to skip ahead: later, the wicked stepsister sought unearned gifts, and dove into the current too soon, while the river ran black.

When she climbed out, cobwebs stitched her lips. Whenever she spoke, snakes and frogs would slither up her throat and out of her mouth, would leave slimy tracks on her chin and clothes, spill squelching at her feet. Anka would squeal and roll on the rug, disgusted and gleeful, and Kiril shuddered. He couldn't help imagining how it would feel, the wet wriggling in his chest.

Yulia arrives with a large clay pitcher and a tub. She spills warm salt water into the mouth of his dented funnel, one that the surgeon had thrown away. Kiril holds up a finger to stop her while it drains. Then again. Again.

Lavage, the surgeon called it. Washing the insides clean. Rinsing away the traces of whatever Anka took, the red-black tonic sticking to the bowl of her, reluctant to let go.

Kiril tosses the funnel aside. It rolls under the bed and makes a soft clinking sound as it strikes the chamber pot. He drags the tub closer, heaves Anka onto her side, and takes the end of the tube between his lips. A lifeline stringing his mouth to her insides, a perverse umbilical cord. He tastes the rubber, the saline.

Suction, the surgeon had explained, wiping his chin. A siphon. Once the liquid crests the bend in the tube, it will flow unabated. Yulia crouches on the bed beside Anka to hold her still, though she isn't moving. It's an unexpectedly intimate sight, her skirts bunched in the bends of her white knees. He's accustomed to her standing straight in a corner, pitcher in hand, stiff as a wax dummy. A strange thought: that she looks oddly human.

Kiril steels himself, and then sucks his cheeks tight around the tube. Suck, siphon, spill. Suck, siphon, spill. At first, there's nothing. Then bile begins to dribble into the waiting pot. The smell: like the rotting citrus peels that topped garbage heaps outside the wealthy city houses in summer.

The Captain comes to the door. "What is this? What's wrong with her?"

"Out," Kiril commands. "Yulia, get him out." He takes her place on the bed, one hand on Anka's shoulder, the other holding the tube. He watches Anka's stomach empty. His shirtfront is wet with salt water and acid, but his mouth is dry with the powdery, acrid taste of the hose.

In the end, the wicked stepsister is cursed forever and never speaks again. In the end, the golden maid marries a prince. In the end, the little boy in the surgeon's kitchen didn't survive. One student timidly dared to ask, and the surgeon glared contemptuously. *I did everything right*, he spat. *Sometimes it's too late.*

In the hall, the Captain is demanding answers. Anka begins to cough, and sweat runs into Kiril's eyes. He plants bruises along her arms and shoulders. "Yulia, I need you! Now!" She slams the door. He heaves Anka towards her, body like water, limbs like sharp sticks.

"Hold her still. Don't let her pull it out. Anka? Anka! Listen to me. Stay calm. You're going to be all right."

They fill and empty her stomach twice more. The Captain pounds on the door, then leaves, then comes back. Anka visits with them, moaning, then sinks back underwater. When Kiril finally frees the tube and flings it aside, it coils to ouroboros, slimy and bubbling.

"Can you hear me?" Kiril asks, and Anka groans. "Anka, talk to me. Yulia, what now?"

"We keep her awake," Yulia says. "Get her up—make her walk. I'll mix something to give her, to help."

"Is it safe?"

A rare crease folds her white forehead. "Don't let her sleep."

She leaves the door open. Kiril hauls Anka's arm over his shoulders, digs hard into her waist to lift her. Her toes skim the floor, refusing her weight. The Captain arrives.

"Explain," he orders.

"She took something. Some kind of poison—I don't know. We have to keep her awake. Anka? Anka!" He shakes her shoulder, pinches her cheek. "Talk to me. What's the name of your friend who just married? What is she called? Uncle, help me."

The Captain studies the scene. Tub like a foul cauldron, floor wet and sour. The rubber hose, a coiled threat. "Poison," he repeats, and then he turns and looks over his shoulder, down the hall. "You think she's been poisoned?"

Anka groans and tries to swat Kiril away. "Hurts," she mumbles, making to dislodge his arm. "Tired."

"You can sleep later, Anka," Kiril says loudly in her ear. She winces and turns her head. Still drugging. He dips into the cup of water on her nightstand and flicks raindrops onto her face, slaps her cheek. "Let's walk now, all right? Walk with me. Tell me about the wedding. What was the groom's name?"

The Captain finds the glass bottle. He pulls it free and stares. A small bomb in his big hand.

"I think we got it out," Kiril says desperately. "Before her body could absorb it. Yulia says we need to keep her awake."

His uncle slams the flask onto the nightstand. He grabs Anka's chin and gives her a hard squeeze. "Stay with us, little bird." He takes Anka's other arm over his shoulders, and like a hunchbacked giant, they circle the room together.

Gradually, they coax her to stand. To stumble over the damp rug. Her eyes are half lidded, and she winces with every step. There's almost no space, the three of them conjoined, circling the tub. More than once Kiril kicks some wooden bottle of perfume or pot of makeup and watches it roll into a corner. They open the windows and let the winter in, cold white beams. They wet her face. Kiril is afraid to let her drink, unsure what Yulia will bring, but when Anka mumbles, "Thirsty," his heart seizes hopefully in his chest.

An hour or more goes by before Yulia returns, carrying a large mug. A bitter, green smell escapes the steam.

"What kept you?" the Captain asks.

"Sit her down," Yulia says. "She needs to drink this, all of it. It will help with what's left. Here." She hands the mug to Kiril, who brings it to Anka's lips.

But the Captain puts out a hand to cover the mug. Anka rolls her head onto Kiril's shoulder, and he has to pinch her arm to rouse her. "What have you been giving her?" the Captain demands.

He left the glass bottle on the nightstand, a crack growing up towards its throat. Yulia blinks at it.

"Do you want her to live?" she asks. "Let her drink."

"You first," he says. He pulls his hand back and closes it into a fist. Yulia keeps her eyes on him as she sips from the cup.

"Uncle, please," Kiril whispers, and the Captain nods.

Anka tries to spit the bitter tea out, but Yulia covers her mouth like a sick kitten's. Slowly, they empty the mug—sip by small sip. After a while, Anka can keep her eyes open. A weary deadness replaces the unconscious lilt of sleep.

"It didn't work," she mumbles.

Yulia silently combs her bedraggled hair.

Hours tick by. They walk Anka again until she complains of dizziness, keep the window open until her teeth chatter with cold. Kiril thinks of Nina, circling the same creaking floorboards, flushed and alive with fear. Yulia removes the vile wooden tub and mops the floor, spritzes cedar and rosemary from a pale green bottle to erase the stink of vomit. Kiril helps her change the bedsheets while Anka slumps in the chair, wrapped in a blanket, staring at the bumps of her knees. All the while, the Captain stands sentinel in the doorway, glowering when asked to step aside. Danger pulses on the threshold, his weight tilting the room.

When the sun sets, Yulia disappears to the kitchen, and announces dinner on the table. To Anka she brings a wooden tray with a bowl of broth. Anka turns her nose up. "It feels like you scraped out my insides," she whispers. Her voice grates.

"This will help," Yulia says. She sits on the bed and guides Anka to lift trembling spoonfuls to her mouth. "Your dinner will get cold," she says to Kiril and the Captain, but the Captain doesn't move, or even acknowledge that she's spoken.

When Anka's spoon scrapes the bottom of the bowl, Yulia takes the tray away and folds her into the covers. "You can rest now," she says. "We can let her sleep."

The Captain kisses Anka's forehead. "Get strong, little bird."

"I'll be back to check on you later," Kiril promises. She looks away.

Downstairs, the table is humbly set for two. Kiril realizes all at once how hungry he is, and how tired.

"If I never tend to another patient in that room, it will be too soon," he says, pulling out his chair.

There's a loud crash of breaking china over his shoulder. The dregs of the yellow soup bleed down the wall as the Captain advances on Yulia. He seizes a fistful of her pale hair and wrenches her head to the side. Her neck is a slim branch— knots of cartilage press up under her skin.

"What did you do?" the Captain demands.

"Uncle!" Kiril grabs his arm. The Captain knocks him aside without breaking his grip. Kiril's thigh meets the sharp corner of the table, and he shouts at the bolt of pain.

"She mixed it herself," Yulia says. Her eyes are watering.

The Captain jerks her head again. "Don't lie," he spits. "I know who you are—why you're here. You've been hiding in my house. I should have turned you out years ago."

"Let her go," Kiril says, but neither of them looks his way. He shoves his body into the tight gap between them and pushes the Captain back with a hand on his chest.

"I said *let her go*."

Surprised, the Captain loosens his grip. White hair slips from his fingers and onto the floor. Kiril holds his arms wide, to make himself a screen. Yulia's breath is a dry wind.

"She almost killed your cousin," the Captain growls.

"Anka did that to herself."

"Do you know what she is, boy? Like a real witch, with her potions—and a murderer, too."

Kiril lifts his chest. "So are you," he says.

The Captain's fist connects hard with his jaw, knocking him into the wall. Kiril's brow strikes the molding, knees slamming into the floor. His uncle aims a kick at his stomach. Not hard, just enough to shrink him. Like he's punctuating a sentence.

The Captain takes the hem of Yulia's apron and wipes Kiril's blood off his knuckles. "You," he says, reeling her in. "Unless you would rather I have you and the old woman hanged, you will leave this village as soon as Anka is well. Do you understand?"

Kiril tries to speak, but the air won't come.

"And if she dies," the Captain goes on, lifting his arm like a blade to Yulia's throat, "I'll kill you myself. Now get out."

She flees the room. The Captain smooths his shirtfront and begins lighting the candles. Kiril sits, slowly. There's a cut on his forehead—blood runs stinging into his eyes. Gingerly, he gets to his feet and takes his napkin from the table.

They eat without speaking. Kiril handles his food awkwardly with one hand, keeping the napkin pressed to his face with the other. Elbow on the table, which the Captain would ordinarily never allow, but tonight he says nothing.

When their plates are empty, the Captain sits mulling over his wine. Finally he empties the cup and turns to Kiril. "I'll ask once more," he says. "Tell me where you've hidden the widow. I want to see her tonight."

Do you want to see? Nina asks. Kiril lifts the napkin to check his wound. Still bleeding. He wipes a dribble from his eyelid.

"I don't know where she is," he says.

The Captain crosses his arms. "She isn't in her home. And I went to your mother's cottage today, but there was no sign. I thought for sure that must be the place."

"You went—" That morning he left another basket, an apology. He didn't know yet what to say when he saw her again, so he didn't knock. He hadn't thought she would just disappear.

The Captain's eyes narrow. Then he chuckles. "I see," he says. "Useless."

He leaves Kiril sitting at the table, tending to his bleeding forehead. The front door slams open and shut. A short time later, Yulia comes in with a tray of supplies to clean and bind the wound. She washes his face with a damp cloth and wrings pink whispers of blood into a bowl of warm water. He has questions, but he's too tired to ask them. Before she leaves, piling the empty dinner dishes onto the tray, he takes her cool hand and holds it to his cheek.

MARGARITA IS IN Anka's room when Kiril returns, his nose dripping and snow melting off his boots. She's asleep in Anka's bed, their fingers braided together. Did the Captain call her here? Anka stares glass-eyed at the ceiling, like an expensive doll. She follows Kiril to his room when he passes, bracing her hand against the wall.

"How do you feel?" he whispers, unraveling his scarf. She

stops in the doorway, a monster held back by a line of salt. Her short nails dig into the jamb.

"Why did you do that," she asks. "You could have just left me."

Kiril tugs his woolen sweater over his head, wincing where it catches on the bulb of his bandage. He unearths his night-clothes from beneath the pillow and changes while Anka watches. "Of course I couldn't. You know that."

She creeps forward until she's right beside him. A nightmare made of living bone, a deep-water nymph. "Kill me now," she says.

"Don't be ridiculous." He pulls back the covers, and Anka crowds close to his elbow. Her breath smells sour.

"You could do it." She grabs his hand. There's still strength in her bones. She puts his palm to her throat and folds his fingers down. "I hate you," she whispers, and waits. Kiril can hear his own heartbeat, feel his pulse in the cut on his forehead. Under his hand, the flow of her blood is sluggish. "The Captain thinks you're worthless, a traitor. And Nina's run away—she'll never want to see you again."

The cottage was empty when he went, the fireplace cold. She left the basket on the table—left all of the furniture behind, but took her sketchbook and the blankets. Her house, too, was an abandoned tomb. The only footsteps in the snow were the Captain's.

Anka presses her hands over Kiril's, squeezing his fingers down. "You're not enough like him to please him," she whispers. "You're too much like him for anyone else to love you."

The words hit like dull slaps. Where rage once flared in him, there's only the stuttering of a dead-wicked candle.

He pulls his hand away and gets into bed. He holds the covers up for her. She starts to cry, tears sliding off her chin and onto the floor. She gets into the bed beside him and nestles into his arm, dampening his shirt. He holds her until she's cried herself out.

"How can you still love him?" she whispers, wiping her nose on the sleeve of her nightdress.

Kiril pets her unwashed head and kisses her temple.

"Don't you?" he asks.

sixteen

THE FOOTSTEPS DRAG from the graveyard to the midwife's squat house, to a cracked door with broken
lock. Snow blows in over the threshold. In the windows, untended flower boxes sprout withered, needly bones. Inside,
Yana arranges a dead rat at the head of the dusty table.

It's lazy, inelegant. She senses her mother's amused disap-
proval. *You can do better.*

"I want to get out of here," Yana murmurs.

She adjusts the rat's position just so—when the morning
light comes through the east window, she wants anyone peeking through the open door to see the red wound first, their
eyes drawn right to it. With the livestock under close watch,
with winter bitterly here, the vampire turns on vermin. In its
desperation, who's to say it won't attack a human being next?
Tired women go swooning into the doctor's salon—who's to
say it hasn't already?

Satisfied, she turns to go, but her way is blocked. The Captain's pale housekeeper has arrived as silently as the snow.

"How did you know which seat was hers?" Yulia asks. Her
gaze is a little off, lingering behind Yana. Yana finds she doesn't
mind—she's looked at often enough.

She turns back to the table and pauses to reposition the rat's back paw. Less like it tried to scramble away, more like it's been carelessly flung aside, already dead. "She lived alone for many years. It shows in the floorboards under her chair."

"Don't worry," Yulia says, gesturing out at the snow. "I didn't leave any new tracks. Why don't we sit?"

"Here?" The cabin has been latched tight for months. It smells—dry rot from the pantry, mold in a pot left full by the fire. Something nested in the midwife's musty bedsheets before scurrying underground for the winter. It's cold enough that the water in the kettle has frozen, and hard to see with only the moon for light.

"There's a long time to sunrise," Yulia says, patting the curved back of a chair. "Sit with me. You're preparing to leave."

"The Captain wanted me to finish the job. He said I could go once I named the vampire."

Yulia shakes her head and sits. "You misunderstand. I didn't come here on his orders."

The door creaks in the wind. "Then Anka sent you." She can't quite keep the hurt from her voice. She'd thought they could go on together from here, that the road ahead would be less empty, less gray—but she was wrong. Yana lies to people, yes, but they aren't her targets. That's what witch hunters do, preying on the poor and maligned.

"No, I sent myself. Come, sit down. When you first arrived, she told me that you do this work because you want to help people—is that true?"

There's a puddle of old candle wax hardened to the table. Yana should leave it, but she can't help herself—she digs at it with her fingernail, starts to scrape it free. "It's true," she says.

"My mother taught me, when I was very young." Like directing the flow of water, she'd once explained. Tending to the riverbanks with little sacrifices to prevent a dangerous flood.

On the midwife's bed, Mama sighs, resettles herself. She doesn't dent the covers. *You look lonely, my little star.*

"What happened to your father?" Yulia asks, looking over Yana's left ear. "Where was he?"

"He got sick and died. We didn't stay long in the city after that. I only remember pieces of it." How long had they lingered? She doesn't know. There were muggy, yellow days when her mother couldn't get out of bed, and Yana was afraid she would fall ill and vanish, too. She watched the ragged orphans on the street corner from behind the curtains. The next thing she remembers is a gray, rib-boned horse named Chamomile, who her mother must have bought for next to nothing. They left the city, walked in the woods. At some point Chamomile disappeared, and they found Magaro.

"Thirteen years ago," Yulia says, "I had a shop in the city—a perfumery on the bridge. Your mother came to see me there. Do you remember?"

Wax sticks under Yana's fingernail, and the seal breaks. She was hoping to get it up in one piece. On the bed, Mama leans forward, elbows resting on her knees. Yana bites her thumbnail, carves wax loose with her lower teeth. "I don't remember," she says, but maybe she does. Afraid of the dark, an unfamiliar place on a night when the streets were shiny and wet. *Everyone is scared when it's dark enough,* Mama assured her. *Even grown people are afraid of ghosts.*

Yulia watches her closely, focused on her face now, unblinking. "I sold perfumes to wealthy people. I also sold other things—to women who needed to escape. Your father beat your mother. He hurt you."

Yana rubs her clicking wrist. Slowly, an aching, rusted gear turns in an old puzzle box. Scent of floor polish and bergamot. She folds her arm to her chest, abandoning the blot of wax. "You sold poisons," she says, and Yulia nods. "You . . . you fled town. Did my mother . . . ?"

"No. I sold to a countess who was betrayed by her maid."

She remembers walking the streets of the city as a small girl, learning about wealth from long dresses and shoes. Jewel-bright ladies swishing past her, followed closely by hemp skirts snagged on shopping baskets. She wondered sometimes what it would be like to have a companion every hour of every day.

Looking off into the dingy room, Yulia says, "I liked your mother. I only met her once, but I thought she was very brave."

Yana feels a prickling in her nose and eyes. "She *was* brave."

But anyone could guess that of the woman who took her child and taught her to make, see, hunt monsters. It was either bravery or madness. But poison—why believe that? "My father got sick," Yana says firmly. "My mother loved him. She wouldn't—"

"I remember you," Yulia interrupts. In the air before her, she draws the wavering line that splits Yana's complexion. "My clients didn't usually bring their children. That was odd. I think she needed you."

"I was only five years old. Why would she need me?"

"Many of the women I saw had been sold to brutal men they despised," Yulia says, voice gentle. "The rich women, especially, who were married to arrange for land and power. When they killed their husbands, they felt hope, nothing else. But just as many of my customers were still in love."

A memory: her parents laughing, Mama burying her nose in his neck as they watched a sunset. Eyes closed dreamily against the glow, a bruise still shiny on her jaw. He would get on his knees sometimes to beg forgiveness—he would do that only for Mama. Even in church he didn't kneel.

"It's the strange thing about humans," Yulia says. "Never just one thing. Never just good or bad, all tender or hard. It's so easy to keep loving a person, even if they hurt you."

"She was heartbroken when he died." Unable to get out of bed, staring vacantly at a picture she'd drawn of him years ago on the back of a yellowing pamphlet. *I'm not sick*, Mama promised, her voice an unfinished echo. *I'll be better soon.*

One day a friend of hers came, whispered something in her ear, and roused her. The guards were hunting the poisoner, Yana realizes now—they must have been looking for her customers. She and Mama left the city that night and didn't return. Years later, Yana found the drawing of her father pasted in the back of the demon book. Sometimes she would look at it when her mother was out of the room. Her father had a square face, a round nose, and a ray of mischief in his eye. He looked up at Yana from the pamphlet with a smile he'd never shown her in real life. The picture vanished after Mama died—Yana found where the page had been cut away at the binding. Did her mother burn it, throw it out? More likely she folded it into her pocket and took it with her.

Yulia leans forward across the table. "She needed you to be

there, in my shop. If she'd been alone, I think she might have stayed until he killed her. I saw that sometimes—she loved him more than her own life. But not more than you."

Her mother had lived long enough to die far from her father, in a monastery carved into the side of a cliff, where the cells had been excavated from gray stone. Narrow wooden bridges crawled across the rock like dead ivy. In a violent November downpour, Yana hauled Mama, half conscious, up the slick planks to an empty room the brothers offered. They couldn't touch a woman, couldn't help her carry her mother, burning with fever, out of the rain. But after Mama died, they buried her, and prayed for her. What is a body freed of its soul? What sin could there be in handling an object?

With her thumb, Yana digs back into the wax on the table. It breaks into delicate shavings. Mama made no deathbed confessions, admitted no murders, no poisons—but she said his name, once, in her sleep. As if to say, *Wait. I'll be there in a moment.* So faintly Yana barely heard it over the sound of the rain. She turned over on her bedroll and squeezed her mother's hand tightly. *Yana*, Mama murmured. A little while later, her grip went slack.

It feels true. Does Yana remember a bouquet of perfumes on a late night? A mysterious bottle? The mind can invent the memories it needs. But it feels true.

Forgive me, Mama whispers. She stands beside Yana's chair, reaching out like she might touch her forehead. *I should have done it sooner.*

Yulia is looking away. Giving her privacy to remember. Yana wipes her eyes and crosses her arms.

"Why are you telling me this?" she asks. "There must be a price on your head."

"A significant sum. The Captain has known for many years. It was better for him to keep me close at hand."

"You could have left."

"There were the children to look after." Yulia reaches forward and brushes the loose scrapings of wax from the table into a neat pile. She sweeps them into her white palm, and they vanish into her apron pocket. "And I fell in love. I fell in love with a stubborn old woman who neighbors with ghosts."

The wax has left behind a pale patch in the wood, like new skin under a peeled scab. Yana adjusts the candlestick to hide it. There's paraffin under her fingernails, thick and uncomfortable.

"What Anka did at the church—"

"Was foolish," Yulia says. "She was desperate."

"I don't hurt people," Yana protests. "That's not what she taught me."

"Do you think it's that simple?"

People still talk about the city poisoner. In taverns, Yana has heard them parsing the mystery of who she was, where she went. Her story traveled far: she was never caught, never tried, never hanged. Some six hundred dead men in her wake, so they say, and she vanished without a trace. Peasants like to imagine her cloaked in glamour, in the courts of emperors and kings, stirring intrigue into little gem bottles that hide in the bodices of ladies-in-waiting and queens. Had she been a visiting devil? A saint in disguise? They say she only sold to forlorn women. She sold them the hope of escape.

Yulia inspects the dead rat on the table from whisker to tail. "What Anka told the villagers was true," she says. "The women of this village—they'd tell you themselves if they weren't terrified. He may not drink the blood of lambs, but he holds all of their lives in his hands."

"You never did anything to stop him."

"The children," Yulia says. "And Minka—she would never leave this place. It isn't always so easy, to help. Anka tried to poison herself today—that's what I came to tell you. She drank all that was left of her medicine at once."

The cold is getting to her, hurting the tips of her fingers. Yana curls her toes in her boots. She thinks about Anka watching her, trusting and drained, while Yana cleaned her teeth. Her mouth was so warm even as the rest of her froze.

"What would you have me do?" she asks, when she can speak again.

"Minka believes you should take Anka with you and run. Now, tonight."

"He would follow," Yana says. "She said he always finds her. That he would just bring her back."

"I think so, too." Yulia reaches into her apron and retrieves a slim book with a leather cover, wine-stained and old. She lays it on the table between them and slides it towards Yana. Now Yana remembers a strange, pale woman kneeling to her child's height, examining her bruised arm by the moonlight.

Yulia gets up and tucks her chair neatly away. Before she goes, she bends eye level with the rat's bloody fur, and adjusts the reach of its front paw. "There," she says. "That looks more real."

She's right—the body looks like it's freshly fallen from a monster's slick maw, a natural little corpse. The morning sun will hit it just right.

SNOW FALLS IN wet waves. Anka and Margarita watch it all day from her window. They play cards for a while, but it reminds Anka too much of the divination games they loved as children, imagining they could see their future in a queen of hearts flanked by spades. Mostly they just sit. Sometimes, Margarita knocks her foot lightly against Anka's. At dusk, Yulia bustles them out of the room so she can freshen the air.

"Put these on," she tells Anka. "Go breathe in the cold." She packs her in socks, sweaters, scarves, gloves, and finally boots and a coat, until she's transformed into a soft woolen ball. She could almost roll herself down the steps.

"Will you stay for dinner?" Yulia asks Margarita, who hesitates.

"Go home to him," Anka says. "I'll be fine tonight."

"I can at least sit with you awhile."

They descend slowly, Anka clinging to Margarita's arm on one side and the banister on the other. They settle on the front stoop. Anka feels small underneath her layers of clothes: her insides scoured, the little soup she's been able to swallow long cold in her belly. Blue night is falling, a silver sliver of moon struggling to shine. The path away from the house is dotted with footsteps, snowed over into strange burrows and caves for icy sprites. Kiril must be at his salon. She wonders if he'll come back tonight. In spite of herself, she misses him. If she's to stay here, maybe they'll make amends before she kills herself. She hasn't decided yet how to do it. Last night, they heard the Captain screaming at Yulia on the far side of the house. They watched from Kiril's window as the Captain stormed out into the yard with a burlap sack that he emptied onto the frozen earth: bundles of herbs, glass tincture bottles, tools for measuring and mixing. He crushed the vials under his boots. He set fire to the whole heap and stood upwind while everything melted together, leaving a gray pit in the snow. It was feathered with hoarfrost by morning.

"It came on so quickly," Margarita says, tugging on her coat. "Winter, I mean."

Under the sinking sun, the landscape looks like an invitation to the grave. One false step, one slip, and your ankle cracks, the snow covers you over, and you vanish until spring. "Are you sure you want to go back tonight?" Anka asks. Big, flat flakes are still falling.

Margarita touches her back. "Do you want me to stay?"

"No, it's all right. You should see Simeon. I'm just worried about you getting home. Maybe Kiril should go with you, when he returns."

At the edge of the tree line, where the path curves, she spies a small flicker of movement. Not her cousin's long gait, but the shiver of a shadow. She gets only a glimpse of Yana before she melts into the old pines. Behind them, the door opens, and candlelight spills onto the steps.

"Are you cold, little bird?"

"No," Anka says. The Captain hands her a cup of hot brandy; it bleeds through her mittens and fogs the air. The smell makes her head spin.

"Drink," he says. To Margarita, "Yulia could use some help inside, if you don't mind—something about the bedsheets."

"Of course." Margarita kisses Anka's cheek. "I'll be right back."

"It's good to see you out of bed," the Captain says, once she's gone.

"Yulia made me. Fresh air."

He crouches down beside her. "She won't be here much longer. But I don't want to send her away until I'm sure you're well. God knows what secrets she'd take with her."

"I don't want you to send her away. I want her to stay."

"That won't be possible."

The brandy burns her tongue. She coughs as it slides down her throat, a hot bead. Kiril hasn't fed her any of the metal pills today, she realizes. Now that he knows she isn't suffering from anemia, there's no point.

"Soon we'll put this ugly business behind us," the Captain says. "She'll be gone and we'll begin the next chapter."

"She had nothing to do with this," Anka says into her cup. "I did it myself."

"I admire your loyalty, little bird, but I recognize her brand of work. It's unbecoming to lie."

"Nightshade," Anka says, gritting her teeth. Her uncle goes still. "And bulrush, and hemlock. Ground in a mortar bowl, mixed with just enough water, steeped and strained. *I did it myself*. A peddler sold me a book of poisons while you were ill. I made experiments with animals to learn. I should have slipped something into your food when you were trapped in your bed, but I was too frightened. A coward."

She scans the trees for signs of Yana, but there's nothing. Inside, the indistinct sounds of Yulia and Margarita speaking, the crunch of an ice shell breaking as they open the window to air the room. If she screamed, they'd hear, but what could they do?

"Anka." The Captain takes her chin between his thumb and forefinger and turns her face to his. The candle flickers between them. She wishes she could spit the flame into his face. "I have been patient with you. For all the years you hid from me, lied to me, I have been forgiving. I understand you're anxious. But you are grown now—a woman. This is what it is to leave your childhood behind: you must do things you do not want to do. You learn to live with them."

Her pulse is a candle—frantic, casting shadows. He pinches her tighter. "Do you think I wanted to go to war? Do you think I wanted to raise two children without a wife? I came to accept my lot. To love you. Your cousin spends his days examining festering sores—do you think it's because he enjoys smelling the rot? He sees the good that comes after.

"You don't know much of this world, Anka, but I do. There is so little good that can be done. You and I—we can right a great wrong together. *The night that cursed the harvests*—this is bigger than the two of us. It will happen." He releases her chin and strokes her cheek, her pink-cold ear. Takes her long braid in his hand. She tries to pull away, but he winds his fist in her hair and hitches her close.

"I will be very plain with you, little bird. I have made terrible mistakes. I need your help to right the worst of them. But if I'm damned, and you won't play your part . . . Do you know how easily a surgeon can lose a finger? How a single spark could burn a bakery to the ground?" He looks pained, eyes bright and pleading. The terrible long months when Simeon and Margarita thought they would never marry, her eyes were like this. The Captain's fist pulses in Anka's hair. "I can take on new debts to redeem my greatest sin. If I have to, I'll wait sixteen more years to learn how I can absolve the next."

Footsteps approach. He releases her and stands, brushing crushed snow from his knees. He smiles at Margarita as she emerges.

"Ah," he says. "Our young Madam Breadmaker—is everything done? Come, I'll escort you back to your husband. No, no, I have business with the butcher's wife in town, and you shouldn't be alone on a night like this." He sweeps her up the path by a hand at the small of her back—she hardly has time to turn and call to Anka that she'll return tomorrow, to sleep well, I love you.

As they round the bend, a rustle of movement above Anka sends a small cascade of snow onto the porch. Yana slips off the lip of the roof and lands silently beside her, dusting off her hands. Anka stares. "But I saw you," she says. "All the way over there."

"I skirted the trees," Yana says, drawing an arc. "And climbed the trellis on the far side of the house. Nobody looks for eavesdroppers on the roof. You should get inside, shouldn't you?" She reaches to help Anka stand.

Yulia nods curtly when she sees them come in together. "In the dining room," she says, and a minute later returns with another place setting. Yana eats quickly. Anka rolls a piece of beetroot over her plate with her fork. Her insides are still too jumbled for food, but there's something new—a dim light in her belly. A frail, fearful drop of hope that welled with the pressure of Yana's fingers on her wrist, tugging her up.

"I'm sorry," Anka says. "I never should have—not without discussing it with you. I just couldn't—couldn't think. I would have said anything to get away from him then."

Yana studies the table, a cracked knot in the wood. "I know. And I shouldn't have disappeared like I did—I was angry. I'm still angry. But I understand."

Anka extends her arm, afraid to breathe until Yana takes her hand. Envelops it in both of hers. She strokes Anka's dry knuckles with her thumb. "Was it true?" the seer asks. "What you said about the peddler? Your experiments?"

Anka's laugh shudders like a sheet in the wind. "No. With you, with the lamb—that was the first time I've killed anything. But I . . . There was something about it, then. It called to me."

She expects Yana to release her hand in disgust, to maybe even rise and leave the table. But she just nods. Like she knew. She'd seen it, and decided not to be afraid.

"I was prepared to finish my work here today," Yana says. "Last night I went to the midwife's cabin, staged it. And then I undid it all."

"Why?" Anka picks up her fork, looks back to her plate. "What happened?"

Yana has removed a knife from her belt and is turning it

over in her fingers: a familiar dagger with a broken tip. She presses the dull point into her index and spins the blade like a slow top, thinking. "I changed my mind," she says. "I still want to help you. And I don't think anymore that the midwife is the best way."

The light inside Anka flares brighter, starting to catch. "If I were to fall sick again, now, he would never believe it." She lowers her voice, listening for Yulia's return from the kitchen. "He might even have Yulia killed. And I can't just run—he'll hurt Margarita. Kiril. Even Simeon."

Yana lays down the knife and reaches for her bag. "You'll need another way," she agrees. "Now we have to make a choice."

seventeen

STEAM RISES FROM a bowl. "Don't breathe it in," Anka
whispers.

All day, she holds her breath. She sweats, hair dark at her
temples. She reads from the book with the red cover. On the
table in the garden cottage, they lay out herbs pilfered from
the apothecary's shelves. A bundle of dried flowers and mushrooms that Yana brought down the hill, wrapped in old cheese-
cloth from Minka's kitchen. They have no pestle, but Margarita
helps her grind the blossoms and gills into powder with the
rounded butt of a knife.

Anka pours boiling water. She stirs. It's good luck, Yana
says, when the steam rises straight into the air like that.

When dinnertime comes, Margarita hugs her so tightly
her ribs bend. Tears tickle her neck and slide under her collar.
Anka doesn't know how to say goodbye. Eventually the door
is opening, wind is sweeping in. Margarita steps out into the
snow, looking back. "This will work," she says. "I'll see you
tomorrow."

"Watch where you're walking," Anka says, feeling the icy
path in her stomach.

Later, back at the house, Yana comes to help her dress.
She climbs through Anka's bedroom window. The night has

turned bitingly clear. "The comet is very bright tonight," she whispers, and kisses Anka's forehead. "What do you need?" Some years ago, she worked as a lady's maid in winter. Her mother grew tired of wandering in the snow and found them work in a country house where the fires always needed tending and the mistress was desperately lonely, eager for new company. "I learned how to attend a lady," Yana explains, weighing a pot of kohl in her fingers. Kiril knocks as she's buttoning Anka's dress.

"Yes," Anka says loudly. Her voice is round and hard in her throat, an egg. She blocks Kiril's path, his view to Yana hiding behind the door.

"You're up." He's surprised. "Have you eaten tonight?"

She nods. A bowl of soup, red with smoked peppers. The Captain made Yulia swallow three spoonfuls before he let Anka eat any of it. It was still hot enough to scald her tongue.

"You look nice," Kiril says, fidgeting. "Aren't you cold?"

Her fist tightens around the knob, fingernails bending on the brass. Early this morning, a desperate patient came to their front door. She'd heard Kiril's voice as he gently led the woman back to the village, before he'd even had his breakfast. *I'm sorry you're in such pain, mistress. I think I can help.*

"I'm going to talk to him," she says. "Once more, to explain myself."

"To explain why you can't marry him."

"Yes."

Kiril exhales. "And what if he doesn't listen? What will you do then?"

Anka nibbles at her lip, then stops. She'll ruin the rouge. "He threatened you," she says. "You and Margarita and Simeon. And Yulia."

A strange wind blows across his expression. There's a cut above his eye; she hasn't asked where it came from. "What does it matter," he asks, "if he threatened me?"

Can he see Yana's shadow? Anka clutches the doorknob tighter. "It matters," she admits.

He reaches out to touch her face, her hair, and she shrinks.

"I don't want to die," she says. "I know that much. I want a different way."

Kiril folds his fingers and lets his hand drop. "I was wrong," he says. "I'm sorry."

Inside her, broken pieces grind together. If she doesn't forgive him, he might carry this for the rest of his life. She really could die tonight, and leave him hungry forever. But she isn't ready. The pang of pity is too dull; her anger still presses sharp grit against the thin balloons of her lungs.

She straightens her spine and takes a step back to shut the door. "Whatever you hear tonight, don't come in. No matter what it is."

He says something as she turns the lock.

"What?" she asks, but he's already leaving. His weight is on the stairs.

Yana's fingers close over hers, tight on the key. Steady, her warm hand. Steady, her even breath.

THEY HAVE ALMOST enough grain to last the winter, but not quite—the cold came on too quickly. Just enough meat in the smokehouses. The Captain has money set aside in the town coffers. He could ride to the valley and buy more supplies if their stores run low. Maybe he should do it anyway, before the freeze creeps down the mountainside and the merchants raise their prices. It would be smart to have reserves. If they're spared illness this year, most of them could make it.

The Captain shuts his ledger and digs his knuckles into his temples. He wasn't made for this. He was happiest at the butcher's: tendons and meat were easy to understand. He took such pleasure in the slick glide of a knife. He was even happy sometimes at war, feeling himself live, burning with the frantic desire to keep living.

He contemplates the bleak walk back to the village. It's late, but he knows women who will open their doors. He wonders where the witch has gone—he misses her claws. Funny, that Kiril is also taken with her. The Captain always thought him soft and shrinking, but maybe he learned some things about women in his time away. He can find a gleam of pride in that.

Anka knocks just as he's preparing to put out the lights. He recognizes her quavering tempo. God help him, his breath catches. Again he's the boy rinsing cleavers behind the shop, manic with want, his chest ready to burst.

"Come," he says, and she opens the door. Lovely as summer, and dressed for it, too, in a light blue frock he brought her from the city last year. Her wrists are pinned with fine pearl buttons. It's a show of goodwill, he understands: the cloth is so light he can trace her bones. She has nowhere to hide a knife, a candlestick.

She's painted her mouth and brushed her hair back, fixed

it with the silver bird comb. She carries a tray with two glasses and a decanter of wine. She should be in bed. She looks so much like her mother, more and more. He wants to trap her in a tight corner and swallow her warble of a voice. But good sense squeezes a fist around his heart and cools his head.

He smiles crookedly. "Have you come to poison me, little bird?"

Anka's teeth click and grind. She'll wear them to dust before she reaches his age. "I came to talk with you," she says, gesturing to the chairs by the fire. She sets the tray on the low table between them.

Her soft, sweet childhood has drained away. He's not sure when it happened. Her hands shake as she pours the wine, but he can see the lady waiting to step forward, out of this ungainly middle. The paint on her lips looks like a woman's—not the excited smear he's seen on giggling children and inexperienced whores. She is an anxious finch perched in her chair, but he knows better than to try and soothe her. Stiffly, she leans forward and nudges one wineglass across the tray.

"You'll forgive me," he says, "if I hesitate to drink this. You were very fierce last night, talking of venomous peddlers."

Anka doesn't laugh. She holds his eye as she brings her glass to her lips and drinks.

He toasts her health. The wine rolls soft and round over his tongue. It glazes his palate with acid and mineral grit as it lingers. He wonders which bottle she asked Yulia to open. She knows what he's been saving, but probably she no longer cares to humor him.

Anka says, "In one of the books you bought me, the heroine

kills the villain with poison in his glass—not in the wine." Her eyes are very bright.

He wipes his mouth with his hand. "Is that what you've done?" he asks carefully.

"No. I only just remembered it."

The wine leaves woodgrain stuck in his throat. He laughs. "What an odd thing you've turned out to be. Your mother was odd, too. Is that how you see me, little bird? As a villain?"

"You hurt people," Anka says quietly.

"You've hurt me." He leans back in his chair. "Does that make you a villain? You've terrified our neighbors with your stories of monsters and murder—"

"You hired Yana to terrify them."

"Our sabotnik provides a unique service—one this village badly needs. Look here." He rises and takes the ledger from the desk. "Do you see this?" Standing behind her, he draws his finger down one column and up the next. She's so small with the book in her hands. She learned to read like this, sitting in this room, while Kiril shrank into a corner and tried to hide his frustration.

"Let us predict the future," the Captain says. "We have three months, four, until the snow starts to melt. Six months at least until anything new is ripe to eat. What if it's a bitter season, and long? What if there's illness, or if the stocks spoil? Do you remember last year? One old woman died—one nobody liked—and it threw them into a panic. They talked of nothing but witchcraft for months, and it was the blacksmith's widow who paid for it."

Anka turns a page in the ledger. "Yana says what matters is the story they tell."

"Yes. A hard winter with no hope—they'll turn on each other in a heartbeat. None of us will survive it. But if the seer gives them a tale of triumph, of their fortitude—that could carry them. Maybe further than you think."

Anka scans the rows of numbers and looks back at him doubtfully. "They'd still be hungry. What difference will it make?"

"A common enemy," he says, "makes all the difference. I saw that in the war. People will tolerate great misery for that." He reaches over her and shuts the book.

"This is a hard place, Anka. They have always needed this. Why do you think they've hated you for so long?" His fingers caress the silver comb. He grazes her soft neck. "Most lovers aren't so unwavering in their devotion."

She's gone rigid. He moves away, towards the grate. He takes up his wine and holds it to the firelight. Watches its color change, its legs growing long as he spins a whirlpool into the plum-dark sea. "You really didn't poison the glass, did you?"

"No," Anka says. "I wish I had."

She'll hate him for a while—he expected it. He understands. It hurts him anyway, the barb lodging in his chest, invisible shrapnel.

"Why?"

"You *hurt* people. You hurt Kiril. The women of this village, Nina—"

"You're talking of things you don't understand, Anka.

You're still young. There's so much you don't know about women and men."

"You've killed—*murdered*—"

"I've done what I had to do. I killed men in the war, because I had to. I killed a man to protect you—I would do it again."

"But my parents—"

"An accident!" His fist strikes the mantel. "A terrible accident. I regret it, Anka, you know I do, and I've been punished for it. But punishment isn't enough. That can't make it right."

There's a single locked drawer in his desk. He retrieves the key from its hiding place, tucked between the wall and the framed photograph of the boys who went to war. He's tried to have few secrets from Anka, but he hid the things that would hurt her.

He unlocks the drawer and tosses her a stack of letters. A dozen of them, tied into a bundle with white string. The drawer is full of stacks like these. "Read any one you like," he says. "They're all the same. No man within a hundred miles will marry you. I've tried, Anka—I really have. Open them—they go back years."

She turns the bundle over but doesn't loosen the knot. "Yana's vampire," she says. "Once word spreads that the village is no longer cursed—"

He kneels on the ground in front of her chair. "Some curses are harder to break," he says. "Believe me, this will not change. I'd rather you don't read them—they're vicious, written by fools, full of superstitions. *But I did this to you*—do you understand? I have to make it right myself."

"What if I don't want to marry?" she asks, lifting her chin.

She looks down on him like a disdainful queen. The rug's rough weave digs at his knees, but he stays. "Not you—not anybody. I'll be a spinster—what then?"

"You've seen what happens to a woman alone. Nina wasn't widowed three months before they made her a witch. Even if the seer calms them, there will be other trouble someday. Life is full of troubles. They could turn on you in half a breath. Anka, I have to protect you from that. I swore that I would."

He's been climbing for years—he sees the summit up ahead, within reach. Pink sunlight is bleeding over the hill.

She rubs the heels of her hands into her eyes. "Too tight," she mumbles, and tugs her comb loose. The bird takes flight and her hair tumbles down over her back. With his head in her lap, he can appreciate the fine details in the silver, the minute care. The rosebush even has tiny thorns.

"Just the thought of it makes me sick," Anka says. "Like that tube is still in me—like I'll choke and vomit all at once. Please, just let me go—I could leave this village and go where nobody knows me. I don't need you to marry me. I don't *want* it. You've been my father. I can't be your wife."

He rises onto his knees and takes her face in his hands. The illness shows through her makeup. Twice before, she tried to leave, and it almost killed her—when he brought her home she looked as bad as this, with hollow cheeks and hollow eyes. He is overcome with tenderness in his heart, love for his cruel, strange little bird. What a woman she will grow to be.

"You will learn," he says, and kisses her.

Anka tries to recoil, but he grips the back of her skull with both hands. Zora could keep him captive with just a smile, just one finger curled in his shirt. He would have followed her any-where. Lying in fields of clover, she liked to stretch her bare limbs long and tell him to choose their path. Down her wrist, over her elbow, to the tight-laced front of her dress. Up along the ticklish arch of her foot, past the damp bend of her knee, to the swell of her thigh. She watched a ladybug climb over her fingers while he worked, her eyes half lidded. It was easy for her—he would never have pulled away.

Anka has her mother's mouth. Thinner features, harder lines, but the same mouth. Firebirds are reborn, again and again. As endless as the sun's rise and the moon's fall. Keep one close enough, for long enough, and you may even live to see it.

Her lips stay tight, but at last she stops struggling. He pulls her in, folding her into his arms. Feeling the frantic wingbeat of her heart, feeling the scream she won't cut loose. Desire pulses through him like hot wax.

You will learn.

He holds her, seeking her heat. He tastes the paint on her lips, smells the spice of her supper, the unfamiliar perfume in her hair. Her arms are rough with gooseflesh; her body trembles and gags.

He holds her tight until the sharp, silver teeth drive hard into the skin of his throat.

WHAT DOES IT mean, to cross a threshold? What is a door? The power to keep out, the power to keep in. Step inside and everything changes—cold air warms, dark turns light. Cross a threshold and your memory is wiped clean. The hard ice on the frozen lake, locked against her. The trees at the burning point, crowded so thick they stopped wandering eyes—they were a door, too. Anka and Margarita went there as children, to feel for the mystical powers of the place. *That's what the altar is,* Yulia told them. *A door between worlds.* A lock waiting for ash and blood.

She stabs the silver comb into the Captain's neck, and she doesn't let go. Turns it like a key. He freezes, doesn't even think to knock her hand away. Long teeth, a hard bite. She slides the comb right to the hilt, to the silver rosebush. Blood wells hot around her fingers. Her uncle's mouth pants into hers. She wants to pull away but she holds. She can't drop it yet. When she was young, he would stand at the door to her bedroom, a candle glowing in his fist. *Good night, little bird.*

He shoves her and the chair slides across the room, the rug crumpling around its wooden legs. Her hand is empty. He falls to the floor, eyes round and white. She has made him afraid. One hand goes to his throat, tries to pull the comb loose, but his fingers slip. Blood in the air, on her skirt. His grip is growing weak; his hand can't close. The silver bird slides through his fingers.

He grabs for her and misses. Anka scrambles backwards out of the chair, knocks it over, her bones rattling. His lips move in a rasp, a gurgle.

Deadly in the blood, Yulia's journal said. *Very quick.* She hadn't let herself imagine it. She'd put it out of her mind as she measured and mixed, as she soaked the teeth, again and again. For hours today, while Yana sat with her at the table in the cottage, squinting. *If you hit right here, that alone might be enough.* She drew a line down her neck. But there would be no second chances. Anka let the comb's teeth grow thick, like a dipped taper, waxy with poison. She didn't think of it as she dressed and painted her face and let Yana carefully, so carefully, slide the silver bird into her hair. It was like a story she'd been reading, a fiction in her head. She imagined herself entering his study, taking her seat. Past that, the vision lost its shape.

The Captain finally gets his grip on the comb and pulls it free. Blood drips down his wrist. It splashes and sizzles in the fire. Blood, to cleanse. Blood, to make passage. His mouth moves again, but his voice is lost—maybe punctured, maybe drowned. His eyes never leave hers. His lips are turning blue.

A shaman, who danced her over hot coals. A father, who rubbed her back when she was sick. A door, barring her way. She unlocks it with silver key and poisoned teeth. She chooses herself. Raw and shaking, she steps through.

eighteen

KIRIL FAILS HER again. When he hears the crash, he streaks towards it. He never thought before how impractical this house is, its two small wings, its parallel stairs. He never knew it could be so loud. He runs down one flight and up another. He passes Yulia in the hall, standing still like an upright clock. Her lips move, counting. The door opens easily when he turns the knob.

The room is a broken mirror, full of fragments. The chair on its side, the upturned table. A crystal decanter rolls across the floor, and a shattered wineglass grins at the fire. Anka crowds back against the Captain's desk, away from where he bleeds into the rug. His eyes are open. His mouth twitches.

Doctor, what do you see? Kiril is kneeling on crushed glass, he is taking the Captain's hand. There is a wound in his uncle's neck, four deep punctures. There is blood, but not so much. There is something hard in the Captain's fist.

"*Don't touch it!*" Anka shrieks. A comb, he sees—his gift to her. It's glued to his uncle's fingers. "Don't touch him."

Bloody spittle foams in the corner of the Captain's mouth. His empty hand shudders along the floor like an injured rodent. His skin is losing color.

In his mind, Kiril is already unrolling bandages, is already calling for Yulia's aid. He feels the blood seeping through the cotton gauze, filling the lines of his palms. His ears ring more loudly than ever. The frantic rush of preservation gallops through him.

"Kiril," Anka whispers. Her voice is settling ash. "Let him go."

He stops short of a cliff, a dry riverbed beneath it. At the bottom he sees Nina—her body a patchwork of bruises stitched together by shallow cuts. He sees Yulia's white neck, bared for a rope. Fire spots dance in front of his eyes, molten silver blotting his vision. His imaginary gauze unrolls across the floor, spinning a white spiderweb trail. The Captain's breath is growing wet and heavy, and the tendons are hard in his neck. Anka—there was a way she looked on the night of the wedding, by the light of the burning coals: like an animal trapped under a human skin, helpless without claws or teeth.

I trust you, he told her tonight, as she closed the door on him. He'd wanted to help.

Kiril's hands are empty, clean. He sits back on his heels.

Anka crawls towards him on all fours. Rouge has smeared down her chin. She reaches out, and he anchors her fingers with his. The Captain's blood slows to a trickle. His pupils are big and stutter between them.

Kiril closes up his imaginary bag. He packs his gauze, his little bottles of alcohol, and clicks the handles shut. Quiet, soft leather. Quiet goodbye. Anka leans numbly against him. Their uncle is inches away, but the air between them is perfect, clear glass.

The Captain's fist unclenches, and they can see the curve of silver wings. Quiet, feathers floating through the air. Then

Anka lets loose a howl—the sob of a beast breaking free, scrambling off the edge of the steep and echoing cliff.

WHEN THEY WERE children and the earthquake split the valley, the ravine was deep and cold even in the summer's heat—they could feel it just by stretching out their hands. They lay on their bellies and peered into the gap, eager for a glimpse of the underworld. They only ever saw the wriggling of displaced worms, and the curl of delicate plant roots seeking a return to the dirt. But if Anka threw a scarf over their heads to block out the sun, they felt like they were staring into another night sky. There were stars in the glitterings of damp earth, in the glossy armor of beetles.

Human beings couldn't pull the land back together. The men of the village couldn't pack the wound. Instead, they stitched the earth with wooden planks to keep the livestock from falling in. Under the boards, they left a void. Sometimes, at twilight, Anka stands alone on the strange parquet in the tall grass and tries to feel the emptiness. Does her body know when she leaves solid ground, when she hovers? Her toes curl, her spine quivers. That's another door, a trap beneath her feet.

IN THE GARDEN cottage, Yana watches Anka sleep. Yulia gave her a calming tea—she's very still, but Yana can't sit for long. She tends the fire and watches Anka breathe. She packs most of her knives away and lays out her hammer. She may conduct a burial tomorrow, or she may need to leave town in a hurry.

She is turning pages in the demon book, looking at the pictures, when her mother appears and kneels by the bed. Mama looks closely at Anka's face. Yana wiped the paint away, but her eyes are still swollen, and her skin is blotchy.

"I made a choice, Mama." There are seers who do this easily, who are no better than witch hunters. "I know it's not how you taught me."

Mama doesn't speak, but she smiles. Yana flips the page to her mother's metamorphosis of a vila: four decapitated faces that transform from bow-lipped maiden to shrieking devil. "Do you remember that inn where we stayed, when you drew this? That awful shrew behind the counter?" But when Yana looks up, her mother is gone.

It's still deep night when Anka stirs. Yana hears the moment she wakes: the texture of her breath goes ragged all at once.

"You're with me," she whispers, coming to sit on the edge of the bed. She touches Anka's clammy cheek. "Do you remember? Kiril carried you. We're in the cottage out back."

This is a vulnerable time, she'd told him. *There may still be other spirits that seek to harm her. I'll look after her tonight.* But he wasn't interested in her excuses; he looked past her as she spoke. A ghost beckoned him away.

Slowly, Anka sits. "Where is he?"

"Your cousin called for the priest, and for Simeon. They took the Captain to the church cellar. We'll speak to the village together when the morning comes."

"That's far away," Anka says to the drawn curtains. Her eyes flick to the door, like it might open.

"I could take you back to the house," Yana offers. "If you want to sleep in your own bed."

Anka's hair whips around her. "No."

Grief wears differently on different bodies. Her mother was heavy, a quiet stone sunk into her pillow. Yana was numb with morning frost, staring hard at her feet so she wouldn't slip on the wet ramp. Anka is a boat, crashing against the surf. She breaks on the rocks. Yana clings to her driftwood bones and kisses her neck.

"There's nobody in there," Anka sobs. Splinters float on the waves.

IN THE MORNING, she wakes with Yana warm against her back, a brown-white hand curled on her hip. There will be a time, Anka thinks, when this is the only place she wants to be. It is a thought for the future, a promise she can't yet feel.

Silver light frames the shutters, and there is a noise outside, a rhythmic crack and tumbling. She slips out into the cold, taking Yana's coat with her. Her blue summer sheath has vanished; she has no memory of it, but someone has dressed her in wool again. It really happened, though. Brown blood rings her fingernails. Her sternum is patched with twigs.

In the gray dawn, Kiril is chopping wood. He's turned his back to the Captain's house. He doesn't notice Anka right away, not until she's stood in the doorway and watched awhile. He pauses to rest against the axe handle, and looks back when he sees her shadow growing over the ground.

"Did you sleep?" she asks. Snow crunches under her slippers. Kiril smacks the axe into the chopping block. His cheeks are red, his sleeves rolled to his elbows. The wood pile is almost to her waist.

"Some," he lies. She can smell his sweat, like the taste of iron pills.

"We don't need more firewood."

He shrugs, but she doesn't want to be in the house, either.

"Look," she says at last, and points up. The moon is a pale stamp on the gloaming sky, like a water ring on a table. The comet sparkles by its crooked tooth.

Kiril nods. He shakes damp hair from his eyes. The cut on his forehead is just starting to heal.

"There was nothing you could have done," Anka says. "I poisoned the comb. Even if you'd bandaged the wound—he still would have died."

"I thought—" Then he stops. Kicks a log that has rolled away from the pile. "There wasn't that much blood." His hand goes to his shoulder. Slowly, he grinds the joint in its socket. Two, three big circles around. She can hear the crackle.

"He was heavy," Kiril says. "You weighed nothing, when I took you out of that room. But he was the heaviest body I've ever carried."

A borrowed memory: Simeon and Kiril heaving the Captain between them, straining like packhorses with hooves sinking into the drifts. The priest in his black robes is a vision of death—he guides them with a lantern through the trees. Anka's body wants to cry again; she feels a pull towards the pit in her chest.

"There was nothing you could have done," she repeats.

"It doesn't matter." Kiril plucks a fallen icicle off the ground and flings it into the distance, where it disappears into the snow. "What matters is I didn't even try. You told me not to come in—I couldn't keep that promise. And then I just sat there and watched him die anyway."

Why do you take the hearts? Anka asked Yana last night, floating on the vast black water. Whenever she closed her eyes, she saw the blood, heard the painful bubbling in his lungs. Her hands itched. She thought of the lamb, the way its body had gone cold almost at once.

Probably it won't make sense, said Yana. She kept stroking Anka's hair, tender and slow. *I do it because there's no real sacrifice without love.*

Snow is starting to seep through her shoes. Anka finds another icicle, shaken from some high bough. She rolls it in her hands, burning as the ice melts. It is a spearhead, a dagger, a needle. She wipes her pink palms on her skirt.

"You're right," she says. She puts her arms around Kiril's neck and rests her temple against his shoulder, the one that will never be quite right again. She threads her fingers through his sweaty hair. Overhead, the comet is fading into the morning— this is the last time either of them will see its bright eye, its fiery horsehair tail. She hugs him tightly.

"It matters that you didn't try."

nineteen

T WO DAYS LATER, the villagers pack the cellar. Women stand on the stairs for a better view.

We could skip it, Yana offered, stroking the mallet's smooth handle. *I can just take the body away.*

They need to see it, Kiril said, answering for both of them. *Do what you came here to do.*

He went with Anka to the ruins of the old kiln. They dug in the snow near the base of the chimney. When she swept the rime away with her mitten, she saw dimples where her father's fingers once pressed the clay into shape.

There is a brick, and there is a mouth.

"Anka spoke true," Yana tells the villagers. "It happened last summer, while your Captain was ill." Forty nights, forty days—he completed the whole transformation undetected. Sometimes, demons can weave charms that veil mortal eyes; his household never knew. He was that skilled at hiding. "Even I took weeks to find him."

She indicates the punctures at his throat. "When he attacked Anka, her only weapon was this comb. You remember your destroyed roses? I told you how delicate the vampire's flesh can be. This small wound was enough to drain his power."

Already, people have been coming to see Anka. Yesterday, they wore the door out with their knocking. Thanking her for what she's done, begging forgiveness for a lifetime of insults. Some women, too, who said nothing but offered gifts: dried flowers, pouches of salt.

"A vampire is hunger made flesh," says Yana, taking up her knife. "He can never be sated. We can only stop him from feeding." For a moment, it looks like the Captain is smiling—a quirk of his lip, a charming half grin. Then the skin splits around the blade, and they see his gray gums. When Yana breaks his jaw, Kiril's inhale is so sharp he whistles.

"Look away," he pleads with Anka. But at the first strike of the hammer, the Captain's front tooth goes flying and skitters to a stop at her feet. Another blow, and his throat swells around the intrusion. She can see the edge of the brick under his blue skin and black stubble, stretching the puncture wounds wide. It's over before she can decide.

After, it's still morning. As they leave the church, Kiril stops in his tracks. Nina is waiting for him, lightly rocking the baby tied in a sling to her breast. Anka hangs back in an archway's shadow.

"You look well," Kiril says. "I was worried."

"I've been on the hill," Nina replies, "with Minka." They walk into the sun. Yulia brings the news daily, she explains. She was sorry to hear—

They stop out of earshot, near the rusty stain on the flagstones. Nina points to the cut above Kiril's eye. She brushes his forehead, and he captures her hand. Kisses her knuckles, which she doesn't pull away. Then he offers his finger to the baby, who grips it in her fat fist. They talk quietly for several minutes, villagers passing and casting curious looks their way.

"She's invited me for supper," he mumbles, when he returns to Anka's side. "Though I told her I may be late." For the rest of the day, whenever he is idle, he absently touches his brow where Nina's fingers skimmed the wound.

In midafternoon, they stop riding. Simeon and Kiril light a fire to melt the dirt. They dig a grave under an ice-glazed linden.

Margarita helps Anka collect brambles while Yulia stitches the shroud closed. When the hole is deep enough, Kiril and Simeon stand their shovels in the loose earth, and she pours water for them to drink. They lower the body in with ropes, and Yana arranges a ring of thorns.

"Do you want to say anything?" she asks.

Anka produces the silver comb. It's stayed cold since she washed it clean, even in her pocket and close to her skin. She drops it into the grave. Then she weighs a handful of wet dirt over the hole. It cakes together in her fingers. "Let's cover him up," she says.

While the men work, Margarita worries over the horizon. "It'll be evening soon—you're sure you won't come back? You can leave in the morning."

"We'll reach the inn a little after nightfall," says Yana. "It's up to you."

Anka wipes Margarita's cheeks with her sleeve. She's ready to go. "It has to be tonight," she says.

When the grave is sealed, they carve his name into the tree. They load the shovels back into an empty cart.

She has kisses for each of them. Margarita and Simeon both cry. Yulia presses the red book into her hands. Kiril helps her mount the mare that he took to the city—the Captain's horse is too big for her, but he might grow into it still. If she ever wants it, the mare knows the way home.

"Write to me," he says. "Short letters." She promises that she will.

YANA LEADS WITH her donkey. She hums when she rides— Anka wonders if she knows that. For now, she holds it close like a secret.

The road steers boldly down the mountain. Nobody chases them. Sometimes a lonely bird wings by overhead, or a hungry squirrel scampers across their path.

Anka finds it easier to breathe as they descend. She has always known the future as a narrowing hallway, crushing her smaller and smaller until the only place she could fit was a bed where she would never sleep. Now she peers down at the world, so big she will peacefully crumble to dust before she can learn all its secrets. There are cities ahead she can't imagine, foods she's never tasted, stories she's never heard. There may be people she'll love who she hasn't met yet, sorrow she never thought she'd weather, joy she can't comprehend. Her days are her own now, big and bright.

Tomorrow, she and Yana will head for the coast. They've decided the sea is a good place to begin.

They leave the snow line behind just as the wind picks up and the night gathers. "It's not far now," Yana calls to her. "Are you all right?"

But Anka doesn't fear the dark; she knows now that it's full. "Yes," she says. Soon, they'll see lit windows up ahead. Until then, they ride with the ghosts.

acknowledgments

Creation is collective.

There would simply be no book without my found sister, Sarah Bird, who championed this novel from the earliest, thinnest draft. To the extent that any of these characters are compelling or complex creatures, Sarah's curiosity and enthusiasm made them so. Over countless tacos and a million and one brunches at the Chelsea Grey Dog, this became a real book, and then a better book. Sarah—*the heart is an arrow*. I love you.

On that long and winding road, Jessica Hatch and Emma Hine were the best traveling companions I could hope for. Thank you for all of the writing weekends past, and for all those yet to come.

Thank you also to my early readers for their crucial insights and smart questions. Their influence made the Captain scarier, Kiril hornier, and the astronomical science more sound. They are Deborah A. Diner, Erik Fredner, Kelsey Lenz, Sean Pagaduan, Rafael Anthony Roa, Anna Robeva, Shenin Sanoba, and Kevin Seney.

Thank you to my incredible agent, Stephanie Delman, and also to Elizabeth Pratt and the whole team at Trellis Literary Management for their invaluable guidance and for placing this book in just the right hands.

My editor at Mariner Books, Jessica Vestuto, understood immediately what this novel was and how best to sharpen its teeth. Also at HarperCollins, I am grateful to Rachel Berquist, Emily Dansky, and Eliza Rosenberry for getting this book to its readers.

In the UK, thank you to Victoria Hobbs for finding me such a perfect home with Elizabeth Foley and Harvill. I am also grateful to Mia Quibell-Smith, Sam Rees-Williams, and Christopher Sturtivant for their efforts in bringing this story to the world.

As a full-time designer, I was more than a little anxious about the visual presentation of my first novel, but I needn't have worried. Jackie Alvarado and Paul Miele-Herndon did absolutely stunning work on the US edition of this book, and Julia Connolly and Kishan Rajani made sure it was equally gorgeous for its UK debut. Thank you all, sincerely, for putting up with me. Close to home, I am grateful to Good Boy Ben Young for his willingness, always, to be my second set of eyes.

Many years ago, Charlotte Wood, John Casteen, and William Little each helped shape me as a writer and a scholar, and their influences reverberate not just through these pages, but in the way that I read the world. (Ask me sometime why this novel is a Western.)

Thank you to Sarah Crossland, who was always a step ahead, blazing a trail through the writing wood that I could follow. I am grateful, too, to my friends and teachers at the New York University Creative Writing Program for lighting the way.

There are also three people who left us before I could share this book with them, but who were nevertheless crucial to its writing. Dr. Jan Perkowski taught me how to study monsters. Sydney Blair believed in me early and completely. And Michael Fetterman inspired me to nurture what matters with the brief time we have.

She Made Herself a Monster was completed during a brief but transformative stay at the Virginia Center for the Creative Arts. I am deeply grateful to the amazing VCCA staff for that gift of time and space.

My grandfather, Stefan Robev, was my first and most ardent champion. I am a writer today because he knew I could be one, and he told me so at every opportunity.

My parents have always supported this dream in every way they could, and never once insisted I should go into mathematics instead. For this and much more, I am profoundly grateful. Thank you also to my brother, Sami, for one crucial afternoon spent wandering around New Orleans, asking the probing questions that unlocked Kiril's arc—and also for being my favorite person to cook with on Thanksgiving, and the best Scrabble partner I know.

The demon-infested church of the village Koprivci is a real place, nestled in the Rhodope Mountains. The murals adorning its walls were painted circa 1840 by my great-great-great-great grandfather, Mina, and his sons, Teofil and Marko. They also painted themselves into the scene as three fez-wearing observers, who now appear briefly in chapter twelve of this book. Thank you to my aunt, Jeni, for introducing us.

To my chosen Family—Shenin, Kelsey, and Caroline: thank you for making sure I never have to go it alone.

And to my partners in particular, thank you for the rituals and the sacred time. P—let's never stop pausing our shows so we can yap. (What grim history have you prepared for me today?) M—thank you for being my best friend. Can't wait to keep telling stories with you for the rest of our lives.

Last but not least: thank you, reader, for sharing your attention with me and my disaster children. I hope you enjoyed our time together, and mind the vamps on your way out.